MASTER OF MONSTER

Book One of Unshriven

JEANETTE BATTISTA

To the monsters. You know who you are.

———

Chapter 1

———

The world is out to get you.

Breaker didn't know where he'd heard that idea before, but he thought it made sense. New Venice certainly sucked the life out of most people that tried to live there. And that was if you were one of the lucky ones. Breaker supposed he counted as one of those.

He noticed a few stragglers out on the streets, some heading to their respectable hotels back on the solid ground of what remained of old New Orleans, others ending their shifts in the shops, cabarets, and bars that catered to those seeking a bit of designer darkness. Buskers and musicians filled the heavy, fetid air with lively music, hustling for the last dollars of the night.

Breaker pushed his spelled glasses up a little higher on his nose and set foot on the bridge that would lead him back to the only place he considered home these days. A faint breeze carried the food smells a few of the street vendors hawked in the nearby square to him, making his stomach growl like a wolf warning off others from their prey. All the more reason to hurry home where he kept the booze, food, and a shower to wash away the sweat that clung to him like a second, moist skin.

A light tug on his elbow drew his attention to the woman who followed forever in his shadow. Seraf pointed her chin at the opposite side of the bridge they were about to cross. It was still early in the morning, the sun not even cresting the horizon, though its light had begun to breach the darkness a little. Seraf had excellent vision regardless of light or the fall of thick black hair that obscured her Infernal eye. Otherwise, she appeared unremarkable: average height, tawny skin, thick dark hair that covered the only remarkable thing about her.

"Inspector Summoner Barrow?" Several figures moved around; he caught the tell-tale bulge of a side-arm. Breaker peered through the gloaming to perform a quick count. He saw four officers with the Inspector Summoner staked out beneath the bridge. "Must be a sting of some kind."

Errol Barrow was one of the new class of cops, a relatively recent special unit designed to deal with dangerous mages and wayward Infernals. When the borders between the various planes of existence weakened after the global cataclysms fifty or so years ago, chaotic magic opened rifts that allowed cross-over between planes. It became apparent pretty damn quick that there needed to be some oversight in place to deal with the various mundane and supernatural threats that followed the appearance of those gates and the denizens that came through them. The Inspector Summoners were still finding their way, but they did help dial down the lawlessness, especially in places as rife with magic as New Venice.

Breaker stopped and leaned both hands on the head of his cane. Exhaustion pulled at him. His knee burned in grinding agony after a night spent crouched on a roof with a magically enhanced camera to catch his client's husband and his fae mistress making the beast with two backs. He wanted a hot shower, an ice pack, and his bed. There was a better than average chance he'd stab anyone who got in the way of this.

Seraf sniffed the air delicately, turning her head to catch the scent. Breaker's senses weren't as keen as Seraf's, but even he could discern the sour taste of unshielded magic hitting the back of his throat like milk past its expiration date. The hair on his arms rose as the energy currents in the area shifted to accommodate the rising power. A mage himself, Breaker's senses attuned to the changes in the magical fields that wrapped the earth in a web of energy. He inched back into the square beside the bridge to give himself space and time to regroup.

Damn. He and Seraf just needed to cross the bridge, and then they'd be on their side of their city, safe in the Mire, the spit of marsh and swampland between New Venice and what passed as New Orleans these days. Doubling back to the last bridge they'd passed added another hour at least before Breaker could get off his feet at the office.

Still, it beat getting stuck in the middle of a Maleficar takedown by the NVPPD.

Breaker signaled to Seraf and turned around to retrace his steps. The air around them ruptured with a sound akin to a sonic boom. The blowback of magical energy nearly knocked Breaker off his feet; if not for Seraf reaching out to steady his shoulder, he would have fallen.

A mage stood at the bridge's center, hands already glowing with eldritch power. Breaker didn't recognize the man, but he could feel the lines of force being called and twisted to malicious intent. His shields surged into being as he began to back up towards a nearby building. Seraf growled low in the back of her throat, the strange noise allowed by her inhuman vocal cords.

I.S. Barrow and his team swarmed out from beneath the bridge as one of the summoners dropped a force warding around the bridge. Blue and red lights flashed off the water and bounced off the sides of buildings some distance away—police boats heading towards the scene.

"Disperse your magic and keep your hands where I can see them," Barrow said, his voice augmented by magic so it would carry through the shielding, the minor distortion testament to the man's skill with that particular spell. "You are under arrest by order of the New Venice Paranormal Police Department."

"Highly unlikely from where I'm standing," Breaker muttered to Seraf. "But it means a lot that they tried."

Seraf snorted her amusement and stepped beside him. He edged further back into the square, more than happy to let her bear the brunt of any physical fall-out from the standoff between police and a Maleficar. His lousy knee shrieked its displeasure. He needed food and rest, which he'd planned on getting until they got caught in the middle of this bullshit.

"Crowley's balls, we have shite luck."

Seraf hummed in agreement.

As they crept back the way they'd come, Breaker watched Barrow's team spread out. The sirens' dopplered howl grew louder as the patrol boats approached. The police led with their guns up, causing Breaker to wonder what kind of shot they were packing. Depending on what this yutz of a mage had at his disposal, the bullets might be highly effective or next to useless.

"You have until the count of thr—," Barrow began, only to be cut off when the bottom of the bridge blew out in a cascade of masonry and dust.

"I don't have eyes on them," another detective called out over the heavily distorted sounds of coughing and cursing.

The bridge shield winked out of existence now that there was no one within it to hold. As Breaker watched NVPPD's finest scramble around to find their collar, Seraf put her arm in front of him, her head swiveling as she surveyed the area.

"See anything?" he asked, coughing as he swallowed a mouthful of billowing rock dust.

Seraf shook her head but froze at the same time that

Breaker's arm broke out in goosebumps. He shuddered at the strangely pleasant tingling in the air. Seraf reached out and dragged Breaker to the ground just as something strafed through the square and unleashed forks of red lightning at the area surrounding the bridge. His shields took a hit as one of the bolts glanced off it. He fed what remained of his waning power into it to stabilize it.

Barrow's team scrambled. "We've got a flying Infernal," one of his squad shouted over their coms.

"They were made," Breaker told Seraf as he scooted on his ass to put his back against a crumbling wall. "That Maleficar was ready for them and then some."

Seraf cocked her head, waiting for his orders. Sweat dripped down his temples, making his hair stick to his forehead. He pushed his glasses higher on his nose and scanned the rooftops. Infernals were human-demon hybrids, the offspring of lab experiments begun immediately after the rifts opened. They'd been an attempt to merge the best of both species into something akin to a super-soldier. The project had failed spectacularly. This third and fourth-generation spawn still held that mixed DNA, making the traits inherited impossible to predict. A winged Infernal was rare, but they couldn't sustain flight for long distances or go very high; the wings were best suited to gliding.

All he wanted was to fall in bed and sleep for a week, but no, he had to stumble into this crap. It served him right for trying to save a little coin instead of springing for the water taxi as Seraf had suggested.

Seraf stood before him, hands at her sides, waiting. He rubbed at his temples, the headache that had been threatening all night deciding to roar to life right then. Just once, he wished she didn't look to him for a decision, that she would think for herself.

He pushed aside the unkind thought. His shoulders

drooped. "The usual drill. Seek and destroy," he told Seraf, voice hollow.

Seraf nodded once, long daggers already in her hands. Her left eye, the one that marked her as Infernal, glowed red, the center swirling like an amber hurricane—he could see its glow through the strands of the coarse black hair that fell across it. She spun and raced to the closest building, leaping effortlessly at the fire escape and pulling herself up. In a matter of seconds, she disappeared over the roofline.

Breaker gained his feet with help from the wall and his cane. His knee throbbed angrily, his body howling in protest. Peering around the corner, he watched Barrow's team spreading out in a search formation. Barrow took point as the tip of the spear, gun drawn. Breaker could feel the heat of the man's magic as he tapped into his summoned fire elemental.

The Maleficar they were hunting must be important for them to have at least three summoners, each with their own summons riding shotgun inside their body. Add an Infernal into the mix, and Breaker wondered just what crime the Maleficar committed, despite knowing that curiosity would likely cost him big. New Venice operated on the 'if it ain't your business, best keep walking' premise. Breaker made a habit of keeping his head down as the best way of ensuring it stayed attached to his neck.

The police boat arrived, slewing around the corner, only to be greeted by a sheet of ice that prevented it from closing further. Breaker tracked the magical lines, tracing them back to the source, only to find it difficult with so many users in a confined area. Barrow had a bead on the Maleficar, aiming his summon's augmented fire magic at a space on Breaker's side of the square. NVPPD began to converge on the area, tightening the cordon.

The sounds of fighting above drew Breaker's gaze to the rooftops. A darker shape passed over, jumping from building to building, wings bulky and tight against its back. A lithe figure followed after. Breaker caught the glint of Seraf's glowing red and amber eye in the dim light of approaching dawn.

Breaker breathed out a blistering curse. A stray blast of ice hit the corner of the building where he sheltered. Running feet, gunshots, and the whine of spells going off set his teeth on edge. He'd hidden in the shadows, but that didn't mean he couldn't catch a stray bolt with his shields as weak as they were.

"Stop!" Barrow's magically augmented command echoed in the square.

They were close. The ozone tang of spent magic grew stronger, pinging Breaker's senses. He waited, like a spider in the center of its web, feeling the vibrations of its prey struggling in the strands. The mage ran in his direction, getting closer to Breaker's hiding place with every step. The Maleficar showed no interest in obeying I.S. Barrow as he swung around and raised his hands for a spell.

Breaker stepped out from the shadows of the building, cane in hand. He swept the top of it—a silver phoenix head, heavy and dense—low, aiming for the man's kneecap. Breaker knew just how painful a shattered knee was, and he knew—intimately—that this cane was more than capable of producing the desired result. The resounding, throbbing crunch as the phoenix impacted flesh and bone reverberated in Breaker's own body. The Maleficar shrieked, dropping to the ground. He writhed and howled, hands clutching his knee, spells forgotten.

Barrow skidded to a halt several yards away, gun trained on the fallen Maleficar. His eyes held a faint amber gleam to them—the summoned elemental riding in him. His team converged; some weapons pointed at their quarry, others pointed at Breaker. He held up his hands, his cane clasped in his right.

"Where's the Infernal? Do we have eyes on the bastard with the wings?" Barrow asked into his coms.

A dark shape hurtled from the rooftops, slamming into the stone tiles of the square. It hit the pavement with a liquid thud, like a balloon filled with hamburger. One wing lay crumpled beneath its body; the other ripped off completely. Breaker allowed himself a faint smile. Seraf had a gift for impeccable timing.

"It would appear so," he told the inspector, pushing his glasses back up his nose primly. Sweat slicked the skin covered by both shirt and jacket like he'd just run a marathon. The humidity made everything feel like an overenthusiastic puppy had licked it.

"Thanks for the help, Unshriven," Barrow said with an irritated frown. "I can only assume Seraf's up there somewhere." He glanced at the roofline as if expecting her to pop up and wave.

Breaker said nothing, knowing it would irritate the detective further. He took pride in everything he'd built with Unshriven Investigations. He'd started the agency at nineteen after barely scraping by on the streets for years. He and Seraf had been a joke back then—two street kids trying to make a living solving other people's problems. But after five years, long hours, and hard work, even the cops respected Unshriven, even if they didn't like them.

"Just happy to do our part, Inspector Summoner. We are terribly civic-minded individuals." He kept his expression even and his delivery deadpan.

"This," Barrow gestured at the sobbing Maleficar being bundled into spelled shackles by the inspector's team, "one of yours?"

Breaker widened his eyes behind his glasses in mock offense, leaning on his cane. "You know I only work with the finest clientele New Venice has to offer," he said haughtily.

"Uh huh." The inspector eyed Breaker with pursed lips.

The sudden icy chill behind him told Breaker that Seraf had used her shadow ability to portal in behind him. She didn't like to rely on it because using those skills significantly drained her magic stores, but she must have been in a hurry to return to him to risk it. Without looking, he signed a welcome to her.

"We were just on our way back to the office via the bridge," he told the detective, giving Seraf a chance to put herself back together. "Finished up a case and were calling it a night when we ran across your op."

Popping his neck, Barrow holstered his gun. The amber glow faded almost entirely from his eyes as the incorporeal elemental sharing mental space with him went back to sleep. "Just passing by then." He lifted his chin in greeting. "'lo, Seraf. We have you to thank for that sad pile of guts that used to be an Infernal?"

She stepped beside Breaker, arms folded across her chest. The glow from her left eye faded slowly. The iron scent of her blood hit his nose, mixed with the strange faint smell of brimstone that all Infernal blood, no matter how far removed from the original line, carried. The other Infernal had gotten a few licks of his own in before Seraf facilitated his swan dive from the roof.

"He tripped," she signed as Breaker translated. "He fell."

"Yeah." Barrow raised a skeptical brow. "An Infernal with wings managed to trip and fall off a roof."

She offered him a mournful look full of mock sadness.

"A veritable tragedy," Breaker said flatly.

The detective shook his head, wearing the expression of a man who didn't get paid enough for this shit and well aware of that fact. "What a fucking mess," he muttered.

Breaker took a step forward, gritting his teeth in pain as his knee folded under him. He staggered, the stones rushing to meet him until Seraf caught him beneath his elbow. Her firm grip steadied him as she took his weight. Biting back a furious curse, he managed to right himself with effort. His body throbbed, desperate for rest. He transferred most of his weight to his cane and leaned away from Seraf.

"If there's nothing else, Inspector, I would like to get home." His bad leg trembled, and Breaker knew he didn't have many more minutes upright. Still, he would make it back to Unshriven without help, no matter how much his body protested. He had his pride.

Barrow waved his hand. "Yeah, yeah, go on. Someone will be around to get a statement from you." He gave a sharp whistle and signaled to one of the patrol boats that had just arrived. "Least I can do is give you a lift home."

Breaker saluted the man with his cane. "Much appreciated, Inspector Barrow. Good evening."

"Good morning," Barrow corrected before he began issuing orders to the newly arrived officer approaching them.

"Let's go, Seraf," Breaker ordered and hobbled to the waiting patrol boat, ignoring the agony that accompanied his every step.

Chapter 2

Breaker limped up the stairs, leaning heavily on his cane and the railing, hauling himself up by sheer will. He wished he'd taken the bedroom on the same floor as the office at times like this. He knew Seraf would gladly trade places with him, even for a night, but he valued his space and privacy too much ever to consider such a thing. He had too little of both for his peace of mind.

"Get me some ice," he ordered, turning his head to look down at her and catching the resigned expression that crossed her face before she could hide it behind a blank stare. "Will you?" The question barely managed to mitigate his dick-ishness.

Seraf nodded and descended the stairs, expression neutral. She glanced back at him once as if worried that he couldn't remain standing without her help. Her concern grated on his already raw nerves, and he set his jaw to block his peevish response. Instead, he closed his eyes and breathed in deeply through his nose, shooing her away with one hand.

Still, she hesitated. Gritting his teeth, Breaker said, "I can get to my room fine, but I would appreciate the ice."

Raising her eyebrows, Seraf glanced up the narrow flight

of stairs, most of which he still had to navigate. She wasn't stupid, though most people assumed so because she didn't speak, and neither of them thought to disabuse anyone of that assumption. Her fingers flashed in a series of signs that, along with her facial expression, amounted to, "Go slow and don't be an idiot." She finally turned and made her way back to the small kitchenette.

Words to live by. Breaker should find some pleasant grandmother and have her embroider it on a sampler to hang above the office desk.

The effort of climbing the stairs had Breaker's shirt sticking to him despite the air conditioning. His bed beckoned him, and Breaker wanted nothing more than to drop onto it and lose himself in sleep, but he smelled disgusting. The stink of the city—a cloying mix of the sweet rot of vegetation, fry oil, alcohol, and piss—clung to his hair, skin, and clothes. He needed to be clean before he slid beneath cool sheets. He placed his spelled glasses on his bedside table, leaned his cane against it, and dragged himself into the bathroom.

He'd replaced the light switch with a dimmer to protect his sensitive eyes. Breaker slid the button to its lowest setting to keep from tripping over anything, still flinching when the lights over the sink flared to life. Breaker stripped off his clothes and left them in a sodden pile by the bathroom door. He'd set them alight, but they were probably too wet to burn between his sweat and the water kicked up by the patrol boat. He'd throw them in the wash later, but for now, he only wanted a shower and sleep.

He kept the water temperature on the cool side, groaning when it hit overheated skin. Quickly soaping his hair and body, Breaker reveled in the intense water pressure that pounded into the tense muscles of his back. His whole body locked up and set him off-balance, a side effect of his busted knee. He rinsed off, pulled a comb through his grey hair to get out the worst of the knots, and turned the water off.

He toweled his hair somewhat dry before wrapping it around his skinny waist and proceeding into the bedroom. The clothes he'd dumped on the floor were gone, and Seraf stood with a towel-wrapped bag of ice in hand. Her blue eye watched him closely as he made his slow and painful way to bed without using his cane. She brushed messy black hair out of her face, giving him a glimpse of her Infernal eye. Breaker looked away quickly.

He breathed a sigh of relief when he collapsed on the bed. Thankfully, Seraf had already pulled back the covers. Settling his leg atop the stacked pillows, Breaker pulled the covers over his lower half and shimmied out of his towel. Seraf handed him the ice and took the towel from him to hang it on the hook behind the door.

Breaker leaned over to reach the drawer of his end table and pulled out a small bottle of painkillers. He swallowed down two, chasing it with the remnants of a warm gin and tonic left to die on his nightstand before getting comfortable.

"You need to dye your hair again," she signed. "The white's showing through."

"I'll do it in the morning." Breaker used dye to color his white hair darker. People with albinism tended to stand out, and he couldn't afford to be memorable. His spelled glasses helped with his light sensitivity and hid the lightness of his eyes. "Later in the morning," he amended as he plugged in his phone and saw the time.

"Get some sleep, Seraf. I'll be fine." He couldn't stand the feeling of her watching him. He needed her to go downstairs if he had any hope of getting some rest.

"You sure?" She spoke aloud and her words, as usual, tripped over her teeth. Human speech eluded her—it had since the day they'd met. She relied on a cribbed together sign language rather than verbal speech, though she used her voice more with him than with anyone else.

She spoke now because he refused to open his eyes to look

at her. "Yes," he snapped, his need to be alone chipping away at his manners. The yawn caught him by surprise. " Go on downstairs. I don't intend to move until lunchtime."

He heard the faint rustle of her clothing as she moved back down the stairs, the only signal she'd left. Her feet were silent on the steps. Seraf moved around the office like a damn ghost. Though useful in the field, it could be off-putting when you were slicing a tomato for a sandwich and she appeared behind you, silent and staring.

He rolled over, regretting it when pain flared in his knee and tried to get the sleep he desperately craved...

...and woke with a strangled cry, fingers clutching the sheets in white-knuckled terror.

"*Pop, don't!*" he'd pled in the nightmare, hands held up in submission. "*Please, I'm sorry!*"

His father's dream response echoed in his head. "*You'd choose that monster over me?*"

Now awake, Breaker shook his head, icy sweat rolling down his neck. He rubbed at his eyes with the heels of his hands, hoping to ease the strain of last night. His abstract gaze fell on the silver phoenix that topped his cane where it sat propped against his nightstand. Breaker broke out in a full-body shudder.

He should have expected the nightmare. He flopped back in bed, throwing one arm across his tired eyes. Mornings like this made him want to break that cane into pieces and burn it to ash. Kneecapping that Maleficar triggered memories Breaker did his best to keep buried.

A faint knock on his bedroom door brought his thoughts back to the present. He moved his arm to peer blearily at the hazy outline of Seraf in his doorway. He wasn't ready to view the world through the clarity of his spelled glasses.

"Morning," he greeted, his voice sounding like something had died in his throat.

Seraf entered, cleaned and dressed for another crappy day

of work for those with questionable morals in New Venice. She pulled her black hair into its usual neat tail, coiling around itself like a serpent affixed to the back of her head. Her standard sweep of hair covered her left eye. With a groan, Breaker reached over and grabbed his glasses so he could see what she had to say.

"Bad night?" she signed, brows furrowed.

He sat up, tenting his knees beneath the sheet so he could lean his forearms on them. He made a noncommittal noise.

"I heard you shout." Her hand signs paired with a gaze that bored into him as if she could peer beneath his skin.

Of course she did. Breaker sighed, dropping his head for a moment. It was too early for this—he hadn't even had his coffee yet. "Just a bad dream." He shrugged. "Nothing I haven't already lived through."

If anything, her expression grew more worried, but Seraf chose to remain silent. That was almost worse. Seraf's silences could turn into soliloquies.

"Is Tamlin here yet?" Breaker cast about him for his watch before realizing he'd left it on the top of the toilet tank.

Seraf nodded and signed, "It's a little after eleven."

Too damned early. No point in wasting the day since he was already awake. "Give me a few minutes to pull myself together, and then we'll go get some coffee."

He waited until she disappeared down the stairs before throwing the sheet off and shakily climbing to his feet, feeling relieved when his knee held with only a lancing surge of pain. It had swollen during the night, but it had been worse. He made his careful way into the bathroom. Though he'd just showered the night before, his nightmare left him feeling filthy and sweat-soaked. A quick rinse would help clear away the remaining clouds of sleep and freshen him up.

Water sluiced down the planes of his body, sliding over the faint ridges of scars from fights lost and won. Breaker kept his gaze and his hands away from the worst of them on his right kneecap. Last night's nightmare clung too close, the feel of it against his skin too vivid. Swallowing, he refused to look down, unwilling to see the ruin of flesh and bone that had hobbled him at fourteen.

Breaker finished drying himself. The only concession to his damaged knee was a soft brace that didn't ruin the line of his pants. He dressed quickly in his usual dark trousers and a dark-striped button-down. He swept the worst of the water from his hair, styled it loosely with his fingers, and placed his glasses firmly back on the bridge of his nose. Breaker glared at his reflection once his vision sharpened to clarity. Seraf was right; the actual color of his hair showed through the grey rinse. He'd need to reapply it tonight. He quickly covered his exposed skin with the magical balm that helped him tolerate the intense sunlight without broiling.

Shrugging into his tailored jacket, Breaker stepped out of the bathroom and took his cane in hand. He always made sure to dress well, despite his somewhat unsavory profession. People tended to give well-dressed people more respect and ask fewer questions of him when they found him in places where he shouldn't be. When tailored clothes didn't stop unwanted attention, the dagger in the sheath at Breaker's back and the magic that flowed through his veins served as deterrents. Failing that, he carried his father's cane.

Taking the stairs slowly, Breaker tested his knee. Once on the landing, he decided the brace to be good enough and proceeded into the main office of Unshriven. He shook his head at the sight of Tamlin's desk. Covered in papers, filing, and bits of office detritus, it was amazing the wood didn't collapse in a heap of paper clips, sticky notes, and binder clips. Unshriven's admin stood at the corkboard hung on the wall behind his desk, sliding another piece of paper into the plastic packet pinned to it. The office cellphone sat in easy reach on the desk. Breaker often wondered how Tamlin found anything in that heap of paper, but the admin had proven enough times that he could put his hand on any scrap of information Breaker needed within two eyeblinks. Breaker stopped worrying about the fae man's filing system and just prayed a stray bus didn't hit him because they'd never figure out his accounting.

"Good morning, 'Lin," Breaker greeted, gaze sweeping over the assistant. Lin looked quite appealing with his lanky frame, black hair, and bottomless grey eyes, and Breaker could appreciate the view even if he had no intention of doing anything about it. He shifted his gaze to the job board. "I'm assuming Seraf passed on the intel for the Body Heat account."

"She did, indeed," the half-fae said in a modulated Scottish burr.

Tamlin had been mortal at some point centuries ago before he'd attracted the attention of the Unseelie Queen of the Fae. She'd spirited the young man away to her realm, where he'd become a welcome distraction for her. He remained a member of her dark court until a former dalliance —now pregnant—dragged him off of his horse and held onto him while the Unseelie Queen turned him into everything she could think of to get his lover to release him. Lin stayed in the mortal realm for a time but found it unsatisfying and eventually returned to the fae realm to live there.

Centuries had passed in an eyeblink. Tamlin would likely still be whiling away his time beneath the dappled shade of the fae forests if the magical bindings separating the realms hadn't unraveled like a pulled thread. He'd been pulled back by errant magic and said he found himself intrigued by all of the changes that had been wrought in his absence, so he'd decided to stay.

Which meant he'd needed a job.

Breaker hadn't been picky when Tamlin had answered their advertisement for an administrative assistant to help with the bookkeeping and filing and making small talk with clients.

Breaker had been looking for someone capable of answering a phone and scrawling a message. He'd gotten a man with fae charm and good looks that drew in female clients like flowers drew bees. The competency with accounting was a bonus. He could not, however, make a decent pot of coffee to save his life.

"I've already called to set up the meeting with the client to detail your findings. Just waiting for her to get back to me." He glanced over his shoulder, assessing Breaker with his cool steel gaze. "Rough night?"

Running a hand through his hair, Breaker frowned. He hadn't thought he looked *that* bad. Still, compared to Tamlin's fastidiously groomed appearance, Breaker must look like he'd been dragged down a few miles of rough road.

"Not all of us are blessed with magic."

"Then what's your excuse?" Tamlin cocked a hip insouciantly and regarded Breaker with raised eyebrows.

Ignoring that dig at his refusal to use his magical abilities for trivial things like glamours, Breaker walked further into the room. He saw Tamlin's eyes narrow as they took in the way he leaned more heavily on his cane than usual, but Seraf's arrival saved Breaker from any further cutting observations.

"Thank Trigestus," he said, adjusting his glasses more firmly on his nose. "Coffee. Now."

"Madame Domino wants you to swing by today," Tamlin called after them. "It's about a job!"

"Let her know we'll stop in shortly," Breaker called back as he once again navigated the steep stairs of the brownstone. Seraf held the door, waiting patiently for him. The deference made him want to smash something with his cane.

He brushed past her with more force than usual and continued into the streets of the Mire. Seraf said nothing, just followed half a step to his right like she always did. Today, he wanted to grind his teeth as they made their way to the coffee shop closest to Unshriven.

The Mire was a spit of marshy land balanced between the flooded streets of New Venice and the hard-packed earth of what remained of New Orleans. Those who had the resources and money moved away from the doomed city well before the newly designated Category 7 Hurricane Iris completely obliterated the topography and reshaped the area's geography. The Quarter was gone, midtown too. The bones of the stadium poked up through the floodwaters like the skeleton of a forgotten sea monster. Parts of the Garden District survived in some form, primarily due to the old, monied families' magic. Those that couldn't afford to evacuate died when Iris hit or later when the magical fields' stability blew wide open and breached the spaces between realms.

The Mire became one of those liminal spaces, a buffer between the drowned world of New Venice where pleasure seekers looked to debauch themselves in whatever way they pleased and those that sought the more accepted diversions of the decent society of New Orleans. The fringe elements thrived in the Mire.

Breaker winced as the bright sunlight accosted him. Even with his spelled glasses that both improved his vision and protected his pale blue eyes from sun damage, the light sensitivity from his albinism still bothered him. He could always move to someplace rainy and overcast, but that probably wouldn't offer him much of a living. As uncomfortable as the heat and light made him, Breaker knew he belonged in New Venice with the rest of the misfits.

It didn't take long to reach Witches' Brew coffee shop, and once again, Seraf held the door open for him. The familiar smell of brewing coffee, roasting beans, and steamed milk hit Breaker's senses. His dark mood lightened considerably with the imminent arrival of caffeine.

A diminutive, green-skinned young woman with a triangular face and disproportionately large, liquid eyes stood behind the counter. She wore a collection of metal in her face and ears, and the tips of her pointed teeth dug slightly into her thin brown lips. Her hair was a similar shade of brown with a texture almost like the bark of a tree.

"Morning, B!" the pixie called, throwing him a luminous smile. "The usual?"

Breaker nodded. "With an addition from the secret menu if you don't mind, Ari."

"Ooh," Ari breathed, skin brightening to a dusky lime with her delight. "What'll it be? A little touch of glamour to make all the ladies swoon?"

He heard Seraf's snort at his shoulder. Ignoring her, Breaker shook his head. "Not today, thanks. Perhaps a touch of good luck to see me through?"

The pixie winked and turned toward the back room only to stop and sneer at Seraf. "Your usual too, Hellspawn?"

"Don't spit it in this time," Seraf signed.

"I wouldn't waste it on you," Ari sassed with a twinkle in her large eyes as she continued on her way.

Seraf rolled her eye and signed to Breaker, "Still as charming as ever."

Breaker slid the money for their drinks across the counter, including a hefty tip for Ari for the bump of faery magic. Most fae who decided to remain permanently in the human realm ended up supplementing their income by finding ways to profit from their natural abilities.

Ari returned a few minutes later, a to-go cup in one hand. A golden glow spilled over the rim as she filled the cup with coffee, topping it off with steamed milk. She blew across the surface of the foam. Breaker saw the golden glow flare before disappearing as the charm sank into the liquid.

"Here you go," Ari said, handing the cup over. She quickly poured another steamer full of milk into a to-go cup, added a bit of cherry-flavored syrup, and stuck it all under the frother. "And yours."

"Thanks, Arinayah," Breaker said with a grateful nod. He

took a sip and groaned as the coffee and milk exploded on his half-asleep tastebuds. "Perfect as always."

"You know it." She swiped the money from the counter, her cut disappearing somewhere on her person while the rest went into the register. "See you later!"

He stepped out into the muted light of late morning. Being an epicenter of one of the realm rifts played havoc on the weather and atmosphere. The city suffocated beneath the usual humid oppression, but the light held a transparent quality akin to a watercolor painting. The Mire stood far enough removed from most of the effects of rift energy—even with the bindings and protections some of its power leaked through—but it was close enough to get the occasional glaring reminder of its proximity.

Seraf took the lead, and Breaker didn't protest. He leaned on his cane more than usual. She could see it even if she didn't say anything, adjusting her pace to his much slower one. He appreciated it almost as much as he resented it. Another constant reminder of the ways they were bound to each other.

He tutted in protest when she stopped at a water taxi stand at the edge of the Mire. Making a sharp downward motion with her arm, Seraf cut off his argument. "I'm paying for it," she signed, a grim expression on her face. "Not up for debate."

He threw his arms up—hands full of coffee and cane— and stepped into the boat. Giving the boatman the closest cross streets to Purgatorio, he settled back in the small plush seat of the gondola. At least he could sit and enjoy his coffee.

Seraf sat opposite him, sipping absently from her cup as she stared at the bridges they passed beneath. She wore what she always did: a pair of worn jeans, a fitted heather grey t-shirt, and a pair of broken-in, black steel-toed boots. She'd left her jacket behind. The black of her hair glistened against the tawny, orange-brown of her skin in the heavy sunshine.

She appeared utterly and frighteningly normal.

Breaker pulled his gaze away from his business partner

and took another deep swig of coffee. The luck charm fizzled at the back of his throat, almost like he'd gargled champagne and the bubbles were still there. It filled him with warmth for a brief moment before dissipating.

Their pilot guided them unerringly along the narrow channels that joined the Mire to New Venice, oars dipping rhythmically into the canal. The water circulated slowly, and the scent of algae bloom and rotting vegetation hung potent in the heavy air. The fetid smell of stagnant water filled Breaker's nostrils. He kept his coffee cup at his mouth to combat the worst of it.

Seraf said nothing, sipping at her cup of cherry-flavored hot milk with relaxed intent. Smells never seemed to bother her, though to be honest, little did. They'd known each other since he was twelve and she was around ten, and he could count on one hand the times he'd seen her truly upset. Did the stoicism come from a genetic difference in Infernals or her life before him? Likely he'd never get an answer. He had enough problems with his own childhood.

It didn't take long before the fringes of New Venice intruded on Breaker's periphery. Gaudy buildings, most lashed to pontoon-like floats and stabilized with powerful spells, appeared like water-borne mirages. Zydeco and jazz music spilled from the open doors, filling the streets with the infectious sound. These were the cheaper establishments: brothels and bars and burlesques, strip clubs, several gay bars, and a few voodoo shops practicing questionable magic. These were the places frequented by tourists interested in a brief respite from their dreary lives or some Spring Break adventure. Musicians and other performers lined the streets, always happy for a tip. This was the face of New Venice that most everyone knew.

The real money lurked deeper in New Venice, at the rotting heart of the city.

Purgatorio sat like a gilded spider just outside the floating city's center. It resembled an old Greek Revival mansion, soaring columns and deep front porches, with balconies on all three floors. It appeared as pristine as a child's jewelry box. A tall, dark man in a white suit stood by the door, sweltering in his tailcoat as he ushered clients inside with a gracious nod of his head.

Breaker levered himself out of the boat with a bit of effort as Seraf paid the boat pilot. He shot his cuffs and smoothed down his jacket, wondering what business the mistress of Purgatorio wished to discuss. Seraf joined him on the dock presently.

He eyed the front door with growing trepidation. Infernals made up most of Purgatorio's roster of talent. Breaker glanced at Seraf, only to find her staring at him. She looked as nonplussed as ever, but he could see her tension showing in the tightening of her shoulders and the tautness of her mouth.

Still, money was money.

"Let's go," he said and proceeded to walk forward, his cane clicking like a timebomb against the spelled cobbles of the street.

Chapter 3

Purgatorio's old plantation house façade did not follow into the interior, although it reminded Breaker of slavery nonetheless. Infernals lounged about in various stages of undress. The trappings and furnishings held a certain Byzantine luxuriousness, a debauched, dissipated languor clinging to the color palette full of arterial reds, rich golds, and tawny bronzes. Heavy, lush draperies dampened sound. The dim lighting allowed for plenty of shadowed alcoves in the large sitting room where at least thirty people—clients and employees—congregated. Large ormolu vases flanked a slate fireplace, holding massive fans of greenery. It was lavish and alien at the same time.

Several human employees circulated among the assembled crowd dressed in the typical white suits of Purgatorio. They carried trays of drinks, bite-sized snacks, or tablets to input requests. A striking marble staircase led to the upper floors. Breaker heard rumors of a basement dungeon where those who wanted to experience something a bit more perverse could indulge those fantasies, but he didn't see a way to get down there from the reception room.

Seraf stiffened beside him, unease coming off of her in waves as she took in the room's occupants. He paused in his steps to lean in close. "You can wait outside if you would rather," he murmured.

She threw him a betrayed glance. Her signing was curt, gestures clipped and powerful. "I'm fine where I am." She gritted her teeth as her gaze skipped from one Infernal to another.

A tall man with more joints in his arms and legs than he should have meandered past, one long arm draped over a dark-haired male patron. Another Infernal, a female with stunted black bat wings sprouting from between her shoulder blades, got pulled onto the laps of two men. A petite blond woman giggled as a male Infernal used his pointed tail to tickle under her chin. Each of them wore only enough for modesty's sake. Breaker could feel Seraf's secondhand embarrassment and disgust.

Breaker went back to scanning the room. He didn't believe for one minute Seraf liked standing there, but he trusted her to know her limitations.

Another tall man, built like a tank and wearing the white suit of the house, stood at the base of the stairs. A crimson and gold sash wound around his trim waist, matching the silk pocket square he wore in his white jacket. Breaker made his careful way over to him, stepping over the legs of a horned Infernal sitting on his knees giving a client a foot massage.

"Absalom Breaker of Unshriven to see Madame Domino. She's expecting me." He assumed 'Lin had gone ahead and made the phone call to confirm the meeting after their departure.

The man went off to fetch the proprietress, and Breaker leaned on his cane, head cocked to the side as he watched the Infernal escorts parade for clients looking for a taste of the strange and dangerous. Seraf pretended to study a tapestry hung along one wall rather than look at her brethren. *There but for the grace of God.*

Except God had nothing to do with it. Tobias Winstead II had bound their fates together.

Other human "talent" stood on display—Madame Domino believed in providing for all tastes and pleasures. A few escorts cast hopeful glances at Breaker, only to find interest elsewhere when Seraf glared at them.

Seraf turned heads. The Infernals in the brothel wore collars imbued with magical wards specific to an Infernal's powers. It kept their abilities dormant and helped level their mercurial moods. Most of Purgatorio's Infernals were under contract with Domino and didn't need such precautions, but collars made patrons more comfortable and were a cost-effective way to prevent accidents.

Breaker tried to imagine a collar on Seraf. He couldn't.

She wore none, and she never would so long as he had any say about it. She was his: partner, penance, responsibility, guilt, pet—whatever she was, she belonged with him. He didn't need a collar or a contract to keep her. They were bound together by blood and secrets and something hot and dark that stretched between them but never broke. No matter how much he'd tried.

Still, seeing an Infernal without a collar had to anger the other collared Infernals. It made the human patrons uncomfortable too. What if she went on a rampage? Gazes skipped nervously from Seraf to him. Breaker kept his face impassive, expression carved of marble. Let them wonder; he had no reason to enlighten them. Mage or not, only the most powerful or deluded dared to control an Infernal without using a collar. Seraf going without a collar made him appear more powerful and dangerous.

More suicidal too.

An acceptable trade-off.

Madame Domino descended the grand staircase amidst

the tinkle of piano keys and low murmurs of patrons. She stepped with the grace of a goddess and the stride of an executioner. A simple black and white domino mask covered the upper half of her face, her mane of silver hair streaming behind her in a plume of heavy curls. She wore a black latex pencil skirt with a kick pleat at the back and a high collared white shirt with a cravat that looked like it belonged on a librarian or an eighteenth-century French dandy. A black brocade vest showed off her narrow waist to great effect.

At the base of the stairs, she beckoned Breaker over with a languid wave of her beringed hand. He crossed the parlor with Seraf at his heels.

"Mr. Breaker," Madame Domino greeted in a voice like diamond dust, all glitter and edges. "How lovely to see you again."

Breaker inclined his body—almost a bow—toward her in greeting. Domino enjoyed the appearance of comportment and manners, and he didn't mind obliging her if it made their business dealings more fruitful. But he never forgot that a vixen curled beneath that genteel exterior with sharp teeth ready to rip out his throat.

"You are looking well, Madame."

"I do, don't I?" Gesturing back up the stairs she'd just descended, she asked, "Shall we retire to my parlor to discuss arrangements?"

"Of course, Madame." Breaker eyed the stairs with barely veiled distaste. He would prefer not to aggravate his knee any more than he had to. Still, he couldn't refuse, especially not when Madame Domino watched his every move with an uncomfortable amount of curiosity. He'd be damned if he'd display any weakness in front of a client.

She turned with a subtle flourish; Madame Domino loved nothing more than making an entrance unless she was making an exit. Breaker appreciated the showmanship even as he wanted to roll his eyes at it. The woman understood her clientele and their expectations.

He'd only taken a step when Domino turned, lips pursed in displeasure. She gazed behind him, her eyes narrow beneath her mask. "I am afraid, my dear," she said, flicking a finger at Seraf, "that your compatriot," she hesitated just enough to drive home the insult, "will need to remain here. Infernals are not allowed in my chambers."

Breaker tightened his hold on his cane, knuckles bleached white at the force of his grip. The subtle insult scraped his already sensitive nerves raw. He managed to keep a tight leash on his temper. Domino knew—hell, everyone in New Venice knew—he and Seraf were a matched set, a packaged deal. They'd run together for years. Where one went, the other followed.

Some days he thought it symbiotic. Others, parasitic.

It was a power play. From the sharp intake of breath behind Breaker, Seraf knew it too. He could feel her anger at the thought of being unable to watch his back. As much as he wanted to challenge Domino, this wasn't the time or place for Breaker to correct Domino and the woman knew that too. They needed the job if they hoped to keep Unshriven running.

Seraf's brief touch on his back pulled him out of his thoughts. She jerked her chin at a spot against the wall, her meaning clear: she'd wait for him there. He nodded and turned back to Domino with his most charming smile and gestured toward the stairs. She watched the two of them closely. Breaker knew she'd been hoping for a scene, a protest of some sort, and he happily vexed her any way he could. He would die petty.

Expression as placid as a still lake, he said, "Of course," he told Madame Domino. "Please lead the way."

He followed Domino to her parlor, watching as she locked the door behind them before she made her way over to an elegant glass and metal bar cart set against the wall between bookshelves.

"Sherry?" she asked, pouring herself a measure into a small glass.

"No, thank you." Breaker stood, waiting for her to take her seat before sitting himself. She might pour from the same bottle, but that didn't mean Domino hadn't laced his glass with some drug. There was no harm in being cautious. He lowered himself carefully into the chair, his cane braced against the arm within easy reach.

Domino settled herself, leaning back to gaze at the garnet-colored liquid in her glass. Breaker waited for her to begin. The waiting was part of the game too. She finally placed her glass on the delicate table beside her and folded her hands primly in her lap. "Now to business."

"You mentioned an issue with an employee in your message." Breaker crossed his bad leg atop his good one to give it some support."

"Yes. A few of mine have gone missing. And they're not only employees," Domino corrected. "Infernals."

Breaker's eyebrows rose in surprise. That shouldn't be possible, not with the collars they wore. "Missing Infernals? Do you think they ran off?"

Her jaw tightened as she gritted her teeth. "No, I do not. I have no idea how they managed it. That is why I am hiring you."

"How many Infernals so far?"

"Three." Domino leaned forward, placing her palms on her knees. "At first, I thought it was just a runaway—Tilda was new and high-spirited. Young." She waved her hand around to indicate the girl's flightiness. "But then we couldn't track her. We never found a body. That was very strange, of course." She rolled her shoulders in a semblance of a shrug. "Business was busy. Tilda was an anomaly—that's what I told myself anyway."

"Until another one disappeared."

Breaker watched Domino's hands closely, unease pooling in his guts. People could hide their expressions, especially when wearing a mask. Hands were impossible to hide and gave away things that faces didn't. Domino had threaded her fingers together, but they shook even as she tightened her grip.

"Two this time, one with a unique look." Domino let out a heavy breath. "I made discrete inquiries among those who . . . collect unusual things." She adjusted the set of her mask over her nose as if it was suddenly too tight. "Sometimes they think it acceptable to poach," here her mouth turned down in a moue of distaste, "and I must instruct them in the error of their ways."

"You don't think that's what happened in this case," Breaker guessed.

Domino hummed in answer. "There's been no sign, no word—nothing. The collars should transmit location, vital stats, any number of things by which we could track them." She spread her hands out. "There's been nothing."

"Is it possible they removed their collars in some way?" There were always rumors of Infernals who managed it, but he'd yet to meet one.

She shook her head. "Impossible." Her gaze met Breaker's. Her eyes were a stormy, almost iridescent green, like an unsettled swamp. "The collars are designed to release a massive amount of magical force should an Infernal attempt to remove it without the proper codes. They'd be dead within moments. A signal would alert us to the tampering so we could recover the body."

Breaker breathed slowly. She had adjusted the collars. Initially, the collars didn't kill, only stunned. Domino kept what she owned. Ruthlessly.

"Could they have kept the collar on and somehow disabled the tracking system?" Breaker maintained his relaxed posture, but inside, his mind screamed. He paid close attention to her reactions, gleaning what information he could.

Domino paused, taking a sip of sherry. Breaker waited with a predator's patience. She'd have to tell him eventually if she wanted to hire him. He could afford to wait. She couldn't.

Finally, she sighed, bringing one hand to try and pinch the bridge of her nose, forgetting that she wore a mask that would interfere. Interesting. Domino must be more bothered by these losses than she let on.

"The collars also are infused with a kind of magical charm. When I say it relaxes them, I mean it. The magic gets into their system and adapts. When they don't have the collar on, the charm can't work." She cut her eyes at the crystal decanter on the bar longingly. "After a day, perhaps two at the outside, the Infernal will begin to develop withdrawal systems that will only grow more severe as time passes. Without a follow-up dose, they'd be in agony."

"So you've made them addicts."

Breaker wisely hadn't accepted the drink; had he held it, the shaking of his hands would have betrayed his anger. He understood the need to monitor Infernals and—in some cases —control, but these methods were extreme. When he tried to imagine Seraf collared in conditions like these, bile rose to the back of his mouth.

Clearing his throat, Breaker mastered his emotions. He was here for a job. If he and Seraf finished this one, they'd have some scratch and Unshriven will have made its reputation. He could put up with a bit of moral discomfort.

"Have any of the other establishments like yours reported similar disappearances?" he asked, keeping his voice carefully neutral.

"Do you truly think I'd let my competition know I can't control or protect my assets?" She gave him a mocking smile.

"Of course," Breaker agreed, "but there are always

rumors." He'd been gathering some himself before he'd come to meet with Madame Domino.

He knew that Domino and the other Grand Dames would do anything to maintain their appearance of strength, with weakness ferreted out and punished harshly. Control of the skin trade was hotly contested. But people got bored, and when they got bored, they talked.

Breaker enjoyed listening.

"There's talk of others," she conceded after a few silent moments.

Two Infernals from Mistress Silk's Exotic Emporium had gone missing in the last month. Another one, this one from Magnificent Opal's joint, hadn't been back to his room in a week. There was no word from Tante Marie's place, but that could be because her assets were spelled to silence when not working.

Breaker hummed, coming to a decision. "Three thousand a week, plus expenses." A pittance, yes, for the kind of work he and Seraf would be doing, but he was building a business. He needed a low rate to be competitive, though not too low that he appeared willing to be taken advantage of.

Domino made a clicking noise in the back of her throat that could have been shock or amusement. Breaker sat in his chair, hands folded and resting on his bad knee, waiting for her answer. He gave her his best smile, infused with fae charm. He hoped she wouldn't haggle. He hated haggling. It cheapened the experience for both parties. He'd much rather steal what he wanted than try to bargain someone down.

"Done," she said after a few moments of consideration.

Breaker nodded. "Any others missing? Non-Infernals? Clients? Normies?"

She shook her head, mouth opening for a reply when a heavy knock interrupted her. "Madame, we've got a situation downstairs," a deep voice said from the other side of the door.

Domino leaped to her feet in an eyeblink, unlocking and

flinging open the door to reveal one of the bodyguards from below. He looked at his boss with a sheepish expression like a child caught looking at their mother's lingerie catalogs. Sounds of people shouting and delicate items breaking carried to the second floor. Domino strode through the door, Breaker following as quickly as his bad knee allowed.

Looking down from the stairway, it took him a minute to make sense of the chaos. Clients streamed out the doors—the rest huddled in the corners of the room in fear. A few bodies were on the ground. He had no idea whether they were dead or just unconscious.

Seraf had her knee planted in the middle of some poor Infernal's back. He lay spread out on the floor like a starfish. Three bodyguards had their tasers trained on Seraf, and a fourth held a dosing injector, likely full of the custom sedative reserved only for Infernals.

Seraf hadn't drawn her daggers, but her hair fell about her face in disarray, down from its neat tail. Damn it. He'd assumed she wouldn't be bothered at Purgatorio, but it looked like something had gotten curious about her.

"Stop!" he shouted, leaning heavily on the remaining luck charm before anyone else could do something stupid. Or stupider.

Touching an Infernal without their—or, more specifically, their contract holder's—permission was tantamount to suicide. Breaker hustled down the stairs as quickly as he could.

Madame Domino waited for him at the bottom, a displeased expression curling her painted lips. She stepped over the unconscious bodies with the bearing of a monarch. "Is there a reason why my salon is in such a state?" She stopped beside the bodyguard holding the injector, glaring at Seraf. Breaker stopped beside her.

"If you would be so good as to have your creature release my employee," Domino said to Breaker, mouth twisted in distaste at the scene, "I would be most pleased."

"Seraf?" The Infernal got up and came to stand at his side. "What happened?"

Breaker's eyes followed her hands, noting body language and facial expressions. She signed, using gestures as familiar to him as words. It was a language made up by the two of them, some of it proper ASL, some shortcuts they'd come up with in the years they'd been together. Most of it came from knowing the other as well as they knew themselves.

When Seraf's flashing hands were once again still, Breaker rubbed his forehead. "She says one of your patrons thought she worked here. He refused to take no for an answer. Got another Infernal to proposition her," he pointed to the spread-eagled Infernal at his feet, "and then things got . . . heated?" At Seraf's scowl, he repeated, "Heated." That seemed the safest word to use. He spent the last of the luck charm, putting a bit more emphasis on his words.

Domino gestured for her majordomo. They conferred for a few minutes. Breaker watched the head nods, tried to read the expressions, but their masks hid most of their faces. Clasping his hands on the silver phoenix of his cane, he ground the butt into the exquisite Persian rug beneath his feet. He did not look at Seraf.

Finally, the two broke apart. "Which patron?" Domino's words fell like a guillotine blade.

Seraf glanced at Breaker for approval. When he nodded, she pointed to one of the unmoving bodies at Domino's feet. She jerked her head; one of her bodyguards hoisted the man over his shoulder and took the client upstairs. Domino might apologize profusely to the man when he woke or have him barred for life from her establishment, and he didn't care. He cared about making sure the job was still a go.

"My apologies for the impudence of my asset," she said to Breaker, ignoring Seraf standing beside him. "In future, perhaps it might be better if your," her gaze slid briefly to Seraf then back to him again, "counterpart waited outside?"

Breaker's fingers twitched around the head of his cane. He counted to ten in Latin before he calmed enough to speak. Infernals didn't get apologies. Seraf appeared oblivious to the treatment. She merely watched him and waited for the signal to leave.

At least Domino hadn't canceled the job. "I'll send a contract around," he told her. "And my apologies for the fuss," he added as an afterthought.

Domino's mouth twisted into a sour frown, but she inclined her head in acknowledgment. That bare apology still made Breaker want to wash his mouth out with lye, but she expected one. Domino could have done far worse to them over Seraf's outburst even though her people—and a patron— had been in the wrong. Breaker was responsible for his Infernal's behavior and he would share in the punishment, though his would be considerably less than hers.

They took their leave of Domino and her establishment. Breaker breathed a sigh of relief when they stood once again on the narrow sidewalk.

"Asshole." Seraf's rarely heard, gravel-rough voice at his side made him jump. She raked her disarrayed hair back into a tail, settling the rest over her Infernal eye.

He wanted to be angry with her. She'd endangered their lives and their livelihood but she also had a right to defend herself from unwanted intrusions on her person. Most people didn't think Infernals deserved bodily autonomy, let alone mental. Breaker was in the minority. He couldn't ignore it when that belief became inconvenient.

"Come on," he told her as he set off down the street. "I need Lin to draw up a contract." Fae were meticulous in their wording; that's why so many of them found work as paralegals in contract law firms.

"What's the job?" Seraf signed.

"Some missing Infernals," he signed back. "Just an easy

find and retrieve." He caught a red splash on the side of her shirt. "Yours or theirs?"

"Both," Seraf signed.

With a sigh, Breaker turned in the direction of the closest water taxi stand. "Let's get started."

Chapter 4

Breaker filled Seraf in quickly as they walked, sketching out the job in broad strokes. Her face clouded the more he spoke until she resembled a walking thunderhead. The foul taste of the apology lingered in Breaker's mouth at the insult to both of them.

"The way I see it, we need a list of all missing Infernals. I'd be curious to see if this extends beyond the bordellos. I'll have Lin start checking the PPD lists."

"Kidnappers? Ransom?" Seraf's fingers spelled out her questions.

Breaker shook his head. He wished it would be that easy, but few things in New Venice ever were. "Nothing so high-brow." He met her gaze, holding it for a long moment as he spoke. "Lots of ways for people to go missing, especially if there's no one to notice." He looked pointedly at a deep silvery scar on her upper arm.

She shifted her free hand to cover it, staring at the tips of her boots as if they held the secrets of the universe. When she didn't sign anything, Breaker continued. "We need to canvas the streets and maybe the shelters—anywhere the vulnerable would congregate and see if anyone is missing. They may have an idea of where our Infernals went." He tapped his index finger to his lips. "It might be worth it to pay a visit to Inspector Summoner Barrow and his merry band of Inspecters."

Shortly after the new police outpost opened in New Venice, they'd gained the moniker and the magic users were officially installed on the police payroll. Breaker always enjoyed clever wordplay, and Inspecters sounded more respectable than Freak Squad.

"The cops? Really?" Seraf signed, rolling her eyes.

"They know all sorts of interesting things," he told her, crossing his arms over his chest. "It's getting them to share that's the problem."

"Good morning!" a faintly Cajun voice called, interrupting their conversation.

Breaker stopped and closed his eyes as he recognized the voice. When he opened them again, he saw Seraf waving as Father Lyle approached the two of them. The man wore his collar though he'd opted for a short-sleeve clergy shirt in deference to the heat. He resembled a linebacker more than a priest, a big man with sandy hair sprinkled generously with silver. Breaker remembered when there was no grey in that hair and fewer lines around his faded denim-blue eyes. He still walked with a limp, though.

"Beautiful day, isn't it?" he greeted them cheerily before peering up at the sky.

"Not particularly," Breaker deadpanned, adjusting his glasses. He shook Father Lyle's hand when the priest offered it. "What brings you to our modern-day Sodom on so fine a day?"

The priest grinned, but his eyes were dark and shadowed by the weight of his calling. "Ministering to those in need," he answered.

Breaker couldn't stop his derisive snort. Father Lyle slanted a look of rebuke at him and said, "It wasn't all that long ago that you were one of those, Absalom." He spread his arms wide as if he meant to hug the entire city. "Everyone deserves a hand extended in amity."

Breaker shared a pointed look with Seraf but kept his opinion to himself. Breaker would have thought the man's attitude a put-on if he hadn't known Father Lyle for years. That was the furthest thing from the truth. The priest genuinely cared about people, not just his parishioners. Breaker and Seraf were proof of that.

He gestured to the nearest pleasure palace and scoffed, "Sinners and Infernals too?" He caught Seraf's scowl in his peripheral vision. She began to sign something, but he turned away to address the good Father. "Would have thought you'd given up on this place by now."

Father Lyle frowned at the edge in his voice, but his response was mild. "Especially those. More than just my small flock make their home here and in the Mire, and everyone deserves another chance. The Divine practices outreach to all souls that flounder in the darkness."

The Church of St. John Divine, or the Divine for short, was the only Catholic church remaining within the confines of the Mire. Built decades before Iris hit, the parish had been waning before the cataclysm, but the church managed to eke enough out of its parishioners to remain. Considered a miracle that the building had survived, Lyle believed it to be a sign that the Lord still had His eyes on the area.

Breaker believed that something had its eyes on New Venice, but it had nothing to do with divinity. Still, despite his faithlessness, he had to admit that Father Lyle's soup kitchen had saved him and Seraf from starvation. The priest had taken an interest in the two of them when they lived on the streets, helping them where and when he could.

The man had been the parish priest for the past thirteen years, and he showed no signs of stopping. He still ran the soup kitchen in New Venice. He was a one-man force for good in a city renowned for vice and inequity. Breaker had called it Sodom, and he wasn't far off the mark. Drugs, guns, sex, magic—anything illegal, unstable, or just generally a bad idea was available for a price in New Venice. Depending on the desperation of the peddler, they were available very cheaply too.

"Where are you two off to this fine afternoon?"

Turning, Breaker motioned for the clergyman to join them. Seraf fell into step behind the two of them, watching their backs. "We're working a job," Breaker told him.

"Oh?"

It was a prompt, an invitation to share as he waited in expectant silence. Breaker had seen Father Lyle use it before —a few times on him. Playing along could get him some information, so he answered.

"A couple of missing working Infernals." Tilting his head, he kept his gaze on Father Lyle as he asked, "You hear anything about that?"

Lyle hummed in the back of his throat, one large hand coming up to rub at his jaw. "Not that I recall." His fingers scratched at the stubble on his chin.

"Anybody new been by?" Breaker narrowed his eyes at that answer. The good Father made it a point to learn the names of everyone who came through his church and charities, and he kept his finger on the pulse of his parish and, by extension, the city itself.

"We've had a few homeless come by the kitchen that I hadn't met before, but they weren't in good enough shape to work the pleasure houses." Lyle took out a handkerchief, mopping the droplets of sweat from his face. "None of them looked to be working kin."

Swallowing his frustration, Breaker breathed out sharply

through his nose. He relaxed his wards enough to sense any untruth in the man's words. Seraf's elbow dug into his side. When Breaker glared at her, she scowled back, upper lip curled in distaste. She cut her gaze to Father Lyle and barely shook her head.

Turning his body away from the priest, Breaker signed quickly. "Just because he hasn't lied to us in the past doesn't mean he isn't now."

Seraf's answer came quickly. "He's not lying. It's just you being paranoid again."

He offered her a rude finger gesture which she returned in kind. Then he signed, "Just because I'm paranoid doesn't mean that people are not out to get me."

Her face clouded with confusion as she tried to make sense of his words. Lyle cleared his throat. "In some circles, it is considered rude to communicate in a language not everyone speaks." Then he grinned and clumsily signed, "Good thing I've been learning ASL."

Seraf's eyes grow round. Breaker had been with her so long that they had their particular language of signs and facial expressions beyond even ASL. Few people outside of their admittedly small inner circle bothered even to try to communicate with Seraf in the way she preferred. Most people assumed she was deaf or damaged in some way even after they learned she was neither. Seraf never expected something like this from anyone besides Breaker.

"Gotcha," Father Lyle signed as he met Seraf's gaze with an impish one of his own.

Breaker remembered sitting at a prep table after the soup kitchen had closed as Father Lyle fed them chocolate pudding cups. It was one of the few times he'd acted like a child his age should. It was one of Seraf's few fond memories as well.

Seraf signed rapidly, a faint smile on her face. For her, she might have been jumping up and down with glee.

Breaker couldn't stop his smile. "Good Lord, woman, control yourself. You're in danger of having an emotion."

She paused in her signing to give him the finger before resuming.

Lyle laughed softly. "I believe I'm familiar with that sign."

Breaker gave them a bit of time to practice, knee twinging as he stepped away. The water taxi dock wavered in the heat haze. To pass the time, he called Lin to give him a heads up about the new case, trading half-hearted barbs with him. He leaned more weight on his cane and tried to get his mind back on the job. He didn't care for reminders of the past beyond the ones he already carried with him. Thinking about the soup kitchen meant thinking about the less pleasant years between the death of his father and the founding of Unshriven.

After a few minutes filled with Father Lyle's admonitions for Seraf to slow down, they joined him. Seraf stared pointedly at his knee though she said nothing. Father Lyle sauntered over, barely a hitch in his step. He'd once said the heat agreed with it; Breaker wished he could say the same.

Father Lyle slowed as they approached the water taxi dock. "Any chance I'll see you back at The Divine? It's been a while, Breaker." He sounded wistful. Almost hopeful.

Breaker plastered a false smile across his face. "Too busy, Padre," he said, swinging his cane with a nonchalance he didn't feel. Father Lyle had been one of the few people who'd helped them when they were new to the streets. He'd let them stay in the sanctuary in bad weather; he'd saved meals for them at the soup kitchen; he'd even accepted Seraf once he'd discovered she was an Infernal.

"Never too busy for the Lord," Father Lyle said, a tight smile on his face.

Breaker planted the tip of his cane against the sidewalk, gloved hand clenched around the silver phoenix. He did not want this reminder, this guilt. No one dished it like the

Catholics. "If the Lord needs a word, then the Lord can make an appointment, just like everyone else who wants to see me."

Father Lyle slowly shook his head, lips pressed tight around the words he wanted to voice. Seraf shifted, watching the two of them as if she expected harsh words. She angled to put herself between the two of them, giving Breaker a significant look as she did so. He ignored her.

"Still too sharp for your own good. I've got a proposition for you then," Lyle said in the smooth voice he typically reserved for his homily.

Breaker tensed. He didn't trust that voice, not in a million years. Priests were damn good—pardon his French—at convincing people to do things that went against their wretched nature. Father Lyle was one of the best. Caution made Breaker hesitate, but curiosity urged him to reply, "Go on."

"Would information about any missing Infernals be worth your time?"

Arms crossed in front of his chest, Breaker growled, "Depends on how accurate and useful such information is."

Lyle nodded, but Breaker could see the faint smirk curling at the corners of his mouth. "If I provide you with information that helps you find these poor souls, you come to a Sunday Mass."

Seraf's elbow found his ribs, making him grunt in pain. Did she take a rasp to sharpen them at night? He glared at her. She glared back, her arms now crossed over her chest, jaw set mulishly. Easy for her—she wouldn't have to attend. All she would have to do was sit in the back garden and wait for him to come out. No matter how comfortable Father Lyle was with her, plenty of parishioners never got past an Infernal's demonic origins. They'd drive her out before the first hymn.

He barely refrained from rolling his eyes. "Fine. If you have reasonably useful information that leads to us finding their whereabouts for my client, I will attend Mass. Once."

"It's a deal."

"Fantastic," Breaker snipped. "I would have thought making deals more in line with the Devil, Father."

"I'll do whatever I have to for the chance to save a soul." He winked. "See you in church, Absalom."

Breaker mouth twitched with his suppressed scowl. "Not if I can help it, Padre."

Chapter 5

"Any calls?" Breaker asked Lin when they returned to the office. Seraf disappeared down the stairs to her floor of the brownstone while he waylaid their admin on the floor that housed their office.

Lin lifted his head from his laptop, watching Breaker struggle with a hand placed on his cocked hip. "You look like shit."

"Calls? As in, were there any?"

Lin rolled cloud-grey eyes and scuttled back to his desk, leaving Breaker to haul his dead ass over to the couch in what served as the waiting area. Grumbling about fae assholes who had forgotten such mundane things as simple politeness, Breaker took his time.

Lin shoved a sweating rocks glass into his hand. Without thinking, Breaker downed the contents. He nearly moaned when the sharp tang of the gin and tonic hit his parched throat. He reevaluated his opinion on fae assholes, especially ones that could make a life-changing G&T.

"Never leave me," Breaker breathed, putting the cold glass to his temple.

"You'll have to up my pay." Lin slid behind his desk and tapped at his laptop.

"I was talking to the gin." He took his half-finished cocktail and slumped over to the couch. He dropped into it with all the grace of a building demolition. Leaning his cane against one arm, Breaker used his free hand to haul his leg up onto the cushions to give his knee a rest.

"Hang on. I'll get some ice for your knee." Lin stood and headed for the kitchen.

Breaker watched him go, sipping absently at his drink. Tamlin moved with an otherworldly grace that drew the eye like a bug zapper did moths. And like said bug zapper, he'd likely kill anyone who got too close. The Fae were feared for a reason.

Closing his eyes, Breaker leaned back against the couch and reveled in the air conditioning that dried the sweat that came from navigating New Venice's swamp during the heat of the day. His shirt had glued itself to his skin with the humidity. He needed about another nine showers to feel clean.

Setting his drink on the floor, Breaker allowed his thoughts to drift. Dee's balls, he was tired. Seeing those Infernals in Madame Domino's bordello forced him to consider things he preferred unexamined. He kept trying to imagine Seraf working in a place like that and couldn't. He knew as sure as he knew his real name that she'd never have given in enough to allow it. She'd have broken since she refused to bend.

An insidious voice whispered in the caverns of his skull. The words it spoke had the same inflection as his father's voice when he'd been alive. *How is where she is now any different?*

At least she's not a sex slave.

Hollow laughter boomed like a church bell in his head. *Semantics. You're too smart for that, Tobias. She is bound to you just as surely as if she wore one of those collars. And you hate her for it.*

Fuck. Off.

Fantastic. Now he argued with his dead father inside his head. One step closer to stripping naked and running through the streets painted purple and carrying a honey-baked ham and a giant bag of marshmallows. Though in this city, he would probably just be considered performance art.

The shock of cold against his tender and swollen knee ripped him from his thoughts. He snapped upright with a pained hiss. Lin gave him an unimpressed look and continued to manipulate the bag of ice until it rested across Breaker's leg.

"Bless you," Breaker said before he thought better of it.

Grey eyes narrowed dangerously, turning the shade of storm clouds. "You take that back."

The Fae did not accept thanks, and to offer it was considered terribly rude. While Breaker hadn't explicitly said the words, the meaning was still there. And while Tamlin wasn't full Fae, he'd been with them long enough to dislike it. Not to mention the Fae weren't big on organized religion unless they were the ones worshipped—and maybe not even then.

"You're a dick?" Breaker took off his glasses and rubbed his gummy eyes. He needed a nap. Maybe then his subconscious and Daddy issues would quiet the fuck down.

"Much better." Lin patted Breaker's shoulder before going back to his desk. "So. Messages."

"That is a thing. That you do. Yes." He sighed, shifting the ice pack to a more comfortable and stable position as he slid lower on the couch.

"Payment's wired on the Single White Female job, I scheduled the follow-up for The Other Woman case so you can go over your findings with the wife, and someone called with a curse-breaking job. I've got all the details." Lin tapped a file folder with one long index finger. "What do you think of calling this one The Ring?"

Breaker grimaced at Lin's horrible naming conventions for each of Unshriven's cases. Lin had missed out on movies during his time with the Fae and did his level best to watch everything filmed. Lin named each case they took after a film with a similar theme as a fun way—his words—to show off his growing knowledge. It amused Seraf; it made Breaker want to douse himself in gasoline and light a match.

He made a 'gimme' motion with one hand. "Let's see it then. Anything else?"

"Madame Domino sent over your retainer." He grabbed a pile of notes along with the case file. "I started that records search you asked of me. I'm still trying to get more information on where those collars come from. But I did run out and pick up a couple of Blue Books for you."

"Good work." Breaker accepted the packets from the admin. He flipped through the Blue Book on the top of the pile.

The Blue Books were put together by a private press and released quarterly. Any of the pleasure houses could feature some or all of their rosters for a price to attract clients. It served as clever advertising and allowed customers to find what they wanted without wasting much time.

Pictures of Infernals stared at him from the pages organized by the pleasure house. A brief note listing physical stats and any 'special skills' accompanied each photo. An online version existed, but the printed Blue Books remained popular, especially for the tourists who kept them for souvenirs.

He set aside the Infernal packet and took up Lin's file folder detailing the new case with reluctance. Breaker never ceased to be amazed at the man's attention to detail; the case notes neatly compiled, the transcript of the phone call typed and notated. It seemed straightforward, but Breaker shied away from such easy judgment—such trust in appearances spelled risk and danger. Nothing was ever as simple as it appeared.

Breaker checked the address and calculated how much time he expected a recon to take. He'd need to stop by his preferred magic shop to pick up supplies, and—he checked the time on his phone—he'd need to do it soon. Unlike the voodoo shops that catered to tourists looking for a dark thrill, the shop he frequented kept banker's hours.

"Would you mind getting Seraf for me, Lin?" he asked, hoping to give his pained leg more time to rest. He needed to take a day off and do nothing but lay in bed with his foot propped on pillows, but that didn't put food on their table or keep a roof over their heads. He supposed he could always visit that lawyer who kept sniffing around every couple of years, but Breaker wanted to make it without help from his father's blood money.

Tamlin watched him with narrowed grey eyes as if he could see beneath Breaker's clothes to the throbbing wreck of his knee. After a moment, he rolled his eyes and headed for the stairs. "You're the best," Breaker told the man instead of thanks.

"Duh." He only went about halfway down the stairs before he shouted, "Seraf! Get your arse up here! The boss needs you."

Breaker frowned. He loathed that word—need. He didn't need Seraf for the errand; Breaker just knew that if he didn't take her with him, she'd follow after once she realized he'd left without her. She'd give him the sad eyes that always made him feel like he'd drowned a kitten or run over a puppy twice.

He downed the rest of the G & T, rolling an ice cube in his mouth. Breaker sucked the chilled juniper flavor from its surface, breathing in deeply. His thoughts roiled beneath the calm façade. His skin prickled with a kind of electricity, and Breaker couldn't shake the feeling of standing at a crossroads. He trusted his hard-won instincts. A divergence loomed ahead, one that would force him to make a choice.

Elbows perched on his knees, Breaker pressed the cool glass against his temple once more. His gaze fell on the packet of information on Domino's case. Tonight. He'd look through it in detail tonight.

It took more effort to climb to his feet than Breaker liked to admit, and he had to lean on his cane, bearing down with most of his weight. He passed Lin as the admin crested the stairs. Lin tugged at a lock of hair at his forehead. "Time for a dye job, boss?"

"Hnnn," Breaker grunted as he continued down the stairs.

Seraf stared up at him as he descended, expression inscrutable. The glow of her half-hidden demonic eye warmed the musty entryway. Giving him the once-over, she snorted and looked away. "Not sure how long this will take, so go ahead and lock up, Lin," he called.

"Right-o!" Lin's reply drifted down the stairs.

"Let's do some shopping," Breaker said, gesturing for Seraf to proceed him out the door and into the muggy late afternoon.

THE BIRD OF HERMES APOTHECARY Shop—Breaker appreciated the lack of the pretentious 'pe' at the end—appeared nondescript. The front door displayed the name in a dignified font, nothing too flowy or blocky, nothing to draw the eye. Somehow the store didn't exist unless you knew to look for it specifically. The plain displays in the front windows —glass jars, gardening implements, and drying herbs hung from wooden ceiling racks—and the stacks upon stacks of complicated wards placed over every inch of the shop dissuaded the attention of the curious and uninitiated.

Breaker knew the store like he knew the contents of his medicine cabinet. If Zoyenatova didn't have it on hand, she would find it—if she couldn't get her hands on it, it meant it couldn't be found. Breaker had been a patron since he'd first discovered his magic, but he hadn't visited Yena's shop in person until he'd been on the streets. He hadn't been able to afford to pay for ingredients, so Yena had allowed him to barter his skills for what he needed, component-wise. Mostly it meant he ran her errands and ferried parcels that smelled and moved strangely to the private residences that requested home delivery.

Walking through the front door felt like coming home.

The shop appeared chaotic to the uninitiated. Display shelves and bookcases of various heights and sizes marched in two rows with an aisle down the center until they reached the middle of the store. A heavy stone-topped table anchored the center of the store, usually covered with numerous spell components and herbal concoctions—nothing dangerous. Yena kept the dangerous stuff in the heavily warded work-room in the back. An old iron pot rack hovered above the table, holding strings of herbs and other, more disturbing, items set out to dry.

Shelving units continued once past the table. The cash-out counter was behind the back of the shop, behind which stood the Cupboard. It didn't have an official name as far as Breaker knew. It was a massive wood and glass monstrosity that resembled a china cabinet. It took up much of the back wall behind the counter. The expensive, rare, and difficult-to-locate ingredients sat behind the spelled and locked doors, as were the truly hazardous components.

Tucked within the shop were small, round tables and slim chairs for people to read or wait while Yena filled their orders. Witch glass globes hung in the windows, throwing fractured colors over the floor when the light was bright. The whole place smelled of earthen things and whatever flavor of tea Yena happened to brew that day.

Seraf touched his elbow to get his attention once they'd entered. She pointed to a stool sitting in the corner, out of the way of foot traffic. From the pocket inside her jacket, she pulled out a battered paperback.

"You borrow that from Lin?" Breaker asked, raising his eyebrows in surprise. Lin read voraciously and indiscriminately—as with movies, he had to make up for all the reading he'd missed while in the Fae realm. He trolled used bookstores like some did hookup websites, swiping right on any title that caught his fancy.

Seraf nodded and held up an Agatha Christie novel Breaker hadn't read. "He's lending me all of them," she signed, expression pleased. Tamlin had been on something of a mystery kick lately.

Breaker managed a pinched smile, a burning sensation settling behind his ribs. He shoved his free hand in his pocket. Seraf had every right to have interests separate from him. Breaker didn't expect her to only follow him around like a robot and then store herself in the closet until he needed her again.

Breaker didn't have a right to get angry that she engaged with something without him. Nodding, he limped away, feeling exposed without her presence at his back like always. They'd been linked together for so long that he always struggled not to resent her protectiveness. He didn't understand why he had such a problem with her absence now. Yena's shop was safe for him. He didn't need Seraf at his back.

"What's with the sour face, brat?" came Yena's Eastern-European accented voice from where she held court at her table. She pronounced brat with an 'o' sound in place of the 'ah' sound. Breaker edged around the rows of shelving until he could see her. "Tch. Leg bothering you?" She turned her head to take in the front of the store. "Where's your *chorabash*?"

Zoyenatova stood barely five feet, looking more like a ballerina than a shopkeeper. Though tiny, her presence filled any space like water filled a container. She had the temper of a dragon protecting its hoard, and, like a dragon, her age was indeterminate. She could have been twenty-five or two hundred and twenty-five. Her knowledge suggested she was older than her unlined face appeared. Her black eyes snapped with mirth as though privately laughing at the world.

Breaker leaned his hip against her table, earning him a vicious frown. He stepped back, resorting to resting his weight on his cane. "She's reading at the front."

Yena snorted, pushing away a few strands of black hair that escaped the loose bun she wore. "What do you need?"

"I can get it. You look in the middle of something. I just wanted to say hello."

She turned her attention back to the collection of jars and plasticine bags filled with things best left unsaid. Yena had warded them to ensure none of her essence leaked into the ingredients. She picked up a beaker of what looked like volcanic ash in her gloved hands. "You come for tea sometime, yeah?" she asked as she added it to the pestle.

"When things quiet down, sure."

Breaker understood the polite dismissal and moved away so Yena could focus on her work. Tea would likely never happen, a convenient lie they kept up for each other. Yena had helped him when he and Seraf had nothing, and it made her feel responsible for him in some small way. She didn't like the feeling, and Breaker had no wish to make her uncomfortable, so he didn't press for a date.

He could sense the presence of a few other people scattered about the long, narrow shop. Only real practitioners came to Hermes. Yena's 'don't notice me' wards deterred more novice clientele. Tourists came to New Venice hoping to catch a glimpse of Louisiana voodoo, some hint of Marie Laveau, a tidbit of thrilling darkness before going back to their everyday lives. Hermes bored the shit out of those people, just the way Yena and her clients wanted it. There were lots of other shops in New Orleans and New Venice that hawked their gris-gris bags stuffed with nothing more magical than oregano or their cloying incense sticks that smelled like a fussy white lady's powder room.

Breaker hadn't met with his cursed client yet, but Lin had gotten enough information to give him a place to start. The difficulty in curse-breaking depended entirely on the caster and the victim's belief in it, always assuming the victim was actually cursed. Many people blamed curses for completely normal issues they were having. Lin had already determined the curse to be genuine, saving Breaker some much-needed time.

Something about the missing Infernals case worried him, and he didn't want to risk drawing unwanted attention to himself before he'd figured out exactly what about it bothered him. He didn't intend to tap into his magic unless he had no other choice. Plus, he didn't want his status as a mage of his power to get around—questions might lead to people looking too closely at his past.

Breaker plucked the various sealed plasticine bags filled with the ingredients he might need: blackthorn, agrimony, stinging nettles, rue, cinquefoil, vetiver. He grabbed a packet of chalk, a box of blessed sea salt, and turned down another aisle to get a batch of purified beeswax candles when he collided with someone coming in the opposite direction.

Off-balance, Breaker bit off a blistering curse as his knee twisted painfully. He managed to right himself with a jerk, core muscles tightening with the effort of keeping his balance, and glared at the man in front of him.

"Sorry," the man said as he bent to pick up the book he'd dropped. "Probably should sit my ass down if I want to read rather than wandering around while I do it." He stood up, his eyes level with Breaker's nose.

"It's fine," Breaker managed to bite out around his gritted teeth. He breathed in slowly, letting the pain break over him like a rock in high tide, waiting for it to recede. It meant he got a snootful of the man's scent, too—ash, burning cedar, and something else. He met the man's gaze and barely suppressed a startle at the dark grey, nearly black eyes, and the fiery red circle around the iris.

A summoner. And one affiliated with fire.

Breaker took in the rest of the man, starting with his wild black hair that stuck out in all directions. It fell to the middle of his broad back and made him look like a hedgehog with the way it bristled. Breaker idly wondered at possible sentience.

A pale hand stretched out. Though not nearly as pale as Breaker's, it stood fair and striking against the starkness of his hair. "Dahrian," he said, pronouncing and emphasizing the 'rye' part of the name instead of the typical 'ree."

"Breaker." after a moment of juggling his ingredients, Breaker took the offered hand. He gave it a firm shake and immediately let go.

Dahrian cocked his head. "Odd name."

Breaker hummed in acknowledgment, offering nothing further. He glanced pointedly at the aisle Dahrian blocked. He still needed to get a set of candles.

At least Dahrian recognized the meaning of his look. He turned his head to follow Breaker's gaze then stepped to the side. "If you tell me what you need, I'll grab it for you. You've got your hands full."

"I'll manage."

"Least I can do after colliding with you." He gazed at Breaker for a moment too long, those remarkable eyes narrowing as Dahrian took in his hair.

Breaker viciously smothered any reaction to the inspection. He hated people studying him most days—his coloring made him stand out, as did his magic if he went unshielded. Being an albino had downsides besides the shitty eyesight and the delicate skin. Some practitioners of certain branches of witchcraft and magic thought albino...parts necessary to some of their spells. Yet another reason to hide his identity behind hair dye and tinted glasses.

Dahrian prowled back down the aisle without waiting to see if Breaker followed after him. It took him a moment to clear his head from all of the thoughts racing through it, and then he made his shambling way to the candles.

"Which set did you need?" Dahrian asked, gazing at the rows and rows of rolled beeswax candles. Plain and enchanted, in every shape, size, and color that any customer might need.

"Those," Breaker answered, jerking his chin at the set of four tapers he needed.

Dahrian stretched to reach the second from the highest shelf and snagged the indicated package.

Breaker barely resisted the urge to smirk at the sight of the hedgehog-haired man standing on tiptoes. "Got 'em. And any time you want to stop grinning like a buffoon would be great."

"Shall I call for a step ladder?" Breaker couldn't help but jibe.

"Only if you want me to call for an ambulance," Dahrian shot back, dropping the candles into Breaker's arms with a sniff. "Exciting plans for tonight?"

"Excuse me?" Breaker's eyebrows shot up in surprise.

Dahrian tilted his head, bird-like, and pointed to the stack of items in Breaker's hand. "Curse breaking, right? You've got a pretty wide array to cover just about anything."

Breaker hummed noncommittally as he made his way to the register to pay. The man was knowledgeable, he'd give him that much. Summoners typically didn't dabble in spellwork—they did not need to. The spirit that they held a contract with made it unnecessary. They lent their power to their summoner directly. Most mages didn't need to bother with a summons—they could manipulate the energy fields that ran through every living thing without the help of another being. The odd mage used their summons like a storage battery, but those were rare. Most mages were wary of the price for such help.

Dahrian trailed after him, filling the silence with mindless chatter. Breaker ignored the man, wondering why the summoner couldn't take the hint and leave him alone. Dahrian didn't strike him as a native; Louisiana folk would talk you to death no matter the resting bitchface you cultivated.

When he arrived at the counter, he dumped his purchases while Yena sifted through them with a weather eye. "I'll also need a railroad spike and a graveyard nail."

Dahrian whistled. "You really aren't taking any chances. What kind of whammy they put on you?"

"Not on me," Breaker said as Yena disappeared into the backroom to collect the things he'd requested. "A client."

"You do work for hire?"

"It would appear that I do." He sounded interested, and Breaker didn't want to turn away a potential client. He dug into his pocket, produced a slim business card holder, and cracked it open. Removing one of the cards—black stock, ivory embossing—Breaker held it out to Dahrian between his index and middle finger.

Dahrian took the card from him, his gaze resting on his face briefly before sliding up to linger on Breaker's white roots peeking out through the silver dye job. He glanced down, turning the card over in his hand. "Unshriven, huh?"

"That's right. People have problems. Unshriven provides solutions."

"What kind of problems?" Dahrian tapped the edge of the card against his pointed chin.

"Any kind you can think of," Breaker said, sliding his money over to Yena as she bagged up the purchases. "We're, ah, a morally flexible workplace."

"Take care, Breaker," Yena said as she passed the bag with his purchases over to him. "And be careful."

"Always am," he said with a wave.

Dahrian fell back into step with him as Breaker headed to

the front of the store. "So, what? You're like a private investigator?"

"Something very like, yes," Breaker answered. He reminded himself that this was a potential client, and he should not insult him more than was necessary to get his point across. He was a professional, after all.

"Then you could f—sweet, salty Christ!" Dahrian jerked away, and his hair spread out from his body like porcupine quills as Seraf ghosted up on Breaker's left side. "Where the fuck did she come from?"

Biting back a smirk, Breaker noticed Seraf's curious expression and signed quickly, "Possible client. Best behavior."

"What's wrong with his hair?" she signed back. "Is it alive?"

"Possibly," he signed in return.

"Can I poke it with a stick to find out?" She mimed the poking procedure.

He took on a scolding expression as he signed his answer. "No. Stick poking is right out. Unless they're dead, in which case, poke all you like. They won't care."

He turned back to Dahrian. "This is my business associate, Seraf."

Dharian's eyes narrowed as his gaze jumped from Seraf and back to Breaker. His eyes took on an abstract look, the red around the iris growing brighter. His summons must be talking to him. Dharian nodded his head once, a low hum sliding between closed lips.

Eventually, he muttered a single word. "Infernal." Then he went back to studying them both.

"Yes, she is." Breaker watched the minute movements in Seraf's body, the twitch tension of muscles held still, ready to attack if provoked. All of her considerable attention focused on Dahrian, who withstood it with better grace than he'd exhibited thus far.

"Good evening," Breaker said as he slipped away with

ease. "If you have a need, come by for a consult. We'll see what we can arrange. We're known for being quite discrete."

That wasn't precisely true, but Breaker didn't mind occasionally stretching the truth to gloss over unpleasant things.

"See you around, Unshriven," Dahrian said, saluting Breaker with the card held in his fingers as he and Seraf stepped out of the shop.

Chapter 6

Breaker stood in the living room of the darkened house, his mage sense extended out from him in concentric circles, lapping at the walls of the structure the way water lapped at the shore of a lake. The homeowner had vacated for the evening, leaving Breaker and Seraf to resolve the problem of her curse. Seraf sat with her back against the front door, watching for anything nasty that might come calling while Breaker focused on other, more important things.

He sank deeper into the watery feel of his magical energy, soaking in his affinity before sending it out in another wave. To the non-magical eye, the house appeared in every way typical. As soon as Breaker had stepped inside the place, though, he'd immediately registered the heaviness, the cloying clutch of despair as whatever was present in the house tried to work its will upon him.

Closing his eyes, Breaker took a different tack. He knew there was something wrong with the energy within the house, but he couldn't pinpoint the location. Energy linked everything on the earth, forming a vast web of connections; the threads in this house shifted strangely, out of alignment with the surrounding strands. He had to determine the exact location of whatever was warping the web before he could do anything to correct it.

He sent his mage-sense out once more, this time as a fall of rain, the drops hitting the threads of energy and soaking into them, sliding down and around them like dew on a spider's web. Breaker stepped through the house slowly, steps unerringly avoiding furniture, as he traced the path to his quarry. He lifted his head, eyes still closed, as he registered the knotty tangle of energy, a dark miasma of angry *intent* bound within it.

Gotcha.

When he opened his eyes, Breaker saw an air vent toward the top of the wall. The source of the energy warp sat somewhere behind that vent. He fetched a sturdy chair from the dining table, pulled on his warded gloves, and opened up the vent. Seraf joined him, standing beside the chair to steady it and him should he need it.

Handing the cover to Seraf, Breaker readied a spike of magelight on the tip of his index finger and held it up to the opening. The vent came loose with barely a tug. Breaker took note of the lack of dust and buildup on the metal and made a note to check the other vents to see if they'd likewise been cleaned or if it was just this one. He had his suspicions.

The winding roil of energy set his insides churning. The damp malevolence of the curse sat strongest just a foot inside the air duct. Breaker allowed the dark energy to slide over him, slick as oil, relieved when it found no purchase on his personal wards.

"I'm going to remove it now," he told Seraf, voice pitched for just the two of them despite the empty house. He didn't have to see her nod to know she had.

Taking a deep breath, Breaker reached inside the opening. For a moment, his hands moved slowly, like they were carving through a wall of sludge. Despair crashed into him, whispering bleak nothings inside his head, urging him to give in to the temptation of oblivion and all of its dark delights. Gritting his teeth, Breaker forced his hands to close around the nexus of the curse and yanked it out of the vent.

Seraf's hands on his waist steadied him as he overbalanced, breath blasting out of him like he'd broken the surface of an icy lake after a long dive. Carefully Breaker climbed down from the chair, gloved hands cupping the cursed object. Seraf followed him to the dining table, where he'd laid out all of his components.

"Okay?" she signed as he found the spelled bag to house the curse.

Breaker nodded. He slid the bundle into the bag and drew the strings tight, slapping a ward around it to be safe. Exhaling, he said, "Nasty bit of work, that."

He'd caught a glimpse of teeth and hair when he'd pulled the thing out, for Crowley's sake. Whoever had created the curse must have been unhinged to use such dangerously personal items.

"I'll unravel it at the office, but I think the client is safe enough for now." He trusted the office wards more than the temporary ones he'd placed house so he could work. Without the nexus in her home filling her with suicidal despair, Breaker expected the client to recover quickly.

"Let's purify everything and get out of here."

He intended to find out who was behind such virulence and make them rethink their choices. Painfully.

THE DARK AMBER liquid glittered beneath the dim pendant lights above the bar. Breaker rolled the nicked rocks glass between his palms, staring into his bourbon, neat, like it held answers to questions he hadn't even voiced. He'd left Unshriven, unable to sleep after dismembering the curse nexus. It had taken a great deal of care and energy to unravel the tangled skein of blood magic, virulence, and obsession that had made up that wad of maliciousness, leaving him jittery with concern.

He already had a suspect—the level of anger and possessiveness within the nexus spoke to an obsessive ex. The protective warding he'd laid down at his client's home, strengthened by the chalk markings and various jars of herbs, blood, urine, and glass buried throughout her yard, would keep her safe while Breaker figured out who cast it. All that was left was to trace the threads of the curse marker he'd found tucked away in an air vent back to its source.

Breaker held the glass up in front of one eye before pressing it to his temple with a sigh. When he'd picked apart the tiny bundle of cloth, teeth, and hair, the sour-milk stench of lost love swirled in the air around him like water going down a drain. He shuddered at the remembrance.

Love.

Breaker sipped at his whisky, thoughts a churning mess. Love was a con game, a series of lies people told each other to stay together until the tether between them finally frayed and snapped, and there weren't enough lies to fix it.

He closed his eyes, setting the glass down on the bar with a faint thump. A memory surfaced, more smell than sight to it. The scent of warm, sun-kissed skin and lemons and cream. Hair that smelled of fresh rain. Soft. She'd been so soft.

He'd flung chubby arms around her neck as she tilted her sun hat to shield his sensitive skin. She'd laughed, the sound like butterflies flaring up from their places in the garden, the faint brush of their wings on the air like music. Only the laugh never reached her eyes. She'd always looked so sad.

And then she was gone. The lemon-sun-warm scent of her replaced with embalming fluid and wet earth. The casket had been closed when he'd toddled up to it. Even then, his father had been speaking with someone that mattered more than his dead wife and grieving son. He remembered crying for his mother, his father looking down on him angrily for pulling him away from his business and—

The presence of someone settling at the bar to his right pulled Breaker out of his reverie. A glance to the side revealed Inspector Summoner Errol Barrow seated on the stool beside him, signaling to the bartender with a raised hand. His pompadour drooped after the long day, pieces falling into his eyes. Breaker sighed and went back to studying the alcohol in his glass.

"Fancy seeing you here," Barrow remarked once the bartender set down his order of Balvenie. "I was beginning to think you didn't have vices like the rest of us commoners."

Breaker recognized the faint taunt in the man's tone. Barrow probably didn't even realize he was doing it by now, so ingrained had it become in dealing with the kind of people that called New Venice home. They were insular, didn't trust cops, and often engaged in illicit activities. Cops were bastards by trade; the Inspecters were just a different kind of bastard. Barrow always pushed, even in conversations where he didn't have to, unconsciously trying to ferret out guilt.

Breaker rolled his shoulders with a sigh. He took another sip of his whisky and said nothing, gaze straight ahead.

Barrow rubbed his eyes before letting loose a tired sigh of his own. "Sorry." He sounded like he meant it. "This fucking day, man."

"Hnnn." Tapping his index finger against the bar, he added, "Right there with you."

Barrow knocked back his Balvenie in one go, a shame for a whisky like that. He asked the bartender for another, then indicated Breaker's half-empty glass and raised his eyebrows. Breaker shrugged, and Barrow signaled the bartender to refill that one too.

"Thanks," Breaker said after a moment of contemplation.

It was Barrow's turn to shrug. "I owed you for taking down that Maleficar."

"We're even," Breaker told him, rolling the heavy glass between his palms absently. "You want to take my statement now?"

"Hells no, I'm off the clock." Barrow took a sip of his refill and slumped, shoulders rounding as he hunched over the bar like an ill-tempered gargoyle. His head swiveled around as he searched the bar. "Where's your other half?"

Breaker's fingers clamped around his glass. "Even Infernals need rest," he told Barrow, keeping his voice level.

No need to tell Barrow that he'd gone out without telling Seraf. He'd cultivated the idea that they were a matched set; where one went, so too did the other. It had been for their protection when they were living rough.

Barrow raised his eyebrows but otherwise let it go. Breaker didn't know what had crawled up his back. His thoughts were twisted things, his mind a forest of shadowy glades and grasping branches that made navigating it painful. The visit to Madame Domino's hadn't set well with him. He couldn't understand why that would be. He was familiar with the pleasure palaces—he'd been in almost all of them for one reason or another. And the case was nothing special—a lot of Infernals went missing.

The image of Domino's new collar floated in his mind, along with all the Infernals wearing them. Bile crawled up his throat, and for a moment, Breaker thought he was going to be sick all over the bar.

His gaze slipped to the right. Barrow sipped on his Balvenie while staring moodily into the middle distance. Now was as good a time as any to get information. Putting thoughts of Seraf out of his head, Breaker cleared his throat.

"You know anything about those special collars some Houses have been putting on their Infernals?"

Barrow set his glass down and leaned into Breaker's space, eyes narrowed. Breaker met his gaze with a flat one of his own, grateful for the light tinting of his spectacles' lenses that made it difficult to discern the exact color of his eyes, especially in the low light of the bar. The inspector's eyes flashed amber as his summons—an air elemental if Breaker recalled right—came to the fore.

"Special? Illegal?" he asked.

Breaker snorted and took a sip of his whisky. "Does it matter? They're on Infernals, so I don't think anyone is likely to complain on their behalf. They're nasty pieces of work though—the collars, I mean." He leaned his elbow on the bar, twisting in his seat so he could look at Barrow head-on.

Barrow shifted, and Breaker could sense the man's internal struggle to keep on enjoying his drink and ignore the threat to those in his precinct or step back into his I.S. shoes. "Tell me about them," he prompted, his voice gruff as the cop in him won.

Breaker did, detailing everything Madame Domino had told him. When Breaker finished, Barrow wore an unpleasant frown. His eyes were practically molten gold. He knocked back the rest of his drink with practiced ease and ran a hand down his face.

"You believe me?" Breaker couldn't help but ask.

Barrow's head came up sharply, dark hair falling across his golden eyes. "Saints above, I wish I didn't."

Breaker imagined he'd seen a lot of abused Infernals in his position, and whether he liked them or not, it had to get to him. The bags beneath the man's eyes had deepened in the time he'd been at the bar. Breaker almost pitied him—almost. Then he remembered how the PPD had treated him the one time he'd gone to them, back when he still believed cops could make a difference. Barrow had chosen his profession. He didn't get to bitch about doing his damned job.

"Look," Breaker said, resting his head on his palm, his elbow still braced on the bar. "A couple of Infernals have gone missing. A client hired me to find them, but I thought you should know. In case you run across them first. They could be in a bad way if what Domino said is true about how those collars operate."

"And also because you hope I'll share whatever I might find with you?" Barrow gave him a disdainful look. "This ain't my first rodeo, Unshriven. I know how quid pro quo works." He pointed a finger at Breaker's nose. Breaker had to fight not to go cross-eyed looking at it, instead keeping his gaze on the detective's eyes.

"I expect you'll do the same." It wasn't a request.

"Of course," Breaker said. He polished off his whisky, laid several bills down on the bar before sliding from his chair. "Always a pleasure, Inspector Barrow."

As he reached for his cane, Barrow stopped him with a hand on his wrist. When Breaker looked up, Barrow wore a haunted expression. "You don't think they're still alive, do you?"

Breaker's pulse thundered in his ears, fingers twitching with the need to reach out for his magic. The urge to drown all of New Venice, finishing what nature had started, was almost too much to resist. Seraf's twelve-year-old face flashed in his memory—the day they'd first met. She'd been small for her age and she didn't know when her actual birthday was, so Breaker was pretty sure she'd lied her way into an extra year. The thought of her in a collar at that age, of what it would have done to her…he shuddered.

He hadn't solved the case yet, but he knew whatever had happened to those Infernals was wrong. "I wouldn't lay any bets on it, but," Breaker gave him a crooked grin, mostly malice, "hope springs Infernal."

<hr>

Chapter 7

<hr>

Breaker slept in, rousing near noon to the smell of cooking. He levered himself up into a sitting position, dragging hands through his freshly dyed hair and yawned luxuriantly. A decent night's work, a few drinks at the bar, and a hot shower were as close to Heaven as he was likely to get, especially since he didn't believe in the place. He'd fallen into a thankfully dreamless sleep as soon as his head hit the pillow.

Slipping a robe over his worn t-shirt and pajama pants, Breaker left his cane behind and went in search of the food that smelled so good.

Seraf stood at the stove, stirring something in a saucepan. Thick crab cakes sizzled in a frying pan alongside bright green asparagus spears. Another pan held something Breaker couldn't see. A battered book sat open on the counter—an old Joy of Cooking that he remembered Seraf fishing out of the trash from a used bookstore in the city. He inhaled deeply, relishing the scents that filled the kitchen. They didn't get much chance to cook these days.

She turned, waving him closer. "Can you get the plates out?" she signed. "It's almost ready." She went back to stirring.

Breaker nodded, leaning over to snag two plates from the

cabinet to the right of her head. As he did so, he saw eggs poaching in gently simmering water. Glancing over her shoulder, he saw the sauce resembled a hollandaise. "Eggs benedict?"

Seraf scrunched her nose. "Sort of," she signed.

Breaker set down the plates and made himself useful by setting out the utensils on the small table. How long had it been since they'd had an actual meal together? He couldn't remember the last time one of them cooked for the other.

A to-go cup from Witches' Brew sat at his spot. He lifted off the lid and smelled his usual order. "You went to get coffee too?"

Seraf shrugged, still stirring the hollandaise with relentless attention. "You were sleeping. I needed to move."

"Any problems?" Seraf was a known quantity in the Mire, but she was still Infernal. With Breaker at her side, she could go—if not unremarked then at least unmolested—most places. When she went out alone, there was always the risk of trouble. She did not wear any obvious signs of a 'controlled' Infernal—no collars, cuffs, spelled tattoos, or warding glyphs inked onto her forehead. She wore nothing that would make the non-magical populace feel better. It didn't matter that Infernals were often at least half-human; people still focused on their more demonic attributes.

Her shoulders bunched beneath the thin fabric of her t-shirt. Breaker scowled. Someone said something to her. Instead of explaining it to him, Seraf shrugged. "It's fine."

Breaker couldn't help but snort. "How many?"

She held up three fingers, hyper-focused on her sauce. Breaker frowned, crossing his arms over his chest. There was nothing he could do about it now, but his impotent anger was harder to ignore. Seraf had learned to ignore the casual harassment that came with being an Infernal long ago, and she could extricate herself from most any situation if she had to, but she shouldn't have to.

"Did you have to--,"

Shaking her head, Seraf began plating the food. "Just comments," she said in her nightmare voice before turning around with two filled plates.

"Wow." Crab cakes rested on perfectly toasted English muffins, topped with asparagus, a poached egg, and then drizzled in hollandaise sauce. "We had all this in the fridge?"

Seraf rolled her eyes, took her plate to the table, and sat down. Picking up her fork, she gestured to the other empty seat and waited. Breaker joined her, still staring in a kind of subdued awe at the food on his plate.

"Is this," he began, then stopped, a sharp pang slicing through his chest.

"The cook used to make it," Seraf signed. "I remembered him making it for special breakfasts."

Breaker nodded and tapped his fork with his index finger. Crabcake benedict had been his father's favorite brunch, and the cook had made it often on the weekends. The few times he'd been forced to eat with his father, Breaker had hated it. Seraf knew that.

"I remember wishing I could have had a bagel," he said with a faint smile.

"You were in training."

"Okay, two bagels." When Seraf gave him a long-suffering glance, he picked up his fork and cut off a piece of the crab cake and English muffin. "Why?"

Seraf put her fork down so she could sign. "Because I thought you would like it, and it sounded delicious. I remember how good it smelled when the cook made it. I wanted to try it."

Of course, she wouldn't have been allowed to eat the same things he and his father did. She was the help—actually less than the help. They, at least, got paid for their work. He took a sip of his coffee, chest tight with guilt.

"Just because your bastard of a father liked something

doesn't mean you can't enjoy it too," Seraf continued. She nudged his plate with her knife. "Try it."

She had a point. It was stupid to avoid good food just because his father was a wanker of the first order. Breaker cut into the food on his plate, noting that Seraf poached the eggs perfectly. He managed to get a bit of everything on his fork and shoveled it into his mouth.

Seraf had outdone herself. He might have moaned after the first bite--he'd never tasted anything so good. He had no idea she was capable of something like this; he knew she'd been teaching herself to cook whenever she had the chance over the years, but this dish took skill beyond the typical throw everything into a pot and call it soup which was all he knew how to do. The sauce was bright and tangy, contrasting nicely with the crab's richness and the toasted muffin's earthiness. Before he was even aware of it, he'd devoured the whole thing and stared mournfully at his empty plate.

"You liked?" Seraf signed, a satisfied smirk on her lips. She still had half her Benedict to go. He debated reaching over and swapping plates but figured she'd stab his hand with her fork.

Breaker sat up straighter with a sniff, tilting his chin in the air. "I still prefer bagels."

"Asshole."

He laughed, feeling lighter than he had in days. It gave him the courage to ask the question that had been on his mind since they'd left Purgatorio. "You ever think about those Infernals? In the collars?"

Her face did that thing where all expression faded until it looked like she was wearing a mask. Her body stiffened, muscles taut beneath the skin, almost like she expected an attack.

"No." Her hands moved slowly, different from the rapid flutter of her typical signing.

Then she shoved her plate at him, giving him the uneaten

half of her breakfast. When Breaker glanced back to her face, it had relaxed back into her regular neutral expression, and he gave her a smile of thanks to hide his unease.

She was lying.

⚠

"WHERE NOW?" Seraf signed as Breaker took a moment to clean his glasses. They'd swung by Opulence to see what they could unearth and come up with nothing good. One missing Infernal was presumed to have run off with a client's help. Opulence was not using Domino's collars yet, but rumors that the owner was considering them made the staff uneasy.

Breaker stopped. Their usual informants had been strangely uninformed about the missing Infernals, though at least he'd gotten the names of two pleasure palaces with disappearances in the last week or so. Neither of them approached the ostentation of Purgatorio; one was an outright dive.

"Taboo. Then we'll hit Mistress Silk's, maybe sniff around the higher-end places."

Seraf rolled her eyes, lip curling in derision. Taboo was one of the worst of New Venice's cat houses—they treated their Infernals poorly, and their testing for diseases was sketchy at best. They catered to the stingiest skinflint customers, offering cheap drinks and even cheaper prostitutes. Rough trade typically ended up there—not real BDSM, just the kind of people who liked to knock others around—and Taboo quickly wore out their employees.

Like most lower rent places, it resided on the first street inside New Venice, within an easy walk of the first water taxi station. Women, men, and Infernals danced in the windows of the upper floors at all hours, casting aside clothing once the sun set. A barker competed with buskers and the din of the crowd on the partially flooded sidewalk to hawk Taboo's wares, practically pulling in tourists and natives alike seeking adventure and an eventual course of antibiotics.

During the day, the lurid paint and signs looked garish against the hazy blue sky. Even though the traffic was light, Breaker knew the pleasure palace never truly closed. He rapped his cane on the door once to announce his presence before opening it.

The stale smell of unwashed bodies, sex, and old incense hit him in the face like a wet slap. He recoiled almost immediately before he mastered himself, throwing a look at Seraf. She wore a sour expression, her eyes narrowing as she scanned the dark hallway.

"Clear," she signed.

Breaker cleared his throat, doing his best not to breathe through his nose. Other smells assaulted him: urine, rotting food, the sick scent of vomit, and old liquor, but he was prepared now. The stench was less intrusive at night, but it was unbearably intense during the day. He walked quickly, twirling his cane to avoid putting the end in something squishy. Seraf stood at his back, closer than usual.

A heavyset man, muscle bleeding to fat, confronted him when he stepped into what passed for a parlor in Taboo. He held out his hand for the "entry" fee. Breaker dropped more than enough to cover him and Seraf before moving inside. Madame Domino's place was all grace, elegance, and impeccable decorating; Taboo held a stage meant to show the merchandise, a few rickety tables and chairs that looked in danger of collapsing from a good sneeze, and a dingy bar off to one side.

Breaker scanned the room. There were no signs of any of the employees, let alone Infernals.

"Only the bar is open now," the lone bartender called in a gruff voice. "What's your poison?"

Breaker slipped his hands behind his back, signing for Seraf to have a look around. The thought of alcohol made him queasy. His stomach wasn't game for day drinking in a place where he could see just how dirty the glasses were.

"Gin," Breaker said, knowing he had to offer something to remain in the bartender's good graces. Plus, it kept the man's attention firmly on him, giving Seraf a chance to snoop.

"Thirteen." The man made a noncommittal noise and snagged a nearly clean rocks glass beneath the bar. He slopped a pour of gin into it, set it on the chipped, chill-spell enhanced bar, and then slid it over to Breaker.

Fair enough. Breaker left the drink where it was and reached into his pocket to pull out two twenties. He slid one across the bar, keeping the other in front of him. "Keep the change. For your trouble."

The bartender deftly pocketed the money, then leaned against the counter, weight on one hand. Breaker tapped the top of the bar with a fingertip, drawing the man's eye. That would give Seraf a chance to fade into shadow and look around the rooms used by the customers.

"Why's the stage dark?"

"Owner decided the talent needed a day off." He shrugged as if he didn't care.

Breaker kept his expression blandly neutral while his brain raced. He knew enough of Taboo's owner, a man by the name of Rossum, to know that shuttering the brothel even for a day was not something he'd ever do unless forced by outside circumstances. Since New Venice operated outside of the laws of New Orleans proper, the routine inspection and violation laws didn't apply to Taboo, and hefty bribes kept any legal crusader's curiosity in check.

"Awful nice of him," Breaker said, moistening his lips with the drink. He should have specified top-shelf—this rotgut was nigh undrinkable. "How come you didn't get the day?"

"I don't fuck for money," the bartender snarled. "Not like those demons." He gave Breaker a challenging look like he

was calling Breaker out for coming into a brothel that special-
ized in that very thing. Breaker ignored it.

"Still, it's a shame that you have to work when they get to
laze around," Breaker commiserated. "Doesn't look like your
boss would lose that much money if he cut you loose for the
day." He made a point of looking around. "Hell, it's so slow,
he could probably handle the bar with no problems."

The bartender sneered. "Rossum'd be useless behind the
bar."

"I hear that." Breaker tipped the drink back to his lips,
only sipping the bare minimum.

"Why'd you come in here if not to fuck one of the
animals?" The bartender didn't sound like he wanted to start a
fight, more like he was genuinely curious.

Breaker shrugged, glass held in his hand. "Personally, I
wouldn't fuck one with someone else's dick." He paused while
the bartender chortled in agreement. "I'm only in town for a
few days, and everyone told me I needed to stop by New
Venice and take in the sights. You were the closest to the
dock." He gestured toward the back door. "The sign had a
picture of an Infernal with scales and claws. I thought he'd
make for a good souvenir photo. Give the guys in the office a
laugh."

"Even if we were open, you wouldn't see Orion. Haven't
seen him around for a few days. Maybe Rossum sold him to
another club."

"Ah well, too bad." Breaker shook his head and set his
drink on the bar. He slipped the twenty back in his pocket. No
need to pay for confirmation of information he already had,
and he didn't want this man remembering him. "Thanks for
the drink."

As Breaker climbed to his feet, the barman leaned over.
"If you want to see the real freaks, you'll check out the fights."

"Fights?" Breaker feigned ignorance. He knew all about
the underground Infernal fighting rings though he'd never

attended one. He didn't want Seraf within a hundred yards of them, and she'd never agree to him going alone. If she was uncomfortable at Purgatorio, he couldn't imagine what she'd feel when watching other Infernals kill each other for an audience betting on the outcome.

The bartender nodded. When he spoke again, his voice was hushed. "Sometimes old whores end up in the ring. They're not good for much else."

"Sure," Breaker agreed and wanted to take a shower with steel wool to get the feeling of disloyalty off him. His skin crawled having to profess solidarity with someone who thought that way—whatever lay between him and Seraf, it wasn't hard to imagine her in a similar situation if things hadn't turned out as they had. He never thought he'd be grateful for his father. Whatever else he'd done, at least he'd brought Seraf into their home where she had a semblance of safety. One of the few good things to come from his father's decisions.

There but for the grace of . . . something and all that drivel. Breaker was certain God had little to do with it.

He listened as the barman gave him directions on finding those in charge of the fights in an alley behind a cabaret called Demi-monde. Someone would show up with a ticket. Breaker took his leave.

It was a relief to step outside into the humid sunlight of late afternoon, even with the oppressive stench. It pressed in on Breaker from all sides, an almost palpable rotting caress. Yet it was still preferable to the inside of Taboo.

Breaker tried to ignore the dull pounding of his bad knee, the constant ache setting his teeth on edge. He strolled over to an iron park bench a block deeper into New Venice. The spicy smell of gumbo, sausage, and onion from a nearby food stall filled his nose, and he leaned his head back to rest.

He raised his head at a flash of light in his periphery, automatically reaching for the water of the canal. The light flashed again. Breaker relaxed as he caught sight of the source. An Infernal hurried down a side street with skin faceted like gemstones. The sunlight reflected off what was not covered by her clothes, breaking into colors like light through a prism. He mentally retraced her path—it was likely she'd come from Taboo. He stood up to follow her.

A strange ripple in the energy lines and an icy breeze brought his head up. Seraf was back. He turned in time to see her brace herself with her hands on her knees before she pushed forward to join him in front of the bench.

"What did you find out?" he asked, still following the jeweled Infernal with his gaze and allowing Seraf the privacy to pull herself back together.

She plopped down on the bench in a graceless sprawl. Breaker waited until the other Infernal was out of sight before joining her. He crossed his legs at the knee and primly rested the cane across them as he waited.

Turning to him, she launched into signing. She scowled as her fingers flickered almost too fast for him to read. "Calm down," he said, catching two of her fingers. Seraf stilled, her body so tense he feared she'd snap in two. She looked pointedly at the fingers caught in his grip. Breaker realized his mistake.

Immediately he let her go. "I want to understand," he explained by way of apology for what amounted to gagging her.

After a moment and a baleful glare, she closed her eyes and exhaled slowly. When she opened them again, she began to sign slower.

Breaker's heart plummeted into his guts as Seraf revealed what she'd seen.

"They're closed because Rossum is putting new collars on all of them," Seraf signed. "They look a lot like the ones Domino uses at Purgatorio to keep her Infernals in line. The one I talked to couldn't tell me much about them other than that they were new and that Rossum had ordered them right after Orion went missing."

"Seems a lot of trouble to go through considering the way he treats his people," Breaker mused. Why bother with expensive hardware—and those collars weren't cheap—when you didn't care what happened to the merchandise wearing it?

"Orion was their big draw," Seraf signed with a frown.

"That says more about the people who frequented the place than I ever wanted to know," Breaker told her.

"Rossum didn't like losing money. Pia said he wanted to make sure it didn't happen again."

Breaker bobbed his good knee up and down to quell the antsy feeling growing inside. Something didn't make sense—several somethings. "Did this Pia have any ideas where Orion might have gone? Was he meeting with someone?" Breaker knew it was a long shot, but he had to ask.

Seraf shook her head. "One day he was there, the next. . ." She made a 'poof' motion with her hands.

Grinding the tip of his cane into the ground, Breaker considered. Taboo had been all but a bust. "Anything else?"

"Pia did say that Orion had a few regulars, but he'd turned away most of them the week before he disappeared."

"Most, but not all?" Breaker raised an eyebrow.

"I asked," Seraf signed. "He never gave names."

"No surprise there." He imagined Infernals would be circumspect with their client list, especially their regulars. Fear of poaching meant secrecy was common. He stood with a pained groan as his knee creaked alarmingly.

"Let's get over to Silk's before the party crowds come out to play," he said. "If we can find a common thread between them, that would be a place to start."

Seraf followed him as he set off at a leisurely pace that mostly hid his limp. Sweat pooled at the small of his back beneath the waistband of his pants. A stagnant breeze barely stirred the ends of his hair. "How much did it cost you?"

Seraf ducked her head. Breaker waited, side-eyeing her. It surprised him when she spoke. Her Infernal vocal cords made human speech difficult. Hearing her was always a shock, the grating rumble of her voice akin to rocks slamming against each other. Still, her voice held power, and something in it touched a deep place inside him that quailed at the sound.

"Donation. Wages of Sin."

Breaker said nothing. He hadn't heard of Wages of Sin, whatever that was. A new outreach? A church or halfway house? Something more sinister? He made a mental note to have Tamlin dig to see what he could find out about it.

"Bartender have anything to say?" she signed.

Breaker filled Seraf in on the conversation, noticing how her shoulders rounded when he spoke about the fight lead. "Don't worry. It's only as a last resort," he assured her. She wrinkled her brow and shoved her hands in her pockets as they walked.

They passed casinos, strip clubs, and Infernal burlesque joints, a few questionable massage parlors, moneylenders, bodegas, and several bail bondsmen offices. Threaded throughout all of these, like pearls on silk string, were voodoo and magic shops, promising love, luck, and lust in various measures. Tarot readers hawked from canoes tethered to the street, avoiding the need for a permit. The heat of the late afternoon sun kept all but the most determined of pleasure-seekers inside, where air conditioning and magic kept the temperatures bearable.

Breaker stopped suddenly, a prickling of unease sliding down his neck. He turned his head, staring first down the side streets before looking up. He saw nothing but that didn't mean someone wasn't watching. Closing his eyes, Breaker knelt and pretended to tie his shoe.

He pressed the fingertips of his right hand to the sidewalk, whispered the words of a spell to focus his will, and sent his magical sense flooding out in a slow wave to see if he could pinpoint who might be spying.

There they were—moving away from their location at a fast clip. The presence was muted and warded. All Breaker could sense was an aura of green, like kudzu vines choking out everything beneath it. He didn't recognize who the person watching them might be. There was something, though. A strange flicker, like a lick of flame that signaled a greater conflagration about to erupt. Breaker didn't understand it, but he memorized the feel of it.

Seraf tapped him on the shoulder. "Breaker? Everything all right?" She cocked her head, gazing at his perfectly tied shoes.

Breaker slowly rose to stand, brushing his hand on the leg of his pants. "Just fine," he told her, not wanting to worry her with news of someone able to hide their magical signature from him. He straightened his jacket, gave her his best rakish smile, and said, "Mistress Silk awaits."

Chapter 8

Mistress Silk's Exotic Emporium was only two streets away from the opulence of Purgatorio, but the difference between the two was remarkable. Purgatorio tried—and succeeded at antebellum charm and all that entailed—while The Emporium doubled down on its name. Glimmerweave fabric banners —magically treated cloth that teased and delighted the eye—fluttered in the thick air, suspended from poles so that the entrance resembled a tent. An onion dome capped the top of the building, and the arched upper windows reminded him of the architecture in old Sinbad movies.

Stepping inside, Breaker took a moment to stare. It was like stepping into A Thousand and One Nights. Infernals, along with the few human women and men present, lounged on vibrantly colored cushions wearing sheer silks that barely covered their assets. Clients sat with them, a few smoking from large, ornate glass pipes set in the center of the low tables strewn throughout the main room. Two winding staircases led to the upper floors. Glass and brass lanterns hung from the ceiling at different heights, illuminating the large room. The smell of incense, tobacco, and human lust hung like a haze over all of it.

A few more customers filtered in behind them, making their way inside. Breaker saw only one or two unoccupied workers. Several customers stood at the bar, sipping drinks and scanning the crowd. A few more spoke with an attractive older Indonesian man at an intricately carved host stand.

Seraf pulled at his shoulder when he took a step. "I'm staying with you," she signed.

Breaker nodded. After what happened in Purgatorio, that seemed the safest bet to avoid unpleasantness. They'd been lucky that he knew Madame Domino—they were acquaintances of longstanding—and he'd sucked down a fae charm boost to boot. Breaker had only met Mistress Silk twice before, and tonight he was not augmented with fae magic. She was unlikely to give them a pass based on an established working relationship.

"Good evening," the concierge greeted Breaker as he approached, a customer-friendly smile plastered on his handsome face. "How may The Emporium entertain you this evening?"

"I hate to inconvenience your Mistress, but Madame Domino suggested I come by." Breaker watched the man's eyes narrow at the mention of Silk's rival. He lowered his voice and leaned in closer, noticing that the concierge's eyes were a stunning shade of deepest brown flecked with iridescent green. An earth summoner, maybe? "It's about her missing Infernal."

The man's fingers dug into the edge of the ornately carved stand so hard Breaker swore he heard the crack of delicate wood snapping. "Who might I say is calling?"

"Absalom Breaker and Seraf of Unshriven." Breaker stepped back, placing both hands on the top of his cane.

A sardonic eyebrow rose as the man's gaze swept over the two of them. Breaker held himself tall and did not look away.

"Very well," the concierge said after a long moment of staring. He raised his hand and beckoned with two fingers. A distinguished younger man wearing a conservative suit appeared and took the concierge's place. Breaker held in a flinch; he hadn't felt anyone using magic, but that didn't mean they hadn't. His paranoia sent his heartbeat galloping. Seraf stood impassively behind and to his right, making him feel safer.

"This way," the concierge instructed. Breaker saw the flash of a brace of throwing knives sheathed in a belt around his waist when he turned. He pointed a finger at it. Seraf nodded.

The man led them down a narrow hallway, far more brightly lit than the rest of the establishment. Breaker could feel the enchantments laid on the place as his magic simmered and bubbled beneath his skin. The sensation of ants crawling over his body made him want to shake like a dog shedding water. He checked his personal warding as he walked beside the concierge.

"Unshriven, eh?" A challenging smirk crossed the concierge's lips. "I've heard of you. Arcane investigators?"

"Something like that, yes." Breaker watched the man from the corner of his eye. He wasn't as tall as Breaker, but he was well-made, strong and lean and at ease in his body.

"Hmph."

"Your name?" Breaker asked.

"Chakrii."

"A pleasure."

Chakrii frowned, sweeping Breaker with another assessing look that easily conveyed just how unimpressed he was. "That remains to be seen."

Breaker smiled, tight-lipped. "Give me a chance. I might surprise you." He could feel Seraf's eyeroll.

"Doubtful." Chakrii's lip curled.

Seraf's low chuckle pulled Chakrii's attention away from Breaker. "Your partner agrees with m—" He broke off as he noticed the swirling amber of her Infernal eye. Breaker watched his gaze flicker from Seraf's face to her neck. His expression tightened at what he didn't find.

Chakrii moved quickly, too quickly for an ordinary human. One of the throwing knives was in his hand, and he swept his arm forward to catch Seraf unaware. She was ready, her hand slamming into his wrist and holding it tight, her other arm braced behind it to keep him from shoving the knife into her eye.

Breaker shoved his cane between them.

Neither moved. Seraf and Chakrii glared at each other, naked blade between them. Chakrii's free hand crept to the small of his back, trying to retrieve another knife.

"Ah ah ah," Breaker scolded, smacking his hand. "And we were getting on so well too. I'd hate to get blood all over the walls."

"Try," Chakrii gritted out from between teeth clenched tight with strain.

Breaker sighed. Nothing for it now. He pulled on the water in the air and imbued it with magical lines of force, molding it with his energy to fashion a kind of liquid prison. He sent it spinning toward Chakrii, watching with a pleased smirk as it settled around the man. The water bars swirled and tightened around him, creating a private birdcage.

Slowly Breaker lowered the cane, gesturing for Seraf to step back from Chakrii. She did so without hesitation. Breaker saw Chakrii's eyes widen as he tried to push against the spell that held him still and bury the knife in her eye.

"She's uncollared!" he snarled, the veins on his neck standing out from the force he used to try and escape the spell. "You endanger everyone in this place, no matter how powerful you are, mage!"

"You think I'm powerful from a simple hold spell?" Breaker preened. "That's sweet."

"Stop flirting," Seraf growled with a disgusted look, "you vain thing."

"I agree with your partner," came a husky voice from farther down the hall. "Do stop flirting with my assistant and release him."

Breaker turned to greet Mistress Silk. She stood silhouetted in the doorway, long dark hair flowing over broad shoulders and down her back. She wore a tuxedo jacket without a shirt beneath it that revealed the gentle curve of her breasts, black cigarette pants, and a pair of bottle-green stilettos that added several inches to her already six-foot-plus height.

"Apologies," he said, grounding the tip of his cane and bowing slightly while he let the hold spell drop. "I was trying to keep the blood spatter to a minimum."

"Noted." She shook her head, then smiled. "Come inside, the pair of you."

Chakrii stepped past Breaker and joined Silk in the doorway. She glanced at him with an expression of fond amusement.

"I assure you I'll be quite safe," she told him.

"If you think I'm leaving you alone with an uncollared Infernal, you have taken leave of your senses. What do you think you'll do—throw a shoe at her?" Chakrii gestured at Silk's feet.

"If her aim is good enough, she could take out an eye," Breaker began, only to receive a snarl from Silk's assistant. Breaker raised his hands in surrender.

"I wouldn't throw these anyway," Silk said. "Do you have any idea how much they cost?" Not waiting for an answer, she waved everyone through the doorway.

As Breaker passed, Silk caught his elbow. "You have five minutes, Unshriven," she warned.

Breaker's eyes were level with her chin. He noted the stubborn jut of her jaw and the simmering anger in her heavily lashed green eyes. The faint jut of her Adam's apple bobbed as she swallowed.

"Understood. I'll be brief."

She dropped his arm and stalked deeper into her reception area. Silk sat in a wine-red leather wingback chair, Chakrii standing behind her. Breaker carefully lowered himself onto an antique velvet sofa. Seraf mirrored Chakrii, guarding Breaker's back. He set his cane beside him and rested his hands on his ankle where it crossed his knee.

"Word on the street is you're missing an Infernal or two," he said, not wasting any time. When Silk simply stared at him, waiting, he continued. "You're not the only one."

She pursed her lips. "I know."

"I've been hired to find out what happened to some of them."

"And you've come to offer your services to me?" Silk leaned forward in her chair, elbow resting on her knee. Her nails were painted the same bottle-green shade as her shoes. "I'm afraid you're was—"

"I've come for information. I'm not looking for another client at the moment." Breaker relaxed until he hit the back of the couch. "I am willing to share my findings should I run across your missing Infernal if you'd answer a few questions for me."

"Perhaps I want the Infernal to stay gone?"

Breaker adjusted his glasses. "You don't. If you did, your man there wouldn't be so jumpy about an uncollared Infernal roaming around. You want him back because that's the only way you know you'll be safe." It was a guess, but Breaker was confident in it.

A tap on his shoulder. When he turned his head, Seraf signed to him.

"It's rude to use a different language in front of people who don't speak it," Silk noted casually, but her gaze devoured Seraf's fingers.

Breaker held up a hand. "Seraf was just reminding me of how this is a courtesy visit, as one professional to another.

We'd prefer your permission to speak with your staff, but it isn't required."

Chakrii made an offended noise on behalf of his employer, but Silk shushed him. She set her full attention on Seraf, weighing her carefully. Breaker was surprisingly proud of how well Seraf withstood the inspection, considering how she loathed being the center of anyone's attention.

"You're an interesting pair, I'll give you that." Silk tapped her fingernail against her cheek. "Very well," she said after a moment of consideration, "I'll play."

"Who is missing?" Breaker asked.

"He goes by the name of Brasius." She gestured toward a desk tucked away in an alcove at the back of the room. Chakrii fetched a sleek silver laptop from it. "He was a crowd favorite, both here and at the fights."

She reached out and accepted the computer from Chakrii. "I'll pull up his picture right now. We always get a picture to include in the Blue Books," she told them without looking up. Most of the higher-end Houses included a picture of their talent in the books so customers knew what they were getting.

"Fights?" Breaker resisted the urge to share a look with Seraf.

"He fought in Dempsey's cage matches."

Breaker heard Seraf's surprised intake of breath. "You knew about it?"

"I allowed it." Silk glanced up, pleased at their surprise. "Infernals must have a stakeholder to provide the upfront money. I provided that in return for ninety percent of the profits." Breaker whistled in appreciation of Silk's mercenary ways. "He got to keep any bonuses he might receive, plus it helped build him a client list." She shrugged. "It's more than most get."

Seraf vibrated with barely checked rage. Breaker lowered his wards to touch his magical resonance to hers, hoping to calm her before she gave in to her fury. He imagined the baleful glow of her eye as her emotions roiled.

"Indeed," Breaker agreed in an even voice. Seraf's anger vanished. Breaker would have been pleased, except he knew it hadn't subsided; Seraf had hidden it, suppressed it so completely it was like it had never been. He chewed at his cheek. He'd talk to her about it after they left Silk's.

"Here we are," she said and turned the laptop around so he could see the screen.

Brasius was a handsome creature. Glowing red lines flowed over his slate grey skin like lava down a volcano. He was heavily muscled, especially his neck because of the thick, curling horns that sprouted from the sides of his head. His eyes were full, gleaming black, giving him an insectoid look. His cheekbones appeared chiseled out of rock, and his measurements were impressive. Breaker could understand how the Infernal was such a crowd-pleaser.

"How long has he been missing?" he asked.

"Nearly a week," Chakrii answered.

"Was he collared?"

Chakrii's flat look would have been insulting if Breaker hadn't expected it. Instead of taking offense, he smiled widely. The man's eye twitched, and Breaker purred internally with satisfaction.

Sometimes being an irritating little shit was its own reward.

"Standard or custom-made?" He shifted his attention to Silk.

"Not those new monstrosities that Domino outfits hers with," she said, crimson lips pulling up in a sneer. "They're effective, but she'll burn out her stable in a few years if that's how she plans to stop the bleeding. Her Infernals will be zombie junkies by the end of it."

Seraf sucked in a harsh breath but otherwise kept quiet. She shifted her weight, and Breaker sent a wave of calm through his resonance before withdrawing behind his wards once more. "So you don't subscribe to her methods," he said, relief lifting the weight from his lungs that he hadn't realized he was carrying.

Silk waved her ringed hand—one on every finger and three on her index. "Too harsh." Breaker raised his eyebrows, surprised she agreed. While not fully human, Infernals weren't animals. They had few—if any—protections. The government couldn't decide what Infernals were, so determining rights violations became difficult, if not impossible. It left them vulnerable.

Her next words dried up the wellspring of goodwill. "Ruins the product. Gets expensive to replace."

Breaker clenched his jaw to keep his words behind his teeth where they belonged. His feelings toward Seraf may be messy and complicated by how they were bound to each other, but he never thought of her as a product. "Right," was the most he could manage in agreement to keep the interview civil.

"Any idea where he might have gone?" he asked, hoping to let that conversational dead-end die a painful and quick death. "Did he have friends? Any contacts outside of the Emporium?"

Silk glanced at Chakrii, who answered. "They are free to come and go as they please," he told them, "though we do keep tabs on them for their own safety."

"Naturally," Breaker said.

Chakrii gave him a glare that promised mayhem as soon as he managed to get Breaker alone. Breaker resisted blowing him a kiss just to see the apoplectic expression on the concierge's face.

"The Infernals who work here are collared so that it is safer for both themselves and their patrons." Chakrii paused. "We keep a dossier on all of our employees to make sure things remain above board."

"And to ensure they aren't skimming or running a scam on you," Breaker added, his grin sharp as a blade. He leaned forward. "Look, I couldn't give two interdimensional fucks about how you keep your people in line. I am just a man trying to do a job. If you don't want to give me anything, just say the word and save us both the time."

Silk held up her hand. "Don't get your briefs in a bunch, Unshriven." She stood gracefully, stalking over to a set of barrister bookcases. She swept her fingertips over the glass door, deactivating the ward on it, and pulled it open. After a few moments of rifling, she retrieved a leather-bound notebook and stepped over to Breaker. She held it out to him, but when he reached up to take it, she pulled it away from his grasp.

"You get five minutes with it. Don't make me regret it." She took her seat. Chakrii poured her a club soda with a twist of lime as she settled in her chair to wait.

As soon as he had the book, Breaker began skimming the pages. He had close to an eidetic memory, his powers of recall uncanny—a good thing when one was a mage and a detective. Seraf leaned over his shoulder, her demonic eye burning amber as she too scanned the pages. Her memory and retention weren't nearly as good as his, but she had an uncanny knack for remembering an important detail or thinking of something in a way Breaker did not.

When he glanced up at Silk after his first pass of the book, he saw her sitting with a bemused expression on her face. When his time was finally up, she signaled to Chakrii. He collected the book. Silk stood once more, the lovely strong bones of her square face set in an impassive expression.

"That should be enough to get you started. Where you go from here is entirely up to you." She tapped a green nail against her red lips. "If you'd like to speak with one of my employees, I would appreciate it if you called here first to give us a heads up and allow us to clear their schedule."

Which gave Silk and her henchman the time to warn the Infernal in question what would happen to them if they didn't tell Breaker what they wanted him to know. Breaker simply smiled, giving a simple nod even though his back had clenched up enough that he expected spasms when he tried to sleep later. There were ways around Silk's request, but it meant wasting time he couldn't afford. The ticking of a count-down clock echoed in Breaker's bones. He needed to find out what had happened to those missing Infernals before there was nothing left to find.

Or before another one went missing.

"Thank you for your help," Breaker said, rising from his seat carefully. "If I find anything out about Brasius, would you like to be informed?"

Silk shrugged. "Do as you like. Once he didn't show up for his shift, I removed him from my roster." She waved her hand as she had just waved Brasius' existence away.

Inhaling sharply, Breaker nodded once before turning on his heel and walking out, not waiting for Chakrii to lead him back to the entrance. Seraf followed in his shadow, silent as always.

Chapter 9

"You're sure about this?" Lin asked Seraf as they prepared to head out to find Dempsey.

Breaker opened his mouth for a sharp answer but fell silent when Seraf nodded emphatically. He frowned at their admin, willing him to shut his fae mouth. Seraf was a bundle of taut muscles and anxious tension on the other side of the reception area. He lowered his wards long enough to feel how the bond they shared roiled with her disquiet before reinforcing them. She didn't want to enter the Infernal fights, but she would because Breaker needed it. It was their best lead on Brasius.

He hadn't even had to ask.

Guilt warred with relief. His head ached. Breaker took comfort that he hadn't had to order her to do it and cursed himself for cowardice.

"We've exhausted almost every other avenue." They'd brainstormed almost nonstop over the past few days. "We know Brasius fought in those cage matches, and some of Domino's probably did as well. If we want to find out what happened to those Infernals, we need a place to start, and this is as good as any."

"It's not your arse that's going in that ring, boss man." Lin said it with a stony smile, his eyes glittering and jagged like smoky quartz.

Breaker squeezed the phoenix of his cane hard, letting the dull ache ground him. Then he set it aside. He was too recognizable with it, and he hadn't bothered with paying for a glamour from Arinaya to have it undone by an accessory. "I am well aware of that, Lin."

Seraf swung around to face him, a question that he knew she'd never ask him in her eyes. She looked nothing like her usual self. "Nothing is going to get out of hand. If things look bad, I'll intervene with some magic, and we'll get out of there. No muss, no fuss."

Tamlin gave him a long, assessing look. Breaker tugged at his cuffs, avoiding the man's gaze. Ages, centuries stood out in the eternally youthful man's eyes, and Breaker felt judged and found wanting in them of late. Breathing deeply, he shoved his doubt aside and straightened his jacket. He'd deal with his *feelings* after this case was over.

Breaker turned on his cloned phone and handed it to Tamlin. "Drop this off after you leave the office for the day." If anything happened, it would look like he was on a stakeout for the evening. Breaker's phone was off and locked in the safe. He'd use a burner if he needed to call anyone tonight.

"I know, I know. It'll be on the rooftop just like you told me."

Breaker thought he heard Seraf sigh as he turned around and opened the back door. Ignoring it, and Lin's admonishment to be careful and his advice to Seraf 'to go for the goolies,' Breaker stepped into the small backyard behind Unshriven and waited for Seraf to join him.

She wore tattered jeans, a pair of old combat boots, and a t-shirt that was far too large on her. Seraf wore her hair out of her face since the glamour made her Infernal eye appear normal. She wore a hooded sweatshirt in place of her usual jacket.

Breaker checked the inside pocket of his jacket for the backup vial of glamour that he'd purchased from Ari earlier in that day. An emergency measure in case they ran into a spell-breaker or something worse, it had cost them the last of their petty cash. Glamours of Ari's power were expensive, so Breaker tried to limit using them.

They took a water taxi into New Venice. Breaker directed the boatman to let them off at the closest cross-streets to Mistress Silk's Emporium. The sun had barely set, but the crowds of tourists, partygoers, and locals filled the streets. A few chartered party barges did laps around the sunken city's canals, stopping to let off its passengers at whatever seedy bar, strip club, or pleasure house caught their fancy.

Thanks to Mistress Silk's contact, they had an in with Dempsey's people and knew the location of the night's fights. Breaker led Seraf to the back entrance of an old warehouse repurposed to a movie theater that hadn't made it and knocked a pattern on the door. The building stood some distance from the main hustle of the tourist sector, in a disreputable, but not outright dangerous, part of town.

After a few moments, a slot opened up in the previously seamless metal door. Breaker kept his magic to himself, but he could feel the warding and protections in place around the building. Some of the work was downright delicate, especially the obfuscation spells, pointing to a practitioner of some skill. Seraf nudged him with her elbow as if he wouldn't have already noticed.

A pair of sunglasses regarded them through the slot. "Yeah?"

Breaker answered with the code Silk's contact had given. "There's a party at Saint's."

"Only sinners invited."

The slot slid closed, once again leaving Breaker with no

indication of its existence. He took a moment to be impressed before sharing a worried look with Seraf. She stood beside him, so tense she was nearly vibrating. Had they gotten the passphrase wrong? Had Silk set them up? Breaker stared hard at the closed door. His expression never revealed the turmoil in his head—he'd learned long ago through painful lessons how to keep his face neutral.

A series of clicks indicated the door unlocking. Breaker stood, ready to pull water to him from the humid air and send it out in deadly spikes. Seraf settled herself in a ready stance as the door swung open. Breaker tensed, expecting an attack.

"You waiting for an engraved invite? Get your asses in here," came an impatient voice.

He glanced at Seraf, eyebrows raised. She frowned, fingers twitching. Her eyes darted to the door, and she licked her lips. Breaker got the message. Even if they were nervous, unsure, there was no going back.

So he stepped forward with Seraf at his back.

BREAKER LEANED against the railing of the upper level of the old theater. He'd made his way there as soon as Seraf had been taken to the locker room to prepare for her match. The vantage point gave him a good view of the ring and the crowds with the bonus of keeping him out of the press of humanity. The cage stood in the center of the room below. It was quieter, less raucous up here, though he expected that to change once the fights got going.

Spectators packed the space surrounding the ring. Breaker observed money change hands as betting chits began on the warm-up match—a battle royal with six Infernals in the cage. The last fighter conscious and standing won. Breaker wouldn't have minded missing it altogether, but he had to gather information, so he sucked up his distaste and mingled.

Most in the upper deck were owners or those that held a vested interest in the fighters on the card. Breaker got a drink from the small bar selling overpriced liquor in the corner just to have something to keep his hands busy and circulated.

He'd only been leaning against the rail for a few minutes before a short and slight man approached him with dusky skin and salt and pepper hair. Breaker nodded at him in greeting before going back to staring at the Infernals in the cage below.

"Fresh meat?" the man asked, and already Breaker disliked him.

"Beg pardon?" Breaker responded with a cool twitch of a dark eyebrow. His glamour gave him olive skin, dark hair, and dark eyes. He still needed his glasses, but he'd changed them out for an old pair with heavy black frames.

"I meant, is this your first time here? I don't recall seeing you around." The man sidled up, resting his crossed arms on the rail and setting his chin atop them. He slanted a heavy glance at Breaker, giving him an easy smile.

Breaker swirled the alcohol in his glass and said, "Yes, it's my first visit. I heard it was a good place to size up Infernals."

"Oh?" The man's gaze swept Breaker once more, probably trying to figure out how much he was worth. "Any particular one in mind?"

Tamping down on the twitch of his lips, Breaker shrugged. Too easy, this one. "I'm a scout. My employer is interested in establishing a fully immersive role-playing experience for those who can afford such things. He's looking for talent that can fill the roles of gladiators, with all that entails." He arched an eyebrow and offered a knowing look to drive home the double meaning of his words.

"I was told to keep an eye out for Brasius," he continued before the man could say anything.

"Brasius?" The man snorted. "Look, let me tell you a few things. Oh, I'm Garrick McGreevy." McGreevy held out his hand.

Grateful for his gloves—he wanted to leave as little trace of his presence as possible—Breaker shook McGreevy's hand. He bit back a sigh when McGreevy clasped his hand so tightly it made his bones grind together and tugged him closer. Resigned, Breaker allowed it.

"Demetrius Stadler," he said, offering a fake name. "What sort of things?"

McGreevy's smile was a greasy, smarmy thing. "He's a whore, for one thing." When Breaker lifted his brows, unimpressed, the man faltered before soldiering on. "And most of what he did in there," he jerked his head toward the cage, "was staged. If he won, it was because his patron paid for that victory."

"Mistress Silk?"

McGreevy shook his head, once again sizing Breaker up. "Seems you've done your homework."

Breaker took the Blue Book from his interior jacket pocket. "It wasn't much of a stretch. He worked in Silk's stable, and I would imagine a champion pit fighter would be quite a draw." He cocked his head. "How can you be sure it wasn't her?"

"Fighters talk." He leaned in, far too close for Breaker's liking, and pointed down to a bat-eared Infernal with a long, heavily muscled tail. "That one's mine." His narrow chest swelled with pride of ownership.

Bile rose at the back of Breaker's throat as the man continued. "Anyway, Titan told me that Brasius was going around bragging that he had some big patron interested in sponsoring him—and it wasn't Silk. Said he was going to be leaving that life behind. Oh, looks like the fight's starting. Keep an eye on my guy."

Breaker made an interested noise and promptly tuned the man out. He stared into the crowd below blindly, deaf to their cheers and screams at the match taking place. His mind worked on the problem before him. Had Silk lied to them? She'd known of the missing Infernals from other houses; was she using those disappearances as a front for her termination of a problematic employee? A rash of disappearances—what's one more?

Drumming his fingers on the rail, he tried to make sense of what he'd discovered so far. Infernals gone missing from at least four pleasure palaces, with several of them boasting more striking demonic traits like wings and horns. Some, but not all, of the missing fought in Dempsey's matches. Clandestine meetings. Donations to some group called the Wages of Sin. The missing Infernals wore collars, yet they were untraceable.

Breaker nearly growled in frustration. He couldn't grasp the shape of it, no matter how hard he tried. That feeling of a ticking clock intensified every time he thought about the case. He and Seraf weren't going to find those Infernals—not alive at least—but that didn't diminish his need to know what happened to them.

If Domino called them off the case, Breaker wasn't sure he would be able to leave it alone.

"Fuck!" McGreevy pounded on the rail, jarring Breaker from the spiral of his thoughts.

He peered over the rail at the cage. Only two Infernals remained conscious within the ring, and neither of them was McGreevy's fighter. One was a woman with skin faceted like cut gemstones. She bared her teeth at the remaining Infernal and beckoned him closer, despite the cracks in her diamond-like skin. She looked familiar, but Breaker couldn't place where he'd seen her before. A collar stretched tight around her neck as she caught her opponent's arm and hip-tossed him onto the floor.

McGreevy held onto the rail with a white-knuckled grip, spitting profanities over the balcony at the crowd and fighters below. Money was already changing hands as bookies called in their bets as the match wound up. The faceted Infernal slammed her boot into her opponent's face several times until he lay still before raising her arms in victory.

"Trilya!" came the roar from the announcer to cheers from the crowd. The Infernal sagged against the men who ushered her out of the cage.

As the cage was made ready for the next fight, Breaker turned to McGreevy. The man's face was red with barely checked anger, sweat beading at his temples and darkening his hair.

"If that idiot took a dive," he began before trailing off and glaring at Breaker. He shoved away from the rail.

"I've got to collect my property," he said after he calmed down. "You're welcome to come."

Breaker stiffened at the man's choice of words. Property. It reminded him too much of how his father thought of people —they weren't people; they were possessions. Shoving aside his personal feelings, Breaker shook his head. "I've got a fighter of my own, so I plan to watch."

"You've got one entered?" the man looked surprised.

"Yes. She's slated for a later match."

McGreevy whistled. "You got a female in one of these things?" He shook his head. "That's ballsy, I'll tell you that."

Breaker frowned. "What do you mean?" He pointed toward the cage Trilya had just exited. "A woman just won."

"That was the warm-up, almost an exhibition match. That's as far as she'll go. But if you've got a broad in a real fight, well." McGreevy's expression turned dark, almost a leer. "Things can get a little out of control, especially when the blood lust gets going. The last time a female Infernal fought here, the—uh—others had a little fun with her before the end."

Breaker kept his face impassive as he answered, "That's interesting. I'm not worried. She's more than capable of taking care of anyone foolish enough to try."

McGreevy snorted and shook his head. "Your funeral, friend. Or hers." He tapped two fingers to his forehead and made his way downstairs, leaving Breaker alone at the rail.

He stared down at the cage, a sour taste flooding his mouth. Seraf. She was walking into that fight with no knowledge of what could await her if she lost. Silk hadn't told them about the dangers of a woman fighting. Why? Had she assumed they knew? Or had there been another, more sinister reason?

The crowd below began to chant the name of one of the Infernal fighters making his way to the cage. The sound was deafening. Breaker increased the strength of his wards, chest constricting. His knee throbbed in time with his rapid heartbeat.

He must warn Seraf. Breaker knew she could take care of herself, but this was somehow different. The idea of her brutalized in such a way made him sick. They'd both experienced their share of beatings when they were young, on the streets, and in their line of work. He clenched his fists as the world spun sickeningly around him. This felt different. He was bound to her just as much as she to him. They were responsible for each other.

He might wish for something different; he might wonder what his life would be like if his father had never brought her into his life, but he never wanted her hurt in such a way.

Taking deep breaths through his nose, Breaker forced back the panic. He focused his attention on a section of the space below, an aisle where people slowly moved to their seats, the exits, or the bar. Letting his gaze rove, he absently noted details: a man in a violently purple suit, a woman with a grey-skinned Infernal on a leash, two young men outfitted in polo shirts and khaki shorts, so out of place as to be laughable. It helped to divorce his attention from his body, allowing him space to recover.

When he was no longer in danger of running shrieking from the venue or hiding in a corner gnawing on his feet, Breaker breathed in the smells of sweat, cologne, and the faintest hint of brimstone-tinged Infernal blood. His body and mind back under his control, he spotted a familiar head of hedgehog-esque hair in the crowd below.

As if aware of Breaker's stare, Dahrian looked up to the balcony. Breaker shrank back, telling himself it was only a coincidence that Dahrian happened to glance over. Not that it mattered; Breaker left the balcony to warn Seraf.

It took the entire next match to make it to the doors Seraf had disappeared through to await her fight. Two massive men with arms the size of pillars stood before them, blocking access. Their faces were about as expressive as stone too. He quickly swept them with an eye for magic but found them entirely normal. Well, their size indicated abnormal, but perhaps they'd been well-fed as children. Or been fed children.

Breaker stepped up to them and said, "I need to speak to my fighter."

The man on the left looked down at him while the other's gaze didn't stray from the corridor. "No one back here but fighters."

"I am her," he swallowed, the word foul on his tongue, "owner."

"That's nice for you."

Breaker cocked his head. "Didn't you hear me?"

The man who'd been silent snarled, "I don't give a fuck if you're her fairy godmother. No one back here but fighters once the matches start. Now get the fuck out of here before we remove you from the premises."

"Or your head from your neck," the other offered helpfully.

Breaker reached for the closest water he could find before he could stop himself, unsurprised when shouts erupted from the nearby bathroom. He let go of his power almost as soon as he realized he'd called it and turned on his heel before the two men got wise to what he'd done.

There was a strict no magic policy inside these walls, and

Breaker had agreed to abide by it as long as the fights were taking place. Usually, he wouldn't hesitate to get what he wanted, but he couldn't afford to get thrown out.

Making his slow way back to the stairs leading to the balcony, Breaker leashed his temper. He needed to think, not descend into blind anger. He'd save his magic for the first sign of trouble for Seraf in the cage.

"Absalom?"

Breaker slewed around, ignoring the painful twinge in his knee as it twisted wrong. Dahrian stood behind him, his dark eyes wide and his head cocked in a curious tilt. His hair was still as much a disaster up close as Breaker remembered from the other day.

Shit. Had his glamour slipped, or was it something else? If Ari had cut corners on the charm, he was going to make it quite clear to her that no one shorted him and got away with it.

"Dahrian No Last Name."

"It is you then. I wasn't sure at first." His smug grin returned. "And it's Ashikaga."

"You can see through glamours?" Breaker whispered, grabbing the man by his upper arm. What the hell was he?

He pulled Dahrian into a less crowded corner, scanning the room to see if anyone had recognized his name. When he turned his gaze back to Dahrian, the man looked pointedly at Breaker's hand on his arm. Breaker let go over him immediately.

"How?" he demanded, voice low and urgent.

"Relax, your glamour is fine," Dahrian hissed. His hair seemed to bristle—Breaker had only heard it described in books; he'd never witnessed anything like it in real life. "I'm not going to fuck anything up for you or your fake face."

Breaker tapped his foot and made a 'hurry up' motion with one hand. Dahrian rolled his eyes and said, "The feel of you hasn't changed."

Breaker gaped, barely managing to keep his jaw from dropping to the floor. "You can sense people's magic?" At least it meant his glamour hadn't faded.

Dahrian shrugged. "More or less. Different people feel different in my head. Everyone has a unique magical signature—sort of like a fingerprint."

"You're a senser," Breaker breathed in, surprised. Sensers were uncommon. He'd never met one before. He wished he could speak longer with Dahrian—he'd love to learn more about this ability since there wasn't much research available on it since it was mostly a passive skill. The leaden weight in his stomach tempered his curiosity. How was he supposed to hide from a senser? He wanted to stay as far away from Dahrian as he could get.

"What are you doing here?"

Dahrian gestured at the audience all around them. "Needlepoint," he deadpanned. "What the hell do you think I'm doing here? A friend of mine wanted to see the fights." He shifted his weight from foot to foot.

Breaker kept his thoughts about the kind of person that wanted to watch a bloodsport like this to himself. "Visitor from out of town?" he guessed, hoping that explained it. Many tourists loved to rack up these types of experiences on their vacations.

Dahrian hummed, turning his head as if searching the crowd. "Never expected to see you in a place like this, Absalom."

"I don't know whether to take that as an insult or a compliment." He pushed past Dahrian, making his way to the stairs. "And the name is Demetrius Stadler."

Dahrian didn't wait for an invitation; he simply fell into step behind him. "But Absalom is such an unusual name, has an old-fashioned sort of elegance to it. It suits you."

Breaker nearly stumbled at his words. He turned his head

to find Dahrian smiling at him. "And you can take the comment however you like."

Frowning at his audacity, Breaker growled, "The name's Demetrius tonight." Why couldn't the man go back to his friend? He needed to focus on the crowd and the matches, not listen to Dahrian ramble about every single thought that entered his head. "Are you following me?"

"Why would I be following you? I'm simply going upstairs for a better view of the proceedings." The dimple in his cheek deepened. "Someone's full of himself."

Breaker gritted his teeth and focused on climbing the narrow stairs without incident.

"So all of this," Dahrian waved his hand to encompass all of Breaker, "is for a job?"

As they crested the stairs, Breaker gave Dahrian a quelling look. "No," he began, leaning close to Dahrian to whisper, "it's for the 'Gram."

"Absalom, you are full of surprises." Dahrian chuckled at the old joke, a sound deep and rich like top shelf bourbon. Breaker ignored the curling warmth in his belly at the sound of that laugh, and made his way back to the railing. Dahrian trailed behind him.

"Demetrius," he insisted.

"Right." He leaned his elbows on the railing and peered down into the crowd.

"Where's your friend? Won't they miss you?" Breaker asked after a few silent moments. *Go away.* Why he didn't say it aloud was something he could analyze later.

"He'll be fine on his own for a few minutes. This place is like catnip to him." The faint smile playing around his lips widened slightly and Dahrian's black eyes seemed to glow amber around the outside of the iris.

Breaker had no idea how to parse that, so he didn't bother.

"Speaking of companions," Dahrian glanced around as

though just realizing something, "where's that woman you were with at Yena's shop? Shouldn't she and her epic bitch face be lurking about ready to jump out at anyone who might want to speak to you?"

"We've swapped," Breaker said drily. "It's my turn to lurk."

Dahrian made a muffled snort, almost as if he were stifling a laugh. Breaker kept his gaze on the cage. Seraf's match should be starting soon.

"Shame. I thought you two were a matched set." There was an edge to his voice, a meaning that Breaker couldn't discern immediately and didn't have the mental energy to waste on it.

Though if there was a sexual meaning to the comment, Breaker might rethink his consideration not to use magic inside the building to drown the man where he stood. "Looking for some kind of subterranean menage a trois, is that it?" Breaker let the distaste bleed into his voice.

Dahrian jerked, face going red. "Wh-what?" he spluttered.

"Because whatever you might think, I run a legitimate business. If you have a problem that needs solving or requires a delicate touch, please come by the office. However, if this odious and rather ham-handed display is your attempt at flirting, or you hope to finagle your way into some kinky fun, I'm afraid you'll be doomed to disappointment. Good evening, Mr. Ashikaga."

Breaker removed himself from the gobsmacked man and went back downstairs. The crush of people was greater here, and the din was deafening. Money changed hands, markers too. He sidled around to a less crowded corner where he could still see the ring and waited. He whispered the words of a simple Blend In spell—no one would notice him unless they touched him—and settled in the corner. A slight risk but one he willingly took to get away from Dahrian.

After a few minutes, he saw Dahrian hurry down the balcony stair. He was easily recognizable by the mass of hair on his head. He scanned the room, his gaze roving over the spot where Breaker stood but didn't find what he was looking for by the expression on his face. Breaker breathed a sigh of relief. Dahrian was a distraction he couldn't afford right now. He silently thanked whoever might be listening for the minimal magic required to stay hidden.

Breaker couldn't help but watch as Dahrian joined the friend he'd mentioned. The man was taller than Breaker and sun-browned as a berry. He had glossy, thick brown hair which he wore to his shoulders. He was built large and broad, like a whisky barrel, and looked just as sturdy. There was something familiar about him even though he'd never met the man before in his life, of that he was sure. Breaker found himself wondering how Dahrian had come to meet this man and if they were really just friends. He stared, unable to shake the feeling that he'd seen Dahrian's friend somewhere before.

"And now," the ring announcer shouted into his mic to be heard over the roar of the assembled crowd, "for our next match! We've got something special for you tonight—a rare bout indeed! A female Infernal versus one of the crowd favorites!"

Breaker swallowed convulsively in a throat gone dry as Seraf stepped into the ring.

Chapter 10

Breaker folded his arms over his chest as Seraf entered the ring. The glamour on her was holding—at least that was something. He wished he had brought his cane if only to give him something to strangle. Maybe their luck would hold.

That thought exited his head like a skydiver jumping out of a perfectly good plane in defiance of gravity when Seraf's opponent entered the cage. The male Infernal was easily a foot taller than Seraf, muscles rippling beneath the negligible coverage of his tank top, which he promptly tore in two to flex better.

Yep. Those indeed were muscles.

Seraf headed to her side of the cage, not bothering with any posturing. Breaker continued to assess her opponent, cursing when he saw the lower half of his body. From the waist down, bronze-colored scales encased the hulking behemoth's body. There were no other outward signs of his demonic DNA, but Breaker doubted those scales were all he possessed. While some of an Infernal's demonic lineage was obvious—like Seraf's eye or Orion's horns—the more dangerous or terrifying aspects of them tended to be less visible.

Thunderous applause, raucous cheers, and beer bottles chucked at the cage greeted the Infernal as he played to the crowd. He raised his arms in triumph and let loose a roar that almost drowned out the excited crowd.

Seraf scanned the spectators, likely looking for him. She wouldn't be able to see him with his Blend-In spell active, but he hoped that she could feel him through their shared bond. She wore an expression that he called Active Bitch Face and Breaker's heart rose at the sight of it. It wouldn't do to underestimate her.

The ring announcer introduced her opponent—undefeated, reigning champion of the fights. His handle was Tiberius the Tyrant. Cute. The crowd erupted in cheers as he swaggered around the perimeter of the cage, stopping to get in Seraf's face. She gave Tiberius her best unimpressed look before the handlers herded him back to his corner. They announced Seraf—Breaker had given her the moniker Morgan le Flay—and once again, the crowd erupted, this time with catcalls, whistles, boos, and more beer bottles slung her way.

A bell rang. Breaker flinched as Tiberius surged into the center of the cage, beelining for Seraf. He was fast for all his bulk. She tracked him, bouncing lightly on the balls of her feet. She put her arms up in a boxer's stance and waited for him to strike first. Tiberius moved into what he presumed to be the blindspot of her Infernal eye and smirked. He punched. Seraf dodged, ducking under his arm and landing a rabbit punch to his kidneys in retaliation.

The crowd screamed, urging them to fight. Well, urging the champion on—most of the public seemed to bet on Tiberius and wanted to see him quickly end the fight. Breaker put the other reason they might want to see Tiberius win out of his mind. He breathed in slowly, concentrating on the scents of spilled beer, sweat, and the stinking mix of colognes and perfumes in a confined space to keep himself calm. Spectators closest to the cage flung their beverages into it, showering the two fighters with liquid. Seraf didn't seem to notice, her gaze never leaving the champion.

Tiberius tried grappling Seraf, but she bobbed out of the way, lashing out in a vicious hook that caught him in the side of the head. Breaker cheered silently. The champion staggered. A chorus of boos sounded from the crowd above them. Tiberius snarled, recovering quickly.

Seraf rolled out of the way as he swatted at her head, trying to box her ears. She came to her feet with a grace Breaker envied. Tiberius had reach, but Seraf was faster and more agile. Tiberius depended on his strength too much, and he telegraphed his next move by the way he tightened his core, something that might have been less obvious if he'd kept his shirt intact.

Things were going well until a beer bottle clocked Seraf in the back of her head. Breaker swallowed back his cry of anger as the crowd roared its approval. It rocked Seraf, causing her to lose focus for a moment.

Fury lit Breaker's blood like a struck match. The angle of the throw and Seraf's position meant that the bottle had come from below. Dempsey's guards surrounded the cage's base; it had come from one of them. Dempsey's reputation was fearsome, especially about those disloyal to him, so if they were trying to influence the match, it was at his order.

Seraf never stood a chance of winning.

Son of a bitch.

Breaker pushed away from his corner and slowly worked through the crowd to get closer to the cage. Heat rose inside him, turning his insides molten. Seraf would not be violated or humiliated in front of an audience, lead or no lead. He would stop the fight before it ever got to it. Breaker owed her too much to allow it.

Tiberius took advantage of Seraf's momentary distraction

and leaped, catching her around the middle and bearing her to the floor. How many of tonight's fights were fixed?

Seraf got her arms up to block the punches to her face. She was at a disadvantage on the ground. Breaker shoved through a gregarious knot of people to get a better look at the action in the cage.

Wrapping her hand over her fist, Seraf hammered the base of Tiberius' skull. The Infernal roared, and his hold loosened for a moment. Seraf couldn't break free before his grip tightened once more.

Seraf threw her head back in a silent yell as the muscles in Tiberius' arms constricted. Breaker's breath sawed in and out of his lungs with a rasp as he watched her struggle. He needed to get closer! Any more pressure and her ribs would crack.

Breaker snarled as Tiberius twisted so he could leer in Seraf's face. He said something to her that Breaker had no hope of hearing over the shouts from the spectators. Seraf didn't appreciate whatever it was he'd said because her hand snapped up, thumb digging deep into his eye.

He released her with a howl, reeling back with his hand over his injured eye. Blood poured down his face. Seraf gained her feet, one arm wrapped around her middle. She lunged at his legs. Tiberius landed on the mat. Scrambling atop him, Seraf attempted to pin his arms with her knees. Tiberius thrashed wildly, roaring like a mad thing. He threw her to the side. Breaker winced when her legs spasmed as she landed on her injured side. It took her a moment to find her feet.

The moment cost her. A hand closed around her throat. Breaker could only watch as Tiberius hoisted her into the air. Tiberius's face was a mess, blood leaking from behind the closed lid of his injured eye.

Seraf grabbed his wrist in both hands and flung her legs up to wrap around his upper arm. Using her body weight as leverage, she twisted. His wrist snapped, the sharp cracking sound swallowed by the outraged shrieks of the audience.

Tiberius dropped her with another yell, his arm limp. Breaker grinned, wishing for him to suffer.

Recovering quickly, Seraf gripped the cage's bars and threw her body upwards so that her calves hit Tiberius's shoulders. She tightened her legs around his neck, reeling him closer to her, hands fisted tight on the bars. Then she began to squeeze.

He clawed at her legs, trying to bite and tear with his teeth when she didn't relent, but he couldn't get a good hold. Seraf kept squeezing, even as the crowd above her hooted and called out abuse and rained trash down on her head. She didn't let up on him until he slumped over, his knees finally giving way in unconsciousness. Breaker shouted in triumph, shoving forward as the screaming died around him.

The crowd sat silent as she dropped her feet back to the floor. Panting, Seraf clutched at her battered ribs. Breaker cursed as the door to the cage crashed open. Four men entered. Their scarred faces twisted in anger as they hemmed Seraf in the center of the ring. She turned in a circle, settling into a fighting stance once more.

Murmurs rose from the watching crowd. A few people started to chant, "Winner!"

The cry swept the audience as more and more took it up. One of the men carried a telescoping baton. He extended with a flick of his wrist. Spectators in the audience began to boo loudly.

Breaker yelled, "Get out of there!" If she stayed in that cage, there was no telling what Dempsey's goons would do to her—though he had a pretty good idea that it ended her body ending up in a canal. With the mood of the crowd changing, violence was likely to erupt.

Seraf's eyes widened at the sound of his voice. Her gaze swept the crowd, passing over him. Breaker's spell was still up so she couldn't see him, but she could hear him.

"Go!" he ordered again.

Her Infernal eye glowed with the power of her demonic blood, illuminating the tired lines of her face. Then she stepped backward and pulled the shadows over her entire body and disappeared inside them.

Breaker smiled darkly when the referee announced her win, and the crowd continued to stare in relative silence, unable to do more than gawk at the space where Seraf once stood.

Chapter 11

Breaker took off to the nearest exit. He and Seraf had agreed on a meet-point before they'd separated in case things went wrong and things had just gone to shit. Breaker moved as quickly as he dared, not wanting to draw attention to his movements. The crowd had begun to chatter, voices growing louder as the audience grew angry.

He didn't know if he should laugh or curse. So much for keeping a low profile.

Breaker was nearly at the back door when someone grabbed his upper arm. He spun, coming face to face with Dahrian. Breaker shrugged him off with effort. "Not now!" he growled, anxious to get going once more.

"That was your girl in the ring!" he whisper-shouted in Breaker's ear. "You in trouble?" Dahrian pulled away to stare at Breaker, his strange eyes looking as if lit with hellfire in the dim light.

"Not if I get out of here quickly." Breaker gave him a pointed look. "Which you are impeding." He moved around him.

Dahrian fell into step beside him. "I'll go with you."

Breaker shook his head, scowling in frustration. He didn't

have time for this! And what was Dahrian playing at? He had only met Breaker once—they weren't even acquaintances. "I don't know you. And I don't need your help."

He broke away and took off at a ragged jog, ignoring the pain in his knee at the jostling. He didn't look back to see if Dahrian followed or not.

There was a guard at the back door. Breaker thought about circling to the front but discarded the idea. He didn't have the time to waste retracing his steps. Instead, he gathered his magic and its strong affinity to water. Breaker pulled at the water inside the pipes threaded through the building. A metallic groaning rent the air, and the guard looked up just in time to get a face full of water from the burst pipe above.

Breaker wasted no time. He sprinted past the spluttering man who was too distracted by the deluge to do more than yell a warning at him. As he tripped into the alley behind the converted warehouse, Breaker wended his way through the trash and a few people taking a break from the over-crowded confines of the building. He nodded at a couple sharing a cigarette before tugging on his sleeves and continuing on his way. He didn't want to draw any further attention to himself.

Breaker was nearly at the alley's mouth when his warning wards flared. His shield spell settled around him at the threat of magical assault. He angled his body to make the smallest possible target as he spun to face the danger and took the brunt of the magical blast of force on his shield.

Four men approached, one of them holding a staff. Breaker took a moment to focus his mage sense on the magic they could bring to bear. Though the staff held a recharging lightning spell, these men had limited power. It had been used once, but Breaker had no idea how many charges it would take to exhaust it. It was a powerful artifact. He was surprised to see it in a flunky's hand. It was powerful enough that Breaker would have expected to find it in Dempsey's hand.

The few people in the general area scattered like cockroaches hiding in a gas station bathroom.

Then Dempsey stepped out from behind one of his men and stared at Breaker like he was something to be found inside a Port-a-Potty. This evening just kept getting better and better.

"Is there a problem, gentlemen?" he asked, tilting his head in curiosity.

"Your little Infernal bitch didn't get with the program." Dempsey's voice was surprisingly mild, the smooth baritone soothing to the ears. "You have trouble getting her to follow orders?"

"Not typically." Breaker stood easy but kept a close eye on the men with Dempsey. He didn't want to risk them flanking him. Outnumbered, he couldn't risk displaying his true power in front of so many unknowns. "Perhaps you didn't offer her the proper motivation." He lifted one shoulder in a lazy shrug.

"Your head still attached to your neck wasn't incentive enough?" Dempsey made a tsking noise. "You need to work on instilling loyalty in your employees."

"I'll take it under advisement."

"Unfortunately, someone has to pay for the money I lost when your Infernal didn't follow instructions." Dempsey raked Breaker with his beady brown gaze. "I've got a couple of houses with clientele that would pay well for someone like her, or you can work it off in pain." His grin was a small, vicious thing. "Either way, I'll have my pound of flesh."

Over my prone corpse. Breaker kept the smile on his face even as his hand rose. He traced an arcane glyph in the air in front of him. He hadn't wanted to call this much attention to their operation tonight, but he was running out of options. Seraf would not be going to a pleasure house, and he was not going to allow anyone to hurt him ever again.

He spoke a word. Heat and blinding light filled the immediate area. A loud crack rent the air, a concussive blast of sound that made Breaker's ears ring.

Taking a deep breath, he blinked his vision clear. "Now then," Breaker said, tone brisk and business-like. "If there are no further complaints, I believe this con--" His voice dried up when he saw the men still standing as if nothing had happened.

His stun spell had failed. Which meant these yahoos were packing serious magic. He expected that kind of protection on Dempsey alone, not on his henchmen. Now that he knew what to look for, Breaker could see the faintest net of magical warding that had sprung up around the five men as he and Dempsey spoke. But none of them had that much talent or natural ability to be able to hide such a high-level ward like it was nothing.

"Warded?" Breaker guessed, taking a step back before he could stop himself. He gritted his teeth; these men would be on that moment of weakness like dogs on a carcass.

Dempsey smiled, a shallow, mirthless thing. "Warded," he confirmed.

"Fuck."

He was going to have to get his hands dirty. His lips curled in irritation. Figured. This case was a pain in the ass in so many ways. He wished he'd never agreed to take it. He was billing Domino for hazard pay. He hoped his glamour lasted.

"You made a huge fucking mistake," one of Dempsey's men growled.

"Not my first, unfortunately." Breaker flicked out a hand, calling power into it, once again drawing down the water that circled restlessly in the air. It came at his beckon, winding around his hand and unrolling in a thin line. He did the same with the other. Breaker broke out a grin as water lashed wildly. "You were saying?"

The men eyed the water whips warily. Breaker kept his rictus of a smile, determined not to show his exhaustion. His reserves still hadn't recovered, and the barest tremor of his hand told anyone with functioning eyes how much a show of power cost him. All he needed was a break in their attention, and then he could get free. He hoped.

Breaker backed up. He snapped a whip at the man closest to him, earning another round of cursing. He responded to every step one of the men took with the snap-crack of the whip. Keeping a particular eye on the one who held the charged staff, he kept the distance between them even. These men weren't magic users of any stripe, seemingly content to wait for the lightning in the staff to recharge.

Three men drew handguns, dull matte black things with short muzzles. The pit bull of firearms; he almost laughed. That alone told him how drained he was. And now, because he'd thought it, Breaker couldn't help but envision pitbull puppy faces on the three gun barrels pointed in his direction. He almost wanted to offer them a Snausage.

Get your thrice-damned head in the game, imbecile!

Swallowing, Breaker edged to the side of the alley, his focus pulling inward. Water once again answered his call as his whips grew shorter. Slivers of water solidified and grew thicker, hardening as they flew through the air at the sharp wave of his hand. They slammed into the muzzles, effectively blocking the bullet's exit path.

Another gesture, this time a pull of his hand backward, and a spoken word had the water's temperature dropping, freezing the metal and turning the water inside the barrel to ice. Two men howled and dropped their weapons as their hands burned at the frigid cold that froze their fingers and ripped off skin. The third managed to get a shot off only to have the gun explode in his hand when the bullet's force had nowhere to go with the barrel blocked. He screamed and fell to his knees, clutching at his ruined hand.

Breaker dodged but not fast enough. An electric bolt slammed into the center of his back, pitching him forward onto the filthy concrete once more. Breaker couldn't even put his hands out to break his fall; his nervous system was too busy twitching as lightning slid through his body. His limbs seized up. His heart stammered its rhythm, thudding erratically like an out-of-time tap dancer. Breaker clenched his jaws around the scream that wanted to tear itself from his throat, though he supposed he didn't have much choice. His body locked up in agony.

The taste of iron and salt flooded his mouth. He'd bitten his tongue. Someone hauled him roughly to his feet, but his brain was too scrambled to take much notice of who. They grabbed his hair, brutally yanking his head back, and he hissed at them through bloody teeth.

How embarrassing. Breaker hadn't expected to die this way. His father would likely kill him for besmirching the family name with his weakness or some such horseshit. Not that his father could say much of anything since he was dead himself, killed by a fourteen-year-old.

Dempsey was speaking. Breaker saw the man's lips moving, but his ears only heard a high whining sound. But he did see a long black oval rocket up from the shadows behind Dempsey and a pale hand smash out of it to bury itself in the man's back. The rest of Seraf followed the fist, Infernal eye glowing wickedly blood-bright, as she stepped from her shadow portal.

"Took you long enough," he muttered as his knees gave out, and he sagged to the ground in exhaustion. A few more men spilled out the back door in time to see Dempsey fall.

Breaker was too rattled to do much more than watch as Seraf took the remaining men apart.

HE STARED AT SERAF, mouth agape.

A knife stuck out of her upper arm. She'd buried her hand to the wrist in one of Dempsey's goons' chest. For his part, the man stared at her arm, mouth opening and closing in silence, like he was fighting to remember the words he wanted to say.

Breaker suspected one of them might have been, "Ow." He would have found the entire situation funny if it wasn't horrifying.

Seraf turned her head to stare down at him. She didn't look good, even taking into account the glamour. As Breaker staggered upright, he took a glance to see if anyone was watching. Thankfully, most everyone seemed to have the good sense to stay away from a magical dust-up like this one.

The man Seraf had impaled on her arm released a breathy moan, almost a whine, and then his eyes glazed over. He fell backward, away from Seraf's hand still buried in his chest cavity. Something came loose from inside him with a wet rubbery snap, and then Seraf had his bloody, shredded heart clutched in her hand.

Okay, that wasn't good.

Lifting the heart to her lips, she sniffed at it curiously. Looking at Breaker, she took a bite of the ropey muscle, chewing absently.

"No, no, no, don't do that." He slapped the bloody muscle out of her hand. "You don't know where it's been."

Blood flowed sluggishly from a deep slash across her ribs and abdomen to end at the opposite hip bone. Breaker slid his arm around her shoulders, bracing her as she listed to the side.

"Break – er," she gasped, face paling as the pain appeared to hit her all at once. She raised one bloody hand to his face to cup his cheek but stopped when she saw it.

Sweat slid down his back to pool in the waistband of his pants. He needed to think of a way out of this, but he took a moment to just breathe in the scent of Seraf's shampoo as he waited for his brain to unscramble from his near electrocution.

"I've got you," he whispered as her legs finally gave way.

He managed to catch and hold her up, despite his bad leg.

She buried her face in his chest, shuddering. She smelled of sweat and fear. She groaned in pain, and Breaker's attention turned to solving their immediate situation.

They were in a world of shit. If Breaker had the time, he likely could have dealt with the bodies in some creative way that would throw the police off—and he had no doubt NVPPD was going to get a call—and obfuscate their part in this shitshow, but Seraf was busy bleeding out all over him, so that had to take precedence.

He pressed the back of his fingers to her dusky cheek. "I know you're tired, but I need you to do something for me." He was an asshole for asking—Breaker knew that, and he'd probably burn in Hell if he believed in such garbage—but he had to ask. "I need you to shadow step us to Doc Grady's. Can you do that? For me?"

She'd push herself beyond the point of sense if she thought it was something he wanted. Seraf shifted, a low, pained noise rising from her throat, and he found himself caught in the slow swirl of her Infernal eye, nearly losing himself in the amber hurricane of it.

"Please, Seraf," he whispered, *bastardbastardbastard* a litany pounding in his head.

Breath hitching in pain, Seraf straightened. A shadow bloomed before her bloody outstretched fingers and widened into a portal. She took a halting step into it. Breaker's grip on her tightened—if he lost hold of her, he'd be trapped in that in-between plane—and he prayed to whatever gods that still listened to the pleas of people like him that she remain conscious long enough to get them out the other side.

Stepping through the shadow realm was jarring. Breaker had traveled with Seraf countless times in their years together, and it never became less strange. It was a place of dim grey light and amorphous shapes, empty and heavy at the same time. Breaker always registered a low hum right on the edge of hearing that never failed to set his teeth on edge.

He didn't belong here, and the place took pains to remind him of that.

One moment they were in that shadow place, the next, Seraf did something that turned everything wrong-side down and twisted it for good measure, and then they were stepping back into the real world Breaker knew. As soon as their feet hit solid ground, Seraf collapsed against him, her breaths rapid and shallow against the side of his neck. Her glamour hadn't survived the trip; he assumed he'd lost his as well.

He raised his head to see the familiar façade of Doc Grady's office. The typically glowing blue neon pill was dark, signaling the place was closed, but that had never stopped Seraf or Breaker before. Hauling Seraf up with the last of his dwindling strength, Breaker pounded on Grady's door.

After several minutes, the door flew open to reveal an older black man, hair going to salt at the temples and speckled through his neatly trimmed beard. His lean body stood wrapped in a threadbare robe that had seen better days. Wrinkles from squinting at the bright sun and working under dim light surrounded his dark brown eyes. His full mouth was set in harsh lines of disapproval that only deepened when he saw Breaker leaning against the railing with Seraf clutched tightly to his side. Breaker knew they looked terrible—he was a hot second away from passing out, and Seraf could have showered in blood.

"I should have known it would be you two chucklefucks," Grady said tiredly, shoulders rounding. "I'd board the place up, except you two would probably follow me wherever I went. Like the clap."

Grady opened his door wide and stepped forward to take Seraf's weight from him. "Come on inside."

Breaker heaved a sigh of relief, staggering at the loss of Seraf's dead weight. He regained his balance and followed the old doctor into his clinic. "Close the door behind you."

Grady took Seraf back into the exam room while Breaker

did as Grady ordered. He threw the locks, closed the blinds on all the windows, and added a softly spoken incantation. Breaker was taking no chances. The obfuscation spell on the door coupled with the scramble glyph he'd sketched in the air would make them harder to track.

He put his back to the door and rested his weight on it for a long moment. He was so damn tired. Some could be blamed on the magic, but the bulk came from his compromised immune system. Raising a hand to rub at his eyes, Breaker froze when he saw the smears of red decorating his palm. Blood. Seraf's blood. The faint brimstone scent mixed with iron turned his stomach. He spent a minute breathing out of his mouth so he didn't throw up.

"Move your ass, boy," Grady called from his examination room. "I have questions," he trailed off, letting Breaker fill in the rest.

Grady was a medical mage. He had medical training just like any doctor, but his skill with healing went beyond stitches and handing out antibiotics. Grady used his magical energy to stimulate healing, knit up wounds, and repair broken bones with touch, concentration, and careful manipulation of energy. Beaker had no idea what made the man set up shop in The Mire; he was just glad he had.

He and Seraf had been coming to Grady for nearly a decade now. He'd kept their secret after that first awful night, and now he was as close to family as either of them had besides each other. Grady must feel something similar for all his complaining since he hadn't barred either of them from the clinic despite his mounting threats.

Breaker straightened with a groan and limped into the exam room. Grady was bent over Seraf, his hands running over her body as he ran a quick diagnostic spell to scan the damage.

"Stab wound to upper left arm," Grady muttered. "Knife still in it too." He glanced over at Breaker. "She gonna want this?" he asked, pointing at the knife sticking out of Seraf's too-pale flesh.

"Highly doubt it. You're free to get rid of it." Breaker hobbled closer as Grady continued his litany of wounds.

"Deep slash across the belly and down to the hip," he said, voice distant. "Likely concussion, various lacerations and contusions, couple of cracked ribs." Grady shook his head in disgust before rounding on Breaker. "What the hell have you been doing, kid?"

"Not a kid," Breaker muttered, refusing to look at Grady. He moved to the head of the bed so he could brush the hair from her face. "Haven't been one for years."

"Then you should damn sure know better!" Grady growled as he gathered supplies. Breaker watched as he filled a syringe.

He stopped Grady before he could inject it into Seraf. "What's in it?"

Grady scowled, clearly wondering if Breaker had suddenly caught a raging case of stupidity. "I could waste the energy sedating her with my magic, or I could spend my limited resources on healing the bulk of this damage and make sure she stays out the old-fashioned way. You want to keep debating my methods while she's losing blood? It's not like I have a stock of Infernal on hand to replace it."

Gritting his teeth, Breaker managed to grind out a reluctant, "Fine."

"Glad you approve." The 'asshole' was unspoken but no less apparent. He emptied the syringe into Seraf with practiced ease, dark eyes watching her for signs of reaction. Then he pressed his hands, alight with the pale yellow glow of magic, to the worst of the Infernal's injuries.

Breaker stared, amazed when Seraf relaxed in infinitesimal increments. How much pain had she been feeling even when unconscious? He had no talent for healing, and even if he'd had any, his father would never have allowed him to pursue it. He could do nothing but watch helplessly as Grady's magic pulled closed that which had been torn open.

Because of him.

He leaned down, pressing his forehead against Seraf's. Her skin was cool, clammy. Her hair smelled of sweat, blood, and the faintest hint of product she used to protect her hair. It was so normal, so human, that Breaker couldn't breathe for a moment.

He'd almost lost this. The smell of Seraf's shampoo. How funny that this is what did him in. He resented her for supporting him, for checking on him when his leg was bothering him, for the way she orbited his life even now. Horror and death had inextricably linked them, and he hated it. He despised that she knew him in all his weakness.

And yet, seeing her like this rocked him.

Closing his eyes, Breaker breathed in slowly and tried to master himself. His hands trembled where they held her head still. "I'm sorry," he mouthed into her hair, knowing she wouldn't hear it but needing to say it anyway. The rawness in his chest refused to lay quietly, prodding him to somehow make the situation better.

He wished he knew how.

They were satellites to each other's planets, with neither of them able to reach escape velocity. They were trapped by each other and with each other, pulled together by each other's gravity. With a sigh, Breaker straightened though he did not stop carding his fingers through Seraf's hair.

He didn't know how much time passed, lost in his dark thoughts. It was only when Grady's tired voice said, "You look like shit," that he paid attention to the world around him.

"You should see the other guy." He bit back a yawn. Crowley, he was tired.

Grady settled a light blanket over Seraf. "I did everything I could. Now it's up to time and rest." He twisted at the waist, the pops of his back sounding like firecrackers in the quiet of the exam room.

He turned to Breaker. "Let's have a look at you."

Breaker shook his head. "I'm fine."

"You're an emotionally constipated moron without the sense God gave a goose is what you are," Grady said, taking Breaker by the arm and leading him over to a second bed and forcing him to sit on it.

Breaker flinched when Grady ran glowing hands above his body. "Magical drainage, shock, exhaustion, is that lightning damage?" Grady shook his head. "Wrenched that knee again too." He used a penlight to have a look at his eyes. "Where are your glasses?" He frowned. "I don't need to know."

Grady examined him quickly. "How are those supplements I gave you working?"

"They help," he conceded, looking away when Grady allowed him. Breaker was more susceptible to illness due to his compromised immune system because of his condition, and living rough through most of his teen years hadn't helped.

"Nightmares bad? You aren't getting enough sleep."

"Leave it." Breaker's voice came out hard and flat. It was the only warning he was willing to offer to Grady.

He saw Grady roll his eyes, but the man held his peace. When the doctor's hands glowed yellow, Breaker thought about protesting before deciding it wasn't worth it. Healing would help, even if a lecture came along with it. He was too fucking tired to argue with Grady anymore.

"Do I need to worry about bad men knocking on my door looking for you?" he asked as he worked.

"Not unless they can track through shadow. And Seraf took out Dempsey and most of his goons anyway, so—"

"Dempsey?" Grady pulled back, eyes wide. "Sweet free-wheeling Jesus, boy! What the actual fuck is wrong with you, Tob--?"

"Do not say that name!" Breaker snarled, cutting him off before he could finish.

"Are you trying to get the both of you killed?"

"It's for a case!"

"That doesn't change the damn question!"

"Then stop asking it when you don't really want the answer!" Breaker snapped his mouth shut, eyes narrowing to slits.

Grady's mouth tightened to a thin line, and Breaker knew he'd gone too far. He shifted where he sat, unwilling to apologize and unable to make things better. Grady just had to push him to the point that his fraying hold on his temper finally broke. He cleared his throat, gaze jumping around the room rather than staying on Grady.

The doctor sighed. "Get some rest. You need it as much as her." Grady turned around and began to clean up the examination room.

Breaker watched the doctor's back as he worked, the set of his shoulders telling him how badly he'd messed up with Grady. Slowly Breaker shrugged out of his suit jacket and slipped out of his shoes. As he settled, Breaker ignored the voice that told him he needed to go back to Unshriven even if it meant waking up Seraf and forcing her to walk. He knew she'd do it if he asked. He didn't know if he was proud or horrified by that fact.

Grady stopped at Seraf's bedside to check on her one last time. He stood there for some time. Breaker watched him. What was he thinking? Did he remember the first time they'd shown up at his doorstep, in worse shape than this? As Breaker watched, Grady's fingers settled on her wrist to seek out a pulse. After a few moments, Grady set Seraf's arm back on the bed. His face settled into harsh lines as he hooked a new IV bag to the stand, swapping out the old, nearly empty one.

The silence was becoming physically painful for Breaker,

the heaviness dragging him down until he thought he would drown from the weight in the air. Grady was angry, angrier than Breaker had ever seen him, and he couldn't understand why that was.

"Do you need anything?" Grady's voice was soft but didn't hide his disappointment as he lowered the lights in the exam room. He sounded sad and a little fond.

"You ever get an Infernal wearing one of those new collars in here?" Breaker asked. Grady turned abruptly to leave, and Breaker knew he'd fucked up again. He wanted to yell with the unfairness of it—he didn't know the right answer, didn't know what the man wanted him to say. He'd never been good with people, and it wasn't improving with age. Had there ever been a right answer?

Grady loosed a disappointed sigh like he wasn't surprised Breaker had failed but had such high hopes in case he surprised him. Then his expression tightened.

"Fuck off, Absalom," Grady told him as he stalked out of the room. "And get some sleep."

Chapter 12

"You kids are going to be the death of me."

The sound of Grady's voice pulled Breaker out of his sleep. He didn't move right away, content instead to float in that half-awake state. Breaker couldn't remember the last time he hadn't jerked into awareness and immediately got to work. There was something to be said for exhaustion.

"You want to tell me what happened last night?"

Ah. Seraf was awake then. Breaker kept his eyes closed and breathing even to allow them privacy. If he were lucky, he'd fall back to sleep.

"Of course, you don't." Breaker bit back a grin, imagining the disappointed headshake and the expression on Grady's face.

A heavy sigh. Then Breaker heard the scratching of a pencil on paper. Grady had learned rudimentary sign language over the years dealing with Seraf, but he didn't know enough for in-depth conversations.

"Him?" A pause in the conversation for a gesture, likely over to the bed Breaker currently occupied. "He's fine. Nothing that a week of rest won't cure. It would help if he took decent care of himself." A pause. "Just knock him unconscious until he stays put."

Breaker wanted to grumble but kept still and quiet. It wasn't like he meant to get so run-down. The expectation to work hard had been drilled into him until he couldn't stop even if he'd wanted to. He remembered all too well what it had been like to be hungry and wet and filthy. They had bills to pay, and they needed to eat. Now they had a place to live, food to eat, a business to run, clean clothes, and fresh water whenever they wanted it. He wasn't willing to give that up.

Grady spoke again, voice placating. "I never said it was your fault. I know you try your best to look after that boy. You always have."

He almost sat up to protest. He didn't need Seraf to look after him, and he hadn't been a boy in years. They both knew that. It wasn't his fault that Seraf couldn't accept the fact that Breaker could take care of himself; she might have been bound to him as protection originally, but his father's death nullified the contract. He loathed her guilt.

"This time, you need to focus on your recovery. Just because I patched you up doesn't mean you're as good as new. I expect you to take it easy."

The weight of their gazes on him made Breaker want to twitch. He managed to hold himself still, feigning sleep. It was a relief when their conversation started again.

"I know, I know," Grady said in a long-suffering voice. "You'll do your best but no promises." The old doctor snorted. "Sometimes I wonder why I bother with the two of you. You both are so hellbent on throwing your lives away it makes me want to slap the stupid out of you."

Breaker had no idea what Seraf wrote, but it must have made a difference because when Grady spoke again, his voice was lighter. "I've got a bag of medicine to send with you. Promise me you'll take what's in it."

A pause as Seraf scribbled on her paper. "Wages of Sin,

hmm?" Grady's fingers drummed the metal side of the bed. "Sounds familiar. Outreach group, I think." Grady made a humming noise. "Yeah, I remember now. Based out of New Venice. They asked me to keep some of their flyers to give out to troubled Infernals that might need their help."

More scribbling. "Yeah, sure. Let me go find one."

Breaker heard Grady leave and figured now was as good a time as any to wake up. He made a point of stretching his arms and groaning, even going so far as smacking his lips. When he opened his eyes, Seraf was staring at him from her bed. By the disdainful expression she wore, he suspected he'd oversold it.

He rubbed at his gritty eyes and wished for his spectacles. He hated the world being blurry. He must have lost them in the fight. "What time is it?"

Seraf signed, "About six a.m."

"How are you feeling?"

A shrug. "Still alive. You?"

"Same." As Breaker got to his feet, he saw the plastic pitcher of cold water sitting on the table between their beds and poured a cup. Breaker handed it to Seraf before pouring himself one. Then he returned to her bed and sat on the edge, gaze fixed on the liquid sloshing against the sides of the cup.

"I'm, um," he took a breath as if that would help him get the words out. "I'm sorry."

He didn't look at her. He couldn't look at her. Had he ever apologized to her before? He didn't think he had in all the years they'd been together. What did that say about him?

A tug on his sleeve. When he glanced up, Seraf watched him with a look of confusion. "What do you have to be sorry for?" she signed.

He stared at the bandages that wrapped her torso and raised his eyebrows. "It was my plan, my idea, that got you those."

"No," she signed back, frowning, "the greedy dickheads

who ran the fights got me these." She cocked her head, loose black hair falling in front of her Infernal eye. "What's going on? It's never bothered you before."

"I've found a set of scrubs for y—ah. I see you're awake." Grady entered with an armful of supplies. He pierced Breaker with a look of warning before turning back to Seraf with an easy smile. "I healed the worst damage, but there's still the superficial stuff to worry about before you're fully healed. I included some antibiotics—not that I think you'll need them—and some additional medical supplies for wound care. Instructions are in there."

He turned to Breaker. "How are you doing with the heat?"

Breaker shrugged. "About the same."

Grady looked like he desperately wanted to punch him and only managed not to by a supreme effort of will. "I've included some supplements for you, as well as more of that special sunscreen. Vision the same or is it getting worse?"

"About the same," he repeated. Breaker twitched at the man's pointed regard. "I'm fine, all right?"

"Oh yes, you appear before me, the picture of good health." Grady shot him a baleful glare. Seraf snorted in laughter.

Breaker gritted his teeth and withstood the teasing; he was probably due for it anyway.

"Sarcasm is not appreciated."

"Just another service I offer. Free of charge." He handed a flyer over to Seraf. "I found it. Hope it helps."

"Thank you," she signed.

"Now I need to get ready for another busy day of young idiots rushing in here to get patched up. If you two could commence with getting the fuck out of my clinic, I'd appreciate it. Chances are good that I'm going to need those beds."

"We'll be out of your hair in no time," Breaker assured him.

Grady rubbed at his balding pate with an expression of

long-suffering patience on his face. Then he gave Breaker the finger. "If I see either of you back here in the next thirty days, I'm going to punch the idiocy straight out of your unresisting bodies. Don't test me."

"Why are you looking only at me?" Breaker asked in mock offense.

"I have no idea what you're talking about."

Breaker caught the wink Grady threw Seraf. She returned a shaky smile.

"I shouldn't have to remind either of you to take it easy, but I'm going to do it anyway because sometimes you're dumber than a sack of hammers." With those encouraging words, Grady swept out of the exam room.

"Need help?" Breaker asked, gesturing to the well-worn scrubs the doctor had provided Seraf.

She shook her head and motioned for him to turn around. Breaker did, doing his best to put himself back to rights. As he rolled up the cuffs of his sleeves, he said, "I wouldn't be surprised if we get paid a visit by New Venice's finest. We say nothing about last night. As far as they are concerned, we were nowhere near Dempsey's." He leaned over to slip on his shoes. "They shouldn't have anything definitive to tie us to the fights, considering the glamour used to disguise us."

A tap on his shoulder had him turning around to see Seraf dressed. Aside from her pallor and the ginger way she moved, she looked as she always did. Her Infernal healing had taken care of the worst of the damage with an assist from Doc Grady.

She signed, "I used my shadow travel."

Breaker nodded. He remembered. And while it was a rare skill, he doubted Seraf was the only Infernal ever to have it, and even if she were, it would only be circumstantial at best if the police had nothing else to tie them to the fights.

"It's fine."

Her expression conveyed her doubt, but Breaker ignored

it. He chucked his jacket into the biohazard bin—there was no saving it—and ran a hand through his greasy hair. Dee, he wanted a shower. He was dreading the walk back to the office without his cane, but it had made sense to leave it behind—it was too recognizable.

Seraf held out the flyer Doc had given her. "This looks like the only lead left," she signed. "One of the Infernals I talked to knew Brasius. And he said a friend of his went missing after contacting Wages of Sin."

Two mentions of it in conjunction with missing or newly collared Infernals. Breaker studied the flyer—a simple thing, really, with a coded message that likely held the location, days, and times. "Then that's where we'll go."

Chapter 13

Errol Barrow was waiting for him at the office when he returned from getting coffee from Witches' Brew. Seraf was downstairs, actually taking it easy. He passed Tamlin his iced coffee with a hit of fae elderflower essence and moonshadow. Breaker had given them the day off after the nightmare of the night before and had slept the entire morning away after a hot shower to get rid of the ingrained dirt and blood.

"If I'd known you were paying us a visit, I would have picked you up a scone, Inspector Summoner," Breaker said as he perched his ass on the arm of a chair and took a sip of his London Fog. Arinayah had talked him into it, and he had to admit it was better than he'd expected. It wasn't his preferred Bitter Like My Heart blend, but it was a pleasant change.

"Where's your Infernal half?" Barrow asked, peering around Breaker as if he expected her to materialize from out of thin air behind him.

"Napping. It's our day off."

The Inspector Summoner gestured at Tamlin. "You don't get the day?"

Tamlin snorted, tossing his black hair out of stormcloudgrey eyes. "Please, I work normal hours. I get weekends and every other Friday off, not like you workaholics. I have a *life*."

Breaker shrugged, hiding his glee behind his typical impassive expression. Tamlin was providing the perfect cover. "Around here, we take what we can get. Can't be picky about when we work if we want to eat." He took another sip of his drink, careful not to scald his tongue. Ari always set warming spells on his to-go orders so they didn't cool too quickly. "But I doubt you came here to talk about nap times. You need my statement from the bridge, yeah?"

Barrow blinked, caught off guard. "Yeah, I guess I could get that now."

Breaker pretended ignorance about what else would bring the Inspector Summoner to Unshriven. Leaning forward with false attentiveness, he kept his gaze open and told Barrow of what he saw of the Maleficar on the bridge several nights ago. He offered concise answers with little personal observation—he'd learned how to spot lies and used the skill to make sure his own were unlikely to be discovered.

He'd had his tells beaten out of him at a young age.

Breaker didn't offer to wake Seraf. He kept Seraf out of it. Technically, he was responsible for her behavior as he'd been the one to give the order that led her to the roof and the Maleficar's Infernal. There was still debate about whether Infernals should even be allowed to testify in court—unsurprising considering the debate still raged on whether to allow Infernals full human rights because of the demonic blood running through their veins. He wasn't interested in making the man's job any easier.

The police had come to his father's house several times when Breaker was a boy. They'd done nothing. Breaker still hadn't forgiven them.

Breaker had finished his tea by the time Barrow had finished his questions. Tossing the to-go cup into the trash, he stood and stretched. "If that's all, Inspector, I think I might follow Seraf's example and have a nap. There's something so," he paused, searching for the word, "decadent about sleeping away one's afternoon."

"Late night?" Barrow sounded nonchalant, but Breaker could pick up the slight fluctuations in his energy. His summons was close, ready to be called on at a moment's notice. That matched the tension in the detective's shoulders and the drawn set of his mouth.

"Stakeout. Seraf and I were perched on a roof for the better part of the night."

"For your collar case?" Breaker shook his head. "Wouldn't have been near Eighth and Bailey, would it?"

Breaker took a moment to respond, as if he were consulting a mental map in his head. So Barrow was here about what happened after the fights last night. He shouldn't have been surprised—the cops always questioned Unshriven when something strange went down in New Venice. They had a reputation for troublemaking and being in the right place at the wrong time.

"No, that's just warehouses. Our client took us closer to the Mire." He cocked his head in curiosity. "Why?"

Tamlin raised a copy of the New Venice Daily. "I don't know why you bother with a subscription if you don't read it."

"I didn't subscribe to it for the news. Consider it a bonus," Breaker snapped at his assistant. He turned back to Barrow. "What happened?"

"Can't say much," Barrow began, running a hand down his face. "You ever hear of Clayton Dempsey?" Then he rolled his eyes at his question. "Stupid. Of course, you have."

"Everyone who runs a business in New Venice has," Breaker said, eyes narrow. "And none of it good. Drugs, curse workings, and the like, yeah?"

The summoner nodded, pointing at the paper Tamlin held out to Breaker. "We found the bodies of him and his crew early this morning. They were floating in a canal adjacent to his fight club. Looks like there was a magical throwdown of some kind."

Breaker skimmed the article, surprised at the swiftness of the reporting. Not the accuracy, that was—as usual—not worth shit. "Territorial scuffle?" he asked Barrow, glancing up from the article.

"Maybe." Barrow ran a hand through his messy pompadour, the tattoos on his arm deep black against his tanned skin as the rolled-up sleeves on his shirt shifted. How long had the man been awake and working?

"He had a place off Bailey where he put on fights. Infernals put in a cage for the amusement of those who paid good money to watch them beat the shit out of each other." Barrow watched him closely.

Breaker continued pretending to read the paper. After a few silent moments, he looked up to find the summoner staring at him. Breaker held the inspector's gaze, his magical energy a still pool of calm water surrounding him. No need to panic. The cop was likely fishing for something to tie him to Dempsey, and Breaker's job was to make sure he found nothing.

"Huh. Maybe some civic-minded Infernal took offense." He stretched, shifting his neck to the side sharply with a loud crack. "Decided to take out the trash." Breaker took off his glasses so he could rub his eyes, hoping Barrow would take the hint. "He was on my list for that collar case I mentioned. His death puts me down a lead."

"You sure you haven't already been by to see him?" Barrow's face set into grim lines.

Here we go. "Pretty damn sure, yeah," Breaker lied placidly. "What makes you think I was?"

"Reports of an Infernal who teleported out of the cage. One moment there, the next gone."

"I think we're all aware I can't teleport. And that I'm not an Infernal."

"Your partner can. I saw it myself with that Maleficar."
Barrow leaned his elbows on his knees, hands clasped in front
of his chin. "You still want to bullshit me, Unshriven?"

Breaker raised a pale brow but otherwise didn't bother to
react. Unruffled, he passed the folded newspaper back to
Tamlin, who was suddenly very busy updating the accounts on
the office laptop.

Barrow was grasping, shooting arrows in the dark in the
hope of hitting anything useful. There were few witnesses, and
Breaker wore Ari's glamour. The only person who could place
him and Seraf at the club was Dahrian.

The strained camaraderie between them evaporated like a
puddle on asphalt beneath the noonday sun. "No bullshit,
Inspector Summoner," he countered evenly. "I'm sure there
are other Infernals with such a power. Seraf doesn't exactly
teleport anyway. And I can vouch for her—she was with me
all night." Not technically a lie. He had been with her all
evening.

"And who can vouch for you?"

"I don't know if you are aware of this, Inspector
Summoner, but the whole point of a stakeout is to remain
unseen." He kept his expression guileless and mild. "Are we
under suspicion for something? Are you charging me with a
crime?" Breaker put on a show of mild affront using his best 'I
need to speak to your manager' voice. He stretched his wrists
out and leaned forward, offering them to Barrow. "Am I," his
voice dropped into a husky register, "under arrest?"

Rolling his eyes, Barrow flopped back in his chair. "For
fuck's sake, I don't have time for this crap." He scrubbed at his
stubbled jaw with a broad palm. "If you were there and saw
anything, I don't suppose you'd tell me, would you?"

"As you said, Inspector," Breaker said, nodding, "if." He'd
won this round, so he threw Barrow a bone. "Look, I had my
cell phone on me all night. You can ping the towers to see
where I was sitting until near dawn." He'd cloned his phone

and had it stashed on the rooftop in question should his whereabouts be questioned. Once he'd turned his original phone off, the cloned one would send up a call to the nearest tower. If they pulled phone records, they'd see that he'd been where he said he was for the better part of the night.

"What happened to your face?"

Breaker didn't possess Infernal durability or healing. It was interesting to study medical applications using magic, and he didn't have Grady's natural skill or the patience to try and learn. Grady had knitted up the worst of his injuries, but superficial bruising remained.

He'd had much worse anyway.

Rolling his eyes, Breaker huffed. "You know my line of work, Inspector. Fraternizing with some entities of less than savory character, both alive and dead, is all part of the job."

"Come again?" Barrow crossed his arms. "Without all the fancy words this time."

Breaker considered refusing to answer but thought better of it. "A poltergeist threw me into a wall."

"Ouch."

"Yes, that's what I said at the time." Breaker stood. "Now, if that's all you had for me, I'd like to take that nap."

The Inspector Summoner stood as well, eyeing Breaker speculatively. "You ever hear of a Tobias Winstead?"

Breaker's insides turned to ice. He cocked his head, needing time to force air into his lungs from the gut punch of that question. "You mean that mage murdered in New Orleans years ago?" Shrugging, he swallowed down his unease. "Who hasn't? It's on the Murder tour."

Barrow's expression twisted into disgust. "Not just him. His kid too."

The knot in Breaker's lungs unwound a bit. "Yeah. Did Dempsey have something to do with that?"

Barrow shook his head. "Not officially. Winstead worked with whoever could afford a mage of his caliber. Dempsey was on the list of suspects, but we were never able to connect him to Winstead beyond a cursory meeting and a few business associates in common."

"Winstead was dirty?" Though he appeared calm, Breaker was only moments from throwing up from anxiety.

"He was a mage for hire, affordable to only the very wealthy and powerful. Some of whom are likely criminals. And he was cunning enough to stay on the right side of the law—at least as far as I know." Barrow rubbed at his jaw. "I can't help but wonder if there's a connection."

"What, like a serial killer or something?"

Breaker scoffed. "Someone hunting people in his circle?"

Now it was Barrow's turn to roll his eyes. Sneering, he answered, "Yeah, because that's all I need." He sighed. "Just watch your back, Unshriven," he said as he left.

Breaker chewed on the inside of his cheek, unsure of what the Inspector Summoner was warning him about but knowing enough to heed it. His stomach clenched. "Always do, Barrow. Always do."

Chapter 14

Breaker stepped out of the back door of Unshriven into the small yard filled with gravel and rocks. Neither he nor Seraf was interested in keeping up with a yard no matter how small, so they'd covered most of it. When Tamlin started as their Man Friday, he'd asked if he could plant herbs in some raised beds against the walls of the fence and Breaker hadn't seen a reason to tell him no. It wasn't like they were using the space for anything anyway. Tamlin filled the yard with the fragrant scent and riotous greenery of herbs, medicinal plants, and possibly some other things that weren't native to this plane. Breaker thought it best not to ask.

He unlatched the gate and slipped into the small alley between his and the next row house on the block, making his way to the street on silent feet. Seraf had slept most of the day away. Breaker had checked on her intermittently, but all she did was nap. He kept his visits short to keep from disturbing her.

Turning left, Breaker made his way toward the nearest canal. Water called to him. Tonight he needed the comfort of the element that spoke most closely to his soul.

Breaker told anyone who asked that he'd decided to build

a business in the Mire because of its easy proximity to New Venice. It was only partially true. The Mire was the closest you could get to New Venice without actually living there, and it was considerably less expensive than the tonier parts of New Orleans. People asked few questions and fewer expected answers. He kept the secret of his affinity to water to himself. It was just another secret, much like his past and real name. Not many people knew him from before he'd been a street kid, and he wanted to keep it that way.

He could feel the water of the canal at the back of his mind as he walked. In the heavy night air, thick with the perfumes of night-blooming jasmine and rotting plant matter, Breaker relaxed in the relative solitude and rare quiet. He 'reached' for the canal, his mind settling as his magical energy melded with the water. Sighing, Breaker tipped his head back and allowed the clean, swirling feel of it to wash over him.

He was a mage, yes, but one with natural energy aligned closely with water. It was different than a summoner who bound an entity with a particular affinity to them via contract in exchange for the use of their power. As a mage, Breaker didn't need to make a deal with an elemental spirit for power; he could focus his energy as well as harness the energy found in the land and people around him to force the laws of the universe to obey him, if only for a short time.

He'd snuck out, hoping to calm his mind enough to sleep for a few hours. Insomnia was a bitch. Every time he closed his eyes, the memory of Seraf in that cage assaulted him. If his brain wanted to be an asshole, a superimposed image of her as a child, dripping with gore, appeared like an appalling phantom behind his closed eyelids.

Grady's harsh words echoed in his head. The doctor was the only one who had any idea who he and Seraf really were. Breaker hadn't had a choice in trusting him—he'd been unconscious and in bad shape when Seraf had carried him to Grady's clinic. When he'd finally woken up to a damaged knee and his father's cane, he'd been too raw to process much of anything. Seraf had told Grady some of what happened while they recuperated. Grady wasn't stupid—he was perfectly capable of putting two and two together and getting four, and that's what he'd done. Breaker hadn't liked anyone knowing his past, but the man had never spoken about it to anyone. As far as Grady was concerned, they were two strays he'd all but adopted.

Stopping at the canal's edge in the shadow of a walking bridge spanning the distance between 'streets,' Breaker rubbed his eyes. He'd left his glasses at home since he didn't have to worry about light sensitivity this late and his poor vision hardly mattered. Stretching out his hand, he traced a sigil in the air then flicked it to hover over the water. It separated into several glowing discs about two feet in diameter. They floated in the air only a few inches above the canal.

He stepped onto the one closest to the bank, then the next, and the next until he stood in the center of the canal. The thing that stood out about Barrow's description of Dempsey's death was that someone had moved the body from the scene. Someone had dumped Dempsey and his men in the canals without arousing any suspicion. Breaker wanted to know how.

Squatting down, he touched the tips of his index and middle fingers against the water's surface. He spoke a word of command, and the water swirled around his fingers, answering his call. Typically water didn't retain information for very long, but Breaker couldn't let something like that stop him. He'd been working on a spell that tapped into water's power of reflection. With enough control and concentration, he should be able to catch a glimpse of the body dump and perhaps gain a clue about who moved them and how.

Taking a deep breath, Breaker emptied his mind of extraneous thoughts. It always surprised him when it worked—his mind moved rapidly, jumping from one idea to the next, never still. However, he'd learned magic at the knee of one of the premier mages in the South. Failure had never been an option.

Breaker merged his consciousness with the canal's, plunging his hand into the water. It was disorienting at first—his idea of his body became fluid as the water within him called to the water without. Breaker's training asserted itself without him having to think about it: his mind snapped back into focus so that the essence of who he was didn't become dissolved in the flowing current.

He reached out again, his hand physically mimicking the mental effort. His fingers sketched out the new sigil he'd created in the air in front of him; a mirroring sigil appeared in eldritch glowing white above the water before sinking below the surface with a flash. As it did so, Breaker shuddered. Before his eyes, the water gave up everything it had 'seen' in a flood of images.

Breaker drowned in information, his mind desperately parsing everything water showed him. It was like drinking from a geyser. His knees buckled from the force of it, the sharp pain when they hit the disc jerking him out of the flow. Taking a deep breath, he dove back in.

He caught sight of Dempsey's face as his body hit the surface of the canal. Breaker didn't understand what the images surrounding it told him. An opening in the earth and stone appeared adjacent to the water. Bodies tumbled out of it to land with separate splashes. It looked like the earth just spat him and his cronies out into the canal.

Breaker's mind whirled with the images and information water had provided him. He surfaced, staggering on the disc that held him and nearly falling into the canal. Reeling, he managed to remain upright. His steps were unsteady as he crossed the discs floating above the water, each one disappearing after he'd stepped off of it until he was once again on solid ground.

The reaction headache hit him like a thunderbolt. He

made it to a metal bench and dropped onto it with a groan, hands fisting against his temples to try and rub away the headache. Breaker didn't mind the migraine; it was a small price to pay for a successful spell and the information he'd gathered.

A hand on his arm had him swinging out in a wild punch. When Breaker opened bleary eyes, Dahrian stood out of reach, a look of concern on his face. Dumbly, Breaker stared up at him, his mind still a mess from what the water showed him. He saw Dahrian's mouth moving, but he couldn't make out the words. They were muffled gibberish. Breaker shook his head.

Dahrian took a few steps closer and squatted in front of him, dark eyes severe when Breaker didn't move.

"What the fuck was that?" he asked in a voice that cleaved Breaker's skull in half.

"Ow," he whispered, still rubbing his temples with his knuckles. "Must you screech?"

"I do not screech!"

"You are doing so right now." Breaker thought about sticking his fingers in his ears to see if that would help. It likely wouldn't stop the pain, but it might go a long way to shutting the infuriating man up. He wished he would go away and leave him in peace.

"I don't know why I bothered." Dahrian climbed to his feet, throwing his hands in the air in frustration. His wild hair spread out from his head strangely. Was Dahrian descended from some kind of sentient hedgehog? "I came to see if you got out okay."

Breaker checked his watch. "At half-past one in the morning?" He narrowed his eyes. "How long were you watching me?"

Dahrian spluttered indignantly like he was in competition for the title for Best Splutterer and wanted to humiliate his opponents for their lack of commitment. After making a noise akin to a boiling tea kettle, he practically shouted, "Don't flatter yourself!"

Breaker couldn't stop the pained sound that passed his lips as his headache pulsed like his brain wanted to burst out of his skull. He surged to his feet, clapping both hands over Dahrian's mouth. "Would you kindly shut the fuck up?" he hissed, eyes narrowed in pain.

Surprisingly, Dahrian subsided. Breaker didn't remove his hands from the summoner until he nodded. Breaker relaxed and buried his fingers in his hair, his elbows braced on his knees and prayed for death. How could one human being be so gods damned loud?

"Bad?" came the whisper beside him as Dahrian settled himself on the bench.

"You have no idea," Breaker whispered.

He jerked when something cold touched the back of his neck at the base of his skull, then groaned at the wash of relief. "What is—what are you doing?"

"It's not much, but I know a little bit of magic outside of summoning. It's just a quick chill spell on my hand. Looks like you could use it."

Breaker didn't say anything, reveling in the relief the cold brought him. After a few minutes, the reaction headache lessened enough so he could open his eyes and straighten in his seat. "Thank you," he said as Dahrian took his hand away.

Then, because he was biologically incapable of accepting kindness, he asked, "Seriously, are you stalking me? First at the shop, then the fights, and now here."

Dahrian reared back in offense. "Wha--? No!" Breaker winced, and he lowered his voice to a more reasonable level. "I mean, no. I just happened to be passing by."

Breaker's bullshit detector went off, alarm bells ringing inside his abused skull. He raised one skeptical eyebrow.

"I had business out this way," Dahrian said, crossing his arms over his chest and staring at the canal.

Breaker shook his head in disbelief, biting back a curse when that threatened to set off his headache again. "Twice, I might put to coincidence. Three times in such a short time, not so much."

Dahrian puffed up, his ridiculous mass of hair looking electrified. Did it have something to do with his summons? He didn't respond to Breaker's hypothesis.

"I could ask the same of you," he said instead. "And just what the hell were you doing in the canal in the middle of the night?"

Breaker had to give the man full marks for changing the subject and leading it away from his actions. However, if Dahrian was hoping to put Breaker on the defensive, he was doomed to disappointment. He simply relaxed back against the bench and glared at the other man as if he were a king looking down on a particularly annoying peasant. "A case," he said.

"You are avoiding my question. And quite poorly, I might add."

"Are you always this much of an asshole?"

"No." Breaker's smile glinted in the moonlight. "Usually I'm worse. Now answer the question: are you following me?"

Dahrian rolled his eyes with a huff. "Yeah. I was."

Breaker narrowed his eyes, already checking his wards. "Why?"

"I saw what happened between you and Dempsey. You left the warehouse so fast I followed after just to make sure you weren't in trouble. I saw them jump you."

"So? You don't know me to be concerned," Breaker scoffed.

"I know that." He shrugged. "I don't know why I did it. You were a familiar face that night or something. I didn't think about it beyond seeing why you were leaving in such a hurry."

Clenching his jaw shut, Breaker breathed in slowly through his nose. Fuck. Here was a witness who could place him and Seraf at the fights and who had witnessed her kill Dempsey. Not good. He pinched the bridge of his nose between his fingers. "How much did you see?"

Cocking his head in a move reminiscent of a curious sparrow, Dahrian drummed his fingers on one knee. "The first time Dempsey used his staff on you. I watched for a few moments before I rushed inside to get Ch—my friend."

It was Breaker's turn to observe Dahrian closely. At least he hadn't seen Breaker biff his stun spell. "Why on earth for?"

Dahrian stared at Breaker as if he'd just sprouted a second, evil head. "To help?"

What had he expected his friend to do? Unless he was a heavy hitter in the magic department, there wasn't much that he could have done to nullify the situation. Plus, it was suicide to go against someone like Dempsey and his organization without disguising themselves. It was better that Dahrian and his friend hadn't interfered. Breaker took care of it.

"Did you make a statement to the police?"

Dahrian drew back as though Breaker had insulted his sainted grandmother. "What do you take me for?" If he'd been an old society matron, he'd have been clutching his pearls.

"A guy who has been skulking around my business for the last week."

Dahrian opened his mouth to reply, then shut it again when Breaker gave him a quelling look. He tilted his head, observing Breaker in a way that made him tense with discomfort. He'd never cared for people studying him too closely.

"I find you intriguing."

Breaker rolled his eyes. "Pull the other one." He'd had a few furtive hookups but nothing resembling a relationship. Breaker's unusual looks attracted a few men, though it typically ended up with them fetishizing him in ways that made him deeply uncomfortable. The less said about his time on the streets and things he'd done to survive, the better.

He'd learned that people didn't like him, let alone find him intriguing enough to follow him around without wanting something from him. Breaker cultivated his prickly personality for that very reason. He was better left alone.

"You don't think you're intriguing?" Dahrian sounded genuinely curious. When Breaker looked at him, Dahrian leaned forward into his space, just shy of uncomfortable.

"Oh, I'm gods damned fascinating." A bitter laugh escaped Breaker before he could stifle it. He wiped the sweat from his brow with the back of his hand and shifted to put more space between them.

Head cocked, Dahrian regarded him with quiet intensity. The hairs on the back of Breaker's neck rose, and he held back a shiver. Dahrian's gaze fell upon him like a spotlight, determined to light up all of the dark corners best left hidden. Breaker hated everything about it.

"What? Do I have a dick drawn on my face or something?"

"Your eyes," Dahrian said, leaning closer.

Breaker instinctively leaned backward; he'd forgotten that he wasn't wearing his glasses. "What about them?"

As if just realizing he was intruding into Breaker's space, Dahrian shifted so they weren't quite so close. "They almost look red in the light."

Breaker glanced up at the mage lamp on the post above them. He should never have left the brownstone. "I have light eyes. They look red because of the blood vessels." Breaker stood. "They're just a pale blue."

Dahrian blinked, almost as if he were taken aback by Breaker's admission. "They look darker with your glasses."

He shrugged. "Okay." The statement hadn't deserved an answer; Breaker didn't understand why he even bothered to give Dahrian one. It would only encourage him.

"Speaking of," Dahrian said, digging into his pocket.

"Here." He held out Breaker's missing pair of glasses, the glamour on them long gone.

Breaker took them before staring into Dahrian's eyes. He couldn't parse what he saw in them. Curiosity certainly, but also something else.

"Thanks." Why had he bothered to pick these up, let alone return them?

He stood, needing to get some space. "It's late. Good night."

Springing to his feet, Dahrian said, "I'll walk with you."

Breaker ran a hand down his face and silently uttered a prayer for patience. As much as he might want to lose his temper, it wasn't professional nor a particularly good look for him. "No need. I would prefer to be alone." He thought he saw Dahrian's eyes shift from side to side. "The quiet will help the headache."

Once again, Dahrian looked like he might protest. Breaker readied himself for an argument, but Dahrian nodded, albeit reluctantly after a few moments. "You're not used to people being nice to you," he said.

Breaker blinked, unable to parse the words that had come from Dahrian's mouth. "Why would they be?"

Dahrian's expression settled into something Breaker didn't recognize. He wasn't interested in sticking around to figure it out either. With a wave of his hand, he turned in the direction of Unshriven and said, "If you want to hire me, come by during business hours. Otherwise, stop bothering me."

Ignoring the twinge in his chest, Breaker made his way home and back to his bed.

Chapter 15

The following day Seraf was much recovered. Breaker sent Tamlin to Witches' Brew to fetch them all enough coffee and pastries to gorge themselves into a carbohydrate coma while he readied the small room that served as their conference room where he typically met with clients. Seraf settled herself in one of the more comfortable chairs around the round table with a ragged sigh.

"How're you feeling?" he asked her as she shifted to find a comfortable position.

"Better," she signed. "Itchy and achy."

"Good." He set the pills that Grady had given her on the table along with a glass of water. "Do you need anything for pain?"

When she shook her head no, Breaker set aside that particular bottle and went to help Tamlin with his bounty. Once they'd settled with their chosen caffeinated beverage and a plate towering with scones, beignets, muffins, and whatever else tickled their fancy from the obscenely large bakery box, Breaker began.

"I didn't find out much," he said around a mouthful of beignet, getting powdered sugar everywhere. "Dempsey fixed the fights, and Brasius was one of the main beneficiaries. He was a big draw for tourists. Dempsey wasn't happy to lose him. Neither was Silk."

"I don't understand," Tamlin said, making notes on a steno pad that he would transcribe into the case file later. "If Brasius wanted to buy his freedom, then making him a champion would only mean he earned out faster, right? Which would go against both Dempsey and Silk's agendas." He took a delicate bite of a lemon blueberry scone and made a happy noise.

Breaker licked the powdered sugar from his fingers before answering. "Depends on the contract he had set up with them. We all know the terms are hardly ever favorable to the Infernal in those things. We also know Silk was taking a huge chunk of his winnings. He wasn't netting a lot from the fights. I'm sure Dempsey took his cut off the top too. He may not have even been close to buying his way out, and we'll likely never know."

Infernals weren't allowed to keep bank accounts in their own names. The best they could hope was to have a trusted friend open one for them, sharing the account, though the non-Infernal would always be primary. They could clean out an Infernal's savings any time they liked, leaving the Infernal with no recourse. Most chose to keep their cash in hidden caches, but that held other dangers.

"I can do a little digging," Tamlin offered. "See if Brasius had savings squirreled away somewhere."

Breaker nodded. A few places online didn't look too hard at the people opening up accounts, but they were sketchy, and the risk of being scammed was high. Still, if Brasius had gone that route, Tamlin would find it for them. Tamlin had taken to computers like a raccoon to trash despite being out of the technological loop for centuries.

Breaker didn't question his luck; he just stood aside and

marveled as the fae man ransacked secure servers with all the gusto of Genghis Khan's invading armies.

"You find anything out, Seraf?"

She set aside her white hot chocolate and nodded. "Talked to a guy named Mook before the fights started," she signed. "We got to talking—he was curious about me not having a collar, I think—and he mentioned a friend of his that worked at Purgatorio and used to fight. He was looking to use the money to buy his way out."

Breaker tapped his fingers on the table in thought. It was a pipe dream. An Infernal could never gain complete independence legally. They were considered too volatile—and often too powerful—to be self-governing. An Infernal descended from demons, born of experimentation. Even a few generations removed, Infernals were still perceived as full-blooded demons and treated as such, like they somehow lacked in morality or intelligence. The most any Infernal could hope for —as far as independence went—was to have a monitoring anklet put on for the rest of their life so that the FBD— Federal Bureau of Demonologists—could track them should they go rogue. Independent Infernals had to register with their local FBD office to make sure they were correctly registered.

Seraf avoided all of this because she'd been bought directly and placed under contract immediately. No one was aware that they had broken the agreement. She could leave any time she wanted—Breaker wasn't holding her—but she'd live a life in the shadows to avoid registration.

"Did this Mook give you a name?"

She shook her head. "He said his friend hadn't been back to the fights in some time. He's worried, though—they'd promised each other they'd leave together."

"You think he knows what might have happened to his friend?" Tamlin glanced up from his note-taking, his voice sad.

"I think he suspects," Seraf signed. "Doesn't want to admit it, though."

"Ahhhh." Lin's grey eyes had gone dark and cloudy, like the sky before a summer thunderstorm. "Shame."

Breaker reached for a sour cream cake donut. He tore off a piece and dipped it in his coffee. "Think you can find this Mook again? Might be worth it to ask him some more questions."

Seraf pinched off a bit of the cranberry muffin and popped it into her mouth. She wiped her fingers clean on a napkin before signing, "Mook mentioned they'd met at Wages of Sin meeting."

Breaker remembered Seraf asking Grady about Wages of Sin when she was recovering. "What is it—some kind of cult?"

Carefully reaching into her pocket, she unfolded a piece of paper. It was a flyer that Grady had given her. "It's a support group for collared Infernals. Said that I should go check it out if I ever get tired of having a contract." Seraf raised her eyebrows at him as she pushed the flyer in his direction.

Breaker picked it up to give it a closer look. "Seems like they're meeting this evening. Shall we pay them a visit?"

HE SHOULDN'T HAVE BEEN SURPRISED that the next meeting of the Wages of Sin outreach group was in the basement of the soup kitchen that Father Lyle helped run. Breaker remembered the times he and Seraf had come by for a hot meal after the kitchen closed from the evening service.

They'd been fourteen, although he never was sure what Seraf's actual age was since she didn't know herself. She'd taken his age as her own just to have something to tell people should they ask. She'd picked her birthday too, a date she'd liked the look of on the calendar. They'd been on the streets for a few months the first time they'd tried the soup kitchen late in its shift, only to find themselves too late and the food gone.

They'd learned that if you wanted to eat, you got in line early and waited. The closer to the front, the more likely it was you'd get fed.

That was all well and good if you were full grown. Most people ignored the homeless and the transient. They didn't want to the reminder that there but for the grace of God and all that horseshit. Being poor was akin to being invisible. The homeless adults could line up around the block, and, aside from a few disdainful looks from passersby, they were left alone.

Children were another matter entirely. People *noticed* children, saw them in ways they couldn't overlook when it came to adults. It was either do-gooders compelled to hold them as examples for their next 'Think of the Children' crusade, or the kind of person who thought to take advantage of children unlikely to be missed. Either way, Breaker didn't like the idea of just standing around in plain sight for hours on end to get a bowl of stew made with suspicious meat.

At least until the gnawing ache in his belly became too much after he and Seraf had been chased from the last of the unlocked restaurant dumpsters weeks before. Urchin gangs controlled certain sections of New Venice, and fights broke out for territory surrounding the best dumpsters. Breaker and Seraf were a gang of two, uninterested in joining any of the gangs who reported to the criminal hierarchy of adults that controlled them. They had few options.

It had been a bad week. Breaker hadn't been fast enough to avoid a run-in with a few street toughs, not with his bad knee being what it was, and Seraf had to chase them off. They'd both gotten more cuts and bruises for their trouble but thankfully, nothing broken. Still, Breaker knew that if they didn't get something to eat soon, they'd be easy pickings for anyone or thing that meant them harm.

Thus Breaker found himself standing third in line on a Wednesday afternoon. Seraf stood with him, eye covered by a bandana. They'd found that most places that offered outreach didn't extend it to Infernals.

He ignored the suspicious and sometimes even hostile looks as more and more people lined up for the evening meal. Breaker kept his magic close, hoping he wouldn't have to use it. So far, he and Seraf had done their best to avoid relying on their respective powers—they would draw too much attention, likely ending with Seraf imprisoned as a rogue Infernal and Breaker sent to a state home. Assuming someone didn't figure out who he was and cash in on the information.

When the doors to the soup kitchen opened, Breaker used the wall to steady himself when he stood up too fast in the heat. Seraf was at his shoulder to brace him if he needed it, but he locked his knees and kept himself on his feet. He wished he had the cane, but he hadn't grown into it, and it was too noticeable anyway. By the time they reached the food line, his hands were shaking.

He and Seraf grabbed plastic trays that reminded him of a cafeteria and made their way down the line. There was white rice scooped into a bowl, red beans with some meat, and another bowl filled with boiled green beans. A piece of bread, no butter. Another bowl of mixed fruit cocktail. He and Seraf took everything on offer with murmured thanks and made their way to a table at the corner of the room, as far out of the way as it was possible to be.

The room filled. Breaker took his time eating, afraid he might get sick if he bolted his food. Seraf had no such worries and did her best to unhinge her jaw so she could swallow everything in one gulp, almost as if she was afraid someone would take the food from her. A few older men and women joined their table, but no one seemed inclined to speak. They shoveled the free meal into their mouths and tried not to make eye contact with each other.

It couldn't last. Of course, it couldn't.

Just as Breaker was reaching for his fruit, saving it for

dessert, a broad hand slapped down on the table beside his tray. Spoon suspended halfway to his lips, he glanced up into the grizzled, flushed face of a man of perhaps fifty, heavyset body collapsing in on itself with the weight of his life and failures.

"What're two kids doing here?" His voice was too loud, tone belligerent. "You've got your own places! Don't take up food for those of us that need it!"

"Newcomers I see. Welcome. Welcome!" Another new voice, this one emphasizing abundant goodwill and joy. Breaker immediately distrusted it and the man speaking.

When neither Breaker nor Seraf said anything, the man stepped into view. Breaker hadn't taken his gaze off the man threatening him, but he caught a glimpse at the newcomer as he stopped at their table. He wore an easy smile on his unre-markable face, blue eyes surrounded by creases from smiling. Nondescript in every way save for the black shirt and priest's white collar he wore.

"Mr. Hallowell," the priest greeted, holding out his hand to get the man to shake, "it's good to see you again."

Hallowell took the hand offered, a flush coloring his cheeks red. He ducked his head, unable to meet the priest's eyes.

"Father Lyle," he muttered.

Breaker watched Hallowell continue to wilt under the priest's regard. "I hope there isn't a problem," Lyle said, a hint of stone in his voice. "There's a limited time you have to eat. It would be a shame to waste the food the Lord has provided."

"Yes, Father. I was just going." He glared at Breaker and Seraf in sullen silence before he walked back to his table.

"Now then." Father Lyle clapped his hands together and focused on the two of them. "Who do we have here?"

Seraf signed to Breaker, "What do we do?" She watched the priest with wary eyes, her whole body tensed to run.

Breaker wasn't sure, but he wasn't about to tell Seraf that.

Thankfully, the priest's eyes widened, and his next words saved him the trouble of responding.

"You are hard of hearing?" Unlike most people who met her, he didn't raise his voice and talk super slow or treat Seraf like she was an idiot. Instead, he shifted so he was facing her head on so she could read his lips more easily.

"She can hear. She just doesn't talk," Breaker told him.

"Mute?" Father Lyle's eyebrows rose in surprise.

"Not exactly." Breaker glanced around and noticed far too many people were interested in their conversation. He tucked himself closer to Seraf, closing their ranks against the angry adults around them. Coming to the soup kitchen was a mistake.

"Brother Benson is going to speak in a few minutes." It was the cost of the meal, Breaker knew. Get free food, listen to a churchman spew all over you, go back to your spot in the gutter. Lyle's next words surprised him. "Perhaps you'd like to come to the kitchen instead."

Father Lyle straightened and gestured for them to get up. Seraf tugged at his shirt, questions in her eyes. Breaker shrugged. The priest might want to throw them out or have them wash dishes to work off their meal. Either way, if it meant not having to listen to a self-righteous man speak about a god who didn't care for his creations, Breaker was okay with it.

He followed the priest, Seraf a half-step behind him. When they were through the swinging door of the kitchen, Breaker realized that his shoulders were tight and hovering somewhere up around his ears. The weight of the stares fell heavy on his back. Now he knew what it was like to be a turtle sticking its head out of its shell.

"Now then," Father Lyle said, turning around and leaning one hip against a stainless steel prep counter. "I don't suppose I have to tell you that this soup kitchen is for adults only. I can only imagine that you two being here is an oversight that I will take up with the nun working the line at the door."

Breaker sighed. At least they got one good meal out of it. He wouldn't have minded making this a weekly thing. Seraf frowned, her face settling into its trademark scowl. It wasn't fair. They didn't have anywhere to go that didn't involve them being separated and investigated, and neither of them could afford that.

"That being said," Lyle continued, expression open and easy to read. "You likely need food, and that I am more than happy to provide. Sound good?"

Breaker shook his head. "Why are you bothering to help us? What's in it for you?" It was impossible to keep the suspicion from his voice; nobody in the Mire or New Venice helped anyone else just because they needed it. Plus, he'd heard tales of Catholic priests; hell, it had been a common joke for decades. Why would Lyle be any different than anyone else, priest or otherwise?

Lyle tucked his hands in the pockets of his pants. "This your first time here?" He ignored Breaker's question to ask one of his own.

Breaker clenched his teeth around his angry words. Adults always did that, as if kids wouldn't notice them pulling that shit. Seraf nodded, but he added, "If it weren't, you'd already know about us."

Lyle didn't rise to the challenge. Instead, he held up a finger and walked to a large pantry to rummage inside it for a few moments. When Lyle returned to them, he held two disposable cups of chocolate pudding and two plastic spoons. He set them on the counter and waited.

Seraf eyed the cups curiously before turning her gaze to Breaker. It was hard to look away from the dessert on offer. The cook his father employed had made the best chocolate mousse Breaker had ever tasted. It had been a treat that he'd whipped up for Breaker's birthdays and holidays like

Christmas and Fat Tuesday. He knew this pre-made, shelf-stable pudding wouldn't be nearly as good, but it had been ages since he'd had anything resembling indulgence.

Still, he held himself back from just grabbing it and shoving it in his face like a starving vampire entering a blood bank. He rocked back and forth on his feet and managed to pull his gaze from the pudding to meet Seraf's questioning face. She signed, "You think it's safe?"

Breaker took a deep breath before reaching out and picking up one of the cups. He peered at it from all sides, searching for signs of tampering. The sealed lid appeared intact, and he couldn't find any holes in the cup itself. The priest watched his inspection with an air of patient amusement.

Finally, Breaker handed Seraf the cup he'd been inspecting and grabbed the second one for himself. He ripped off the top with a nod to her and dug in with the spoon provided. Seraf quickly followed, shoving a huge spoonful into her mouth. She made a noise that Breaker had never heard before in her entire repertoire of sounds as if she'd never tasted anything so good in her life. While he savored his pudding, trying to make it last as long as possible, Seraf ate hers in an eyeblink.

"Thanks," Breaker acknowledged grudgingly. He dipped his spoon into each corner, eating from the outside edges in, every spoonful methodical. Seraf had discarded the spoon and ran her finger along the inside of the cup to get the last of the pudding out.

"You're welcome," Lyle said, an indulgent smile on his face that immediately made Breaker wary. "And you're right. I know it's your first time here." He tilted his head as he stared at Seraf's frantic attempts to stick her entire hand in the cup. "Just as you know that this soup kitchen is adults only."

Breaker took the cup away from her after a moment before going back to his. Seraf made a sound like a dying whale, a disappointed pout on her face. Who would have believed an Infernal could be so childish over a pudding cup?

"Thought we'd chance it," he said, dipping his spoon in again.

"Where are your parents?" When Breaker just kept eating his pudding in small spoonfuls, Father Lyle rubbed at his temples. "There are places for children. Places designed to help you."

Lyle eyed them up and down. Breaker knew what he saw: two dirty, unkempt teenagers, barely out of childhood in clothes that were threadbare and likely getting too small with hair that needed cutting. "You shouldn't be out on the streets by yourselves."

Breaker stared at the priest, his spoon tucked in his mouth. "You going to turn us in?"

"Honestly? I'm tempted." His expression said that he might decide otherwise if they could convince him not to.

He ignored the icy claws that sank into his guts. He hadn't figured out how to alter his fingerprints, so if the cops took them in, they'd find out who he was and, worse, what Seraf was. He couldn't risk either of those things. He put the half-finished pudding cup down and pointed at the priest with the spoon held in his fist.

"You really think the police can help us?" He chuckled softly. Seraf watched with interest, as still as a statue. "Think CPS is going to make a difference? All they're going to do is separate us and throw us in some kind of orphan home if they can't find foster parents greedy enough to take us for the money."

He spun the spoon between his fingers. "You think we're safer in the system?" Breaker snorted. "Better off dead than that. Faster ways to go too."

"It wouldn't be like that," the priest protested.

"It wouldn't?" Breaker jabbed the spoon at him again, satisfied when Lyle flinched before he could stop himself. He cocked his head, a cruel smirk on his face. "I thought priests weren't supposed to lie."

Father Lyle palmed his chin. Breaker waited, trying not to bounce from foot to foot. He stood in thought for several minutes while Breaker finished his pudding and Seraf washed the remains of the sticky snack from her hands at the large kitchen sink.

Finally, the priest sighed and straightened. "You're right."

"Yes, I know." Breaker couldn't stop his shit-eating grin from appearing and didn't feel like trying. "I usually am."

He knew he was being an ass. Seraf would scold him for it later. He was just so damn tired of running, hiding, of pretending to be less than he was, than they both were. He wasn't some kid who didn't know how the world worked—he'd seen and done things that most his age would never experience. He was sick of hiding his magic for fear that the men his father had angered would come after him. The last thing he needed was some do-gooder coming in to offer solutions to problems he didn't understand, all so he could assuage his conscience.

"You're also an irritating little shit."

Seraf giggled, a sound Breaker hadn't heard in, well, he couldn't remember the last time he'd heard it. She clapped her hand over her mouth as her face turned a surprising shade of pink.

"I didn't think priests could swear," he said through the sour twist of his mouth.

Lyle folded his arms over his chest, looking like he was willing to match Breaker stubborn for stubborn. "I try not to, but there are times it's called for." He shrugged. Breaker saw the mischief dancing in his eyes. "It's not like we get a swearendectomy after seminary."

Breaker found himself smiling. A small one that sat strangely on his face for being genuine. Seeing it, Lyle smiled too.

"Okay," he said after a moment. "You obviously can't be served in the food line anymore—it's for the adults. Come around here tomorrow, an hour after we've finished serving. I'll have something for the two of you then."

Breaker's smile dropped. "Yeah, like the cops."

The priest turned serious, staring intently at him. "You have my word that I won't report you to the police. Just come to the side door, and I'll have some hot food for you both." He glanced at Seraf. "Will you do that for me?"

Seraf nodded before checking with Breaker.

"No promises," he snapped, grabbing her wrist to pull her out of the kitchen and back through the dining hall.

"Go out the back," Lyle said, stopping him. "Father Benson is giving the homily and I hate to interrupt him."

Breaker had a feeling his suggestion had nothing to do with preaching. Still, he wasn't going to complain. He didn't want to run into Hallowell again. Best to leave so no one could follow them. Lyle showed them the door leading to a back street bordering one of the canals. Breaker went with little fuss, towing Seraf behind him.

"See you tomorrow," the priest said before closing the door behind him.

"We'll see," Breaker had said to the closed door.

OF COURSE, they'd gone back the next day, despite Breaker's reservations. Father Lyle had answered the kitchen door on Seraf's second knock while he'd kept a lookout in case this was a trap for feral children, like Animal Control sometimes did for feral cats when they threatened to overrun the tourist-laden streets. The priest wore another of his short sleeve black shirts with the collar—Breaker made a note to look up its name when they next visited the library in the Mire—and slacks, this time topped with an apron that had an alligator in a chef's hat stirring a giant pot of gumbo.

"Come on in," he said, gesturing them inside. "I'm glad you decided to come back."

"Seraf wanted more pudding," Breaker said as he slipped past the priest, careful not to touch him.

"Whatever the reason, I'm still pleased to see you both."

"Thank you," Seraf signed.

"Oh, I know that one!" Father Lyle sounded delighted. He slowly signed, "You're welcome." He beamed with pride.

Seraf nodded then ducked her head down, almost shy, when the priest made the sign for "Hello."

"Unfortunately, we've just exhausted the little I was able to retain of it, so I'll have to rely on this young man to translate for me." Father Lyle moved as though to clap Breaker on the shoulder, but Breaker stepped out of the way and deeper into the kitchen, well out of reach.

Two plates of food sat on the counter for them, silverware and napkins set beside each. Breaker tentatively sniffed at the contents. His stomach rumbled in complaint while his mouth watered at the scent. Mashed potatoes and meatloaf swimming in gravy. Steamed broccoli. Cornbread drenched in butter. It wasn't anything like what the cooks at his father's mansion made, but it smelled like Heaven nevertheless.

"This doesn't look like normal soup kitchen food." He wavered, stepping closer to the counter where the plate sat, pulled to the food like he was a magnet and it was True North.

"That's because it isn't. It's what I made myself for dinner. Or rather, the nice lady who cooks for me at the rectory made for my dinner." Father Lyle waved at the plates and silverware. "Go on, dig in."

Seraf didn't wait any longer, but Breaker hesitated. "Your dinner?" he couldn't help but ask, unsure of the answer he wanted. Had the man given them his dinner? Did he want to have that knowledge?

"I ate already. These were leftovers." Father Lyle went to the refrigerator. "The woman makes enough to feed an army—she's used to cooking for ten people. Lemonade?"

Seraf nodded enthusiastically, demolishing the meatloaf like a Category Seven hurricane demolished coastal cities. Breaker took a bite of it and nearly wept in bliss. It was hot, full of flavor, and had a crunchy bit at the top. The potatoes were rich and smooth, heavy with butter. He'd never liked broccoli, and yet he'd devoured every bit that was on his plate. Through it all, Father Lyle stood back and watched after setting down their glasses of lemonade.

"You know my name but I still don't know yours," he said as Breaker mopped up gravy with his cornbread, unwilling to waste a drop. "Might I know them?"

Maybe it was the food coma he was nearly slipping into, or perhaps it was that Lyle hadn't called the police or CPS on them. Whatever the reason, he responded with the names they'd decided on for themselves when he'd woken up at Doc Grady's. "I'm Absalom. She's Seraf."

"A pleasure to meet you both properly." Plates cleaned, Lyle picked them up and began washing them in the sink. "And your parents? Did they mistreat you in some way?"

Breaker shared a look with Seraf, mind whirling. The lassitude permeating his body at having a good, home-cooked meal in who knows how long evaporated like morning fog off the water.

"We don't have any," he told him, voice terse.

"You both sprang fully formed from someone's head like Athena, eh?" Lyle dried the dishes, chuckling.

"Exactly. My dad is Zeus." Keep it light and easy, don't say too much.

Seraf's expression had gone soft and placid, like the surface of a still lake. It was almost like she'd disconnected from a part of herself. Breaker wished he could do that; it would make lying so much easier.

"That makes you a demigod then? Let's see, which one are you?" Father Lyle pretended to think about it. "Hercules?"

"You found me out. Now you're going to want me to clean your stable, right?"

"How long have you been on the street?" the priest laughed, delighted. He put away the dishes, went to the pantry, and fetched three chocolate pudding cups and three spoons.

Breaker took one and passed it and a spoon to Seraf before accepting his own. "I'm not sure. A couple of months." Breaker knew precisely how long they'd been living rough down to the day. No need to give the good Father too much information about who he really was.

"I want to help you."

"We don't need your help." When the priest looked pointedly at the pudding cup in his hand, Breaker set it down on the counter with the spoon. "A hot meal is nice, and the pudding is a treat, but we can do without them. Though if you're offering them freely, we're happy to have them."

That was the closest he would come to begging ever again in his life. Even that made him feel dirty, as if he needed to scrub the concession from his skin before it corrupted him. *Weak*—that was his father's voice, hard and cold with the word clipped like they were when he was spell-drunk.

Father Lyle stared at him for a long moment, taking his measure. Breaker met his gaze, adamant in his resolve. There would be no strings here, no matter how Lyle might try to bind them. If he wanted to help them so badly, he would do it freely, without expectations and guilt trips.

Lyle reached over and pushed the pudding back at Breaker. "Understood," he murmured and went back to eating his pudding.

Chapter 16

Breaker poured purified water from his thermos into the small shallow bowl he'd brought with him and whispered the incantation over it. After uttering the final syllable, he breathed atop the water. As the ripples settled back to stillness, an image of the meeting room emerged. It was slightly distorted from both the glass of the locket he was looking through and the water's surface tension, but it was clear enough for what he needed.

Pulling out his pocket watch, Breaker noted that Seraf had another hour, maybe an hour and a half, left on the shift spell he'd placed on her. It wasn't as comprehensive as Ari's glamours, but time was short. He hoped that would give Seraf enough time to get them a lead.

The first part of the meeting went just like any other: the welcome, introduction of newcomers, stories exchanged, support given. Breaker ignored most of the blather in favor of memorizing the faces in the room. There was no one he recognized. Even the young man leading it didn't seem familiar. Each of the Infernals and the humans present were unknowns. Seraf made sure to give him plenty of good looks at their faces as the other attendees welcomed her.

With that business out of the way, the group began to split

up into smaller sets of conversations, making Seraf make the rounds. Her cover story was a suitably harrowing one; she'd been the one to decide on it and come up with all the horrific little details. He tried not to let the similarities to her history bother him. If she was calm about it, he would do likewise.

Seraf's remoteness made him doubt the times he'd witnessed her depth of care for him. It didn't make sense how she could be so warm one moment and then coldly practically the next. Sometimes, he wondered if there was a grain of truth to the belief that Infernals could not feel genuine human emotions. Was it the instability present in all Infernals?

"How did you hear about us?" Ah, the human leader of the support group—Philip?—had cornered Seraf near the refreshment table. His voice was muffled and slightly distorted as though speaking through a tube. He was an earnest individual, all big brown eyes and hopeful expressions. Breaker sneered, glad the viewing was only one-way. Had he ever been so optimistic? That wasn't quite the word, and he didn't want to think more about it to find the right one. He rubbed at his knee and focused on the conversation.

"A friend," Seraf grated, her ruined voice part of her cover. Her former master had done damage to her vocal cords during her abuse. "He used to work at Taboo."

The man was good. There was barely a flicker in his concerned, pitying expression, but Breaker caught it. "What was his name? I may remember him."

"Orion," she said, loud enough to be overheard by anyone interested in eavesdropping.

A subtle flinch. Philip brought his hand to his face and began to tap a finger to his chin to cover it. Breaker grinned. There was something there, something they could push. This guy knew something about Orion's disappearance. Breaker wished Seraf would turn her body so he could see if anyone else had reacted to the missing Infernal's name.

"Orion, hmmm?" He closed his eyes as if searching his

memories. "Looked a bit...draconic?" Seraf must have nodded because he continued. "Yes, he came for a few months, and then he stopped." The man shrugged. "It happens. I hope he found what he was looking for even if it wasn't here."

For a man fronting a support group, he sounded remarkably unconcerned. He could be telling the truth—Breaker imagined that collared Infernals wouldn't be able to stay long—but his gut told Breaker otherwise. He hunkered closer to the dish of water.

"He's missing."

Philip raised his eyebrows in feigned surprise. "That can't be right. He's collared if I remember correctly."

Now it was Seraf's turn to shrug. Philip's expression slid into concern, and he reached forward with one hand. Breaker bared his teeth at the thought of him touching Seraf. She stepped back, and his hand fell to his side. Only then did Breaker relax.

"I'm sure there's no need for worry," the group leader said in a tone so false it made Breaker want to grind his teeth to nubs. He glanced behind him before turning back to Seraf with an apologetic look. "I'm sorry, it seems I'm needed elsewhere. I hope we'll see you again."

He hurried off as if a cohort of demons had just appeared, wearing nothing but jockstraps and chocolate sprinkles.

Seraf turned to find someone else to talk to, and Breaker gritted his teeth against the dizzy swoop of it. When the image steadied, he saw a few of the group attendees casting furtive looks in Seraf's direction, but no one seemed willing to come up to her. Breaker checked his watch; time was almost up.

The meeting broke up. The group leader wished everyone a good night. The attendees headed to the door, Seraf among them as Breaker watched through the water. They'd gotten one lead; it was better than nothing, even if it left his mouth sour with disappointment.

"Hey." Someone behind her stopped Seraf as she was almost to the front door.

When Seraf turned, Breaker saw a female Infernal whom he hadn't seen at the meeting. Her faceted skin glinted like gemstones beneath the crappy hallway lighting. She had a diffused, rosy hue around her petite frame. Breaker realized it was due to the lights reflecting off her skin. Even her hair was a blushing, barely-there pink shade. Her eyes were sharply slanted, a complete glistening black with no whites visible. She smiled at Seraf, and her teeth were jagged like rocky crags. She had a collar around her neck.

Seraf made an inquiring noise. The young woman beckoned Seraf to come closer before pulling her into the bathroom reserved for Infernals.

"I'm Trilya," she said after she'd opened all the stall doors to make sure they were alone. "You know Orion?"

Seraf raised a hand and made a so-so gesture. "You know him too?" she asked.

Trilya shook her head. "Only through here," she said, shifting from foot to foot. She kept lifting her chin to check the bathroom door over Seraf's shoulder. "I didn't talk to him much, but I listened and I watched."

Licking her lips, Trilya leaned in close to whisper, "I think he got out."

"Why do you think that?"Seraf tilted her head. "How did he do it?"

"You don't know?" Trilya scowled in frustration. "Damn!"

"He never told me about his plans." Seraf's voice was hard edges and brittle shards, her words shuddering down Breaker's spine like nails on a chalkboard.

"He was meeting someone," Trilya said. "From here, I think." She huffed and pointed a faceted finger at Seraf's chest. "I was hoping it would be you."

"Sorry. Tonight was my first meeting. I thought someone might have word of him."

Trilya paced, gesturing wildly at the collar she wore. "He was supposed to help me get rid of this! And now I'm stuck!"

"How long was he coming here?" Seraf asked, cutting through the growing anxiety. "Before he mentioned getting out?"

Trilya stopped, her mouth open in readiness to rant. Closing it, she tilted her head to the side in thought. "Maybe, I don't know, five months? I'd been coming for nearly a year at that point, and I remember welcoming him. He didn't seem to want to be here. Didn't share anything, held himself apart, that sort of thing." Her voice turned thoughtful. "I wasn't even sure he'd come back after his first time."

She shook her head in disbelief. "But he did. Phil spoke to him after his third meeting and his attitude seemed to change."

Breaker rechecked his pocket watch and cursed. They had perhaps five minutes before the spell faded.

Seraf seemed to realize that too. "I have to go," she told Trilya. "Can we meet tomorrow? Tell me when and where, and I'll be there."

Trilya looked like she wanted to protest, but Seraf must have done something because she nodded. "Sure. Afternoon?"

"Fine."

"Two o'clock. Where?"

"The Divine. You know where that is?" Seraf asked.

"Yeah, everyone with eyes knows where it is." Trilya's lips curled in a smile as hard as her skin. "I got it."

Seraf hurried out of the bathroom, leaving Trilya behind. Breaker muttered another incantation, and the image faded from the water. He dumped out the contents of the basin, wiped it dry, and tucked it into his backpack. He had just risen to his feet with the help of his cane when Seraf skidded around the corner as the disguise faded.

He handed her a shirt to put on over the one she wore, a

ball cap, and different shoes. "The Divine?" he whispered, checking to make sure they were alone as she changed.

"It was the first place I thought of," she signed with a shrug.

"We'll have to make sure Father Lyle is occupied," he said as they set off for the office.

Chapter 17

Breaker and Seraf approached the front of the Divine leisurely, scouting the place. Seraf carried a backpack with a set of spare clothes for her cover. They'd arrived well ahead of the meeting with Trilya to make sure they weren't walking into a trap. Breaker's knee buckled as they climbed the wide, shallow steps that led to the front doors. Seraf caught his arm even though he had his cane.

"I'm fine," he snapped, shaking her off in his embarrassment. She held up her hands and stepped back as he steadied himself.

"I'll go talk to Father Lyle, let him know I stopped by," he said when the throbbing pain subsided to a dull ache.

"And maybe distract him so he doesn't interrupt?" Seraf signed.

He adjusted his glasses rather than answer her. "Do a sweep of the grounds. I'll check inside."

They still had nearly an hour before the meet, more than enough time for Breaker to find an out-of-the-way spot where he could scry on the meeting. He exhaled as the cool silence of the church settled over him. The darkness soothed his tired, sun-sensitive eyes.

There was no mass today and no confessional hours so it was just him. The narthex and nave were empty. He suspected Lyle would be in the church's office or possibly working in the small grounds adjacent to the church. Perhaps he was out ministering to the community, going on home visits to succor the sick or infirm, or whatever do-gooder bullshit he got up to when he wasn't behind the altar or confessional screen.

Breaker bypassed the baptismal font and paced up the outer aisle, checking each row of pews for homeless people looking to sleep out the heat of the day. He froze as the smell of blood and shit hit his nose, filling the sacred space like smoke from a censer. His heart sped up in his chest, but he continued up the aisle after a moment. He strengthened his wards, just in case.

As he approached the raised dais of the altar, he noticed a figure standing in front of a podium. He couldn't tell much detail from where he stood. They weren't moving, but Breaker couldn't make out more with his poor eyesight and the distance.

His footsteps echoed in the emptiness of the vaulted chamber. Breaker moved slowly, no longer worried about the pews. "Hello?" he called, the hair on the back of his neck standing on end at the absolute stillness of the person before the lectern.

The angle of his approach allowed him a clear view of the floor beneath the pulpit, and his steps faltered. Thick puddles of red spread across the floor of the dais and spilled over the edge. Breaker stopped, gaze searching the sanctuary for signs of anyone else, before moving closer still.

The heavy scent of butchered meat hit like a physical blow. Breaker's stomach heaved. He swallowed heavily and kept his coffee where it belonged. *Callthecopscallthecopscallthecops* ran through his head on repeat, but he ignored it in favor of seeing who it was.

His curiosity would get him in trouble one day. He easily

imagined Seraf's disgusted eyeroll and subsequent scolding about his lack of self-preservation instincts.

He was still a dozen feet from the altar when he got a clear view of the lectern and the body lashed to it. Ropes secured the limp arms—they stretched wide in invitation. The blood came from the slash across the throat, cut so deep that the head sagged forward drunkenly. Blood drenched the figure's front; the spray had even hit parts of the first pew.

Atop the bent head was something metal. Breaker stopped just shy of the blood pool, but he was close enough to see that it was an Infernal collar, one with a ring of thin needles lining the inside of it. The collar sat upon the Infernal's head, a mockery of a crown. As Breaker swept the sanctuary again, his gaze settled on the carved wooden crucifix affixed to the wall behind the altar. The position of the Infernal on the lectern mimicked Jesus' position on the cross, and the collar was the crown of thorns.

His gaze dropped back to the dead Infernal, shuddering when recognition hit him. Icy sweat broke out on the back of his neck, and he rubbed a hand across his mouth to keep from shouting in panic.

It was Trilya.

"Fuck my entire life," Breaker muttered.

Then he looked up at the crucifix. "No offense, Jesus."

"HOW DO you always happen to be adjacent to every shitshow that goes on in New Venice?" Inspector Summoner Barrow asked as the NVPPD swarmed up and down the steps of the Divine like ants invading a picnic. Even though the Divine wasn't in New Venice, the crime involved an Infernal.

"It's the only way I get to see you," Breaker deadpanned from his seat on the steps. Seraf sat next to him, watching Father Lyle give one of Barrow's colleagues a statement.

"Honestly, I feel like I'm the only one trying in this relationship."

Barrow ignored the comment, all business. "How long between you finding the body and calling it in?"

"Maybe a minute and a half, two minutes."

"Did you touch anything?"

Breaker gave the detective his most withering look. "I licked every single pew. Twice." When Barrow scowled, he held up his hands in surrender. "I know the drill. I made sure not to touch anything, and I've already let the forensics teams have a go at my shoes for footprint matching. I did my best to leave the scene undisturbed."

"What were you doing here? You don't seem like the church-going type."

Breaker nodded. "You're correct. Father Lyle's an old friend. He asked us to come by for a visit a couple of weeks ago. Figured today was as good a day as any. No mass scheduled."

Barrow shifted so he could take the measure of the good Father. "He'll corroborate this?"

"Yes, of course he will." The best thing about all this was the priest didn't even have to lie. Breaker had promised Lyle he'd stop by. He'd just never said when.

Barrow turned to Seraf. "Where were you when Tweedle Dim over here found the body?"

She slowly began to sign, allowing Breaker to translate easily. "I was looking in the yard for Father Lyle. Found him and helped him plant a few things before the yelling started."

"You recognize the Infernal? Ever met her before?"

Breaker shook his head. "Never met her before in my life." Technically it was true. He'd seen her at the fights and through the scrying but had never interacted with her.

Barrow didn't ask if Seraf knew her, likely assuming Breaker spoke for them both. Another time such an assumption would anger him—today, it was a boon he would use to his advantage.

"Clear the way. Coming out!"

Breaker climbed to his feet, using the pillar he'd been leaning against for support. Seraf reached out to help him. He waved her away with a scowl. Barrow stepped over to the doors to clear the way for the gurney that held Trilya's body.

Father Lyle drifted over to them. The lines on the man's face had deepened, the upset at the desecration of his sanctuary carved deep in his flesh. Breaker observed him as he watched the gurney with the black body bag make its slow, rattling way to the ambulance boat parked in the canal nearby. The priest bowed his head, murmuring the words of a prayer with his hands clasped in front of his waist. Father Lyle lifted his head and stared into the middle distance when he finished, mouth twisted.

Breaker shared a concerned look with Seraf. As much as Breaker loathed to admit it, Father Lyle was one of the good ones. He'd been one of the few to help them when they'd been living on the streets. He'd made sure they got hot meals when he could, that they had clothes when their old ones wore out. He'd looked out for them, and while he'd asked them to come to Mass—or Breaker to do so anyway, Infernals weren't allowed—he'd never made his help contingent on Breaker's attendance. For this to happen in Father Lyle's church, under his very nose—it had to rock the man. Rage bubbled inside Breaker at whoever had desecrated the priest's holy space. He didn't deserve it.

"Sorry about this, padre," Breaker muttered as he came to stand beside the man. Seraf joined on his other side.

Lyle flinched as if he hadn't even been aware of their presence. "It's not your fault," the priest said, his eyes shiny with unshed tears. "I just pray that she's at peace." He sighed and met Breaker's gaze. "How are you doing?"

He blinked, shocked at the question. "Fine?"

Lyle clapped a broad hand on Breaker's shoulder with a force that nearly staggered him. "You were the one to find the unfortunate creature. It had to be a shock."

What the hell could Breaker say? He'd seen worse? That Trilya's dead body wasn't even in the Top Five Horrible Things that he'd witnessed—and most of those had been before his voice deepened? Seraf shifted, and suddenly she was shorter and smaller, her face still round with childhood. Blood coated her, long knives in her hands dripping red all over the Turkish rug of his father's study.

Blinking the memory from his eyes, Breaker shrugged. "I suppose that's one way to put it." He rubbed the toe of his shoe on the step. "What are you going to do now?"

Father Lyle stuck his hands in his pockets, rocking back and forth on his feet. "Officer Deveraux offered the name of an excellent cleaning service which, ah, specializes in this kind of thing. I suppose I will give them a call."

"Are you closing the church?" he asked, knowing how much that would pain Lyle.

"I'm going to have to for the time being, I think." He gestured at the doors. "It's an active crime scene."

"Did you see her go in?"

Father Lyle shook his head. "No. I had no idea anyone was even in the sanctuary. Typically Mrs. Tremaine is around, but she ran to Slidell to check on her mother. So I was the only one on the grounds."

"And you didn't hear anything? It seems unlikely that she didn't make some kind of noise."

"The police already asked me these questions, Absalom," Father Lyle chided. Seraf twisted around to give him a pointed glare. She'd always been partial to Lyle. Must have been all the chocolate pudding cups he'd given them when they were younger.

"Sorry, Father. Habit of being a private investigator, I expect."

Father Lyle offered a weak smile. "It's quite all right, Absalom." He took a handkerchief from his pocket and dabbed at the sweat beading his temples. "I know you are only trying to help."

Breaker thought he was beyond feeling guilt for some of the questionable things he did but damn if he wasn't wrong.

Seeing the priest shaken yet still thinking the best of him almost made him want to go to confession. He clenched his fingers around his cane so that the edges of the phoenix dug into his palm until the unpleasant feeling passed.

"Is there anything we can do?" Seraf signed.

Father Lyle watched her hands intently, and his face broke into a benignly serene smile. "No, my dear. There is nothing for you or Absalom to do now. Though I do appreciate the offer."

She nodded and threw a pointed look at Breaker, who stared at her dumbly. His brain refused to work. Maybe the sight of Trilya had shaken him more than he'd thought.

"So to what do I owe the pleasure of your visit?" he asked the both of them. "I expected to see you at Mass."

Breaker shook his head ruefully. The man would never stop trying to woo him into his congregation. Breaker had no desire to associate with the folks that typically attended church, especially when Seraf couldn't come in with him. The first time the upper echelon caught sight of her eye, they'd have a litter of kittens. He'd pay good money to see that.

"No can do, Father. I need my beauty sleep."

"We offer several Masses at all different times of the day," he pressed.

"Right now, it looks like you won't be offering much of anything," Breaker jabbed, grinning to take the sting out of his words. Seraf reached around and smacked him on the side of his head.

"God isn't just in His house. He's everywhere at every

time." Lyle managed a wink at Seraf. "If you attended Mass, you'd know that."

"You're impossible." Breaker couldn't help but admire the man's tenacity.

"Ineffable," he countered.

Breaker held up his hands in surrender. "We were in the area working on a case." Still not technically a lie. "Figured we'd stop by to keep you from bitching at us the next time you saw us."

"And instead, you got this." Lyle shook his head. "I am sorry your day ended here."

Breaker shrugged. What did Father Lyle expect him to say? "Totally fine, don't worry about us, we come across butchered Infernals every day and twice on Tuesdays?" He removed his glasses and cleaned the lens with a cloth he kept in his pocket. The heat must be getting to him, making him irritable.

"This doesn't get you out of Mass," the priest told him, a small private smile quirking his lips.

Breaker just dropped his head into his hand with a groan. Figured with the way his luck ran.

Chapter 18

It was evening by the time they trudged up the stairs of the office. Breaker wanted nothing more than a shower and cold G&T after all that time spent in the humidity answering questions about an Infernal he didn't know. As he cleared the landing, he caught sight of Lin leaning back in his office chair, booted feet propped up on the desk. The half-fae looked like he was catching forty winks.

"Good to see you're earning your keep," Breaker greeted, one shoulder propped against the wall.

Lin didn't startle or jerk. Instead, he pried open one mercury-colored eye and assessed the situation before closing it again. "Madame Domino called," he said in his laziest drawl.

"She want an update?"

"Another of her Infernals went missing."

Breaker cursed. He should go immediately to see what he could find out, but he didn't have energy after the afternoon's events. Seraf stood at his side, eyeing him quizzically before taking him by the elbow and frog-marching him over to the sofa against the wall. She pushed on his shoulders until he had no choice but to sit.

"We can call her," she signed when he looked up at her. "You're tapped out."

He wanted to disagree with her, wanted to prove that she was wrong. Unfortunately, Seraf wasn't, and he was too damn tired to pretend. He nodded and leaned back, resting his head on the sofa and letting the pains of his body fall away.

Vaguely, he heard Lin contact Purgatorio and ask to speak with Domino. After a bit of a song and dance, Lin used his fae compulsion, and in less than a minute, Madame Domino had picked up the call.

"How may I assist you?" Her voice was buttery rich and smoky, like a good fleur de sel caramel. It wouldn't stay that way for long.

"It's Unshriven. You had another Infernal disappearance?"

"Yes, one of my best too." Gone were the honeyed tones used to seduce. Here was the businesswoman. "I need him found."

"When was the last time you saw him?"

As Domino answered his questions, Breaker listened with half an ear. Something about this case still wasn't coming together for him. How did Trilya figure into it—what did she know that would make someone kill her? As much as Inspector Summoner Barrow thought they might be dealing with a killer with a grudge against Infernals, Breaker thought otherwise. There wasn't the expected randomness to these disappearances that spoke of opportunistic attacks. These required planning, especially when dealing with the collars.

The Infernal in question—named Pascal—was much sought after for his looks and skills. He was avian-natured and had what amounted to almost peacock-colored wings. Domino said she would email a picture of him with all pertinent information to them within the hour.

"He's been missing since yesterday evening. He had the day off but was supposed to join us for the stage show in the evening." She paused as if waiting for a question, then continued when no one spoke. "I thought perhaps he'd gotten too involved with whomever he was with and would turn up at the House eventually."

"Except he didn't."

"He didn't," she agreed wearily. "The people I could spare checked all of his usual haunts, but there's been no sign of him."

Rubbing a hand over his face, Breaker bit back a yawn. "All right. I'll leverage my contacts and see what I can turn up. It would help if you can give me a list of known associates, clients, anybody he might have had contact with."

"You'll have it within the hour."

"Thanks."

He signaled to Lin and dropped his head back on the sofa with a groan. "I was hoping for some sleep."

Lin leaned forward, a tin box held out. He met Breaker's gaze with an overly severe expression only marred by the slight twist at the corner of his mouth. "Can I offer you a mint in these trying times?"

"You are such an asshole." Breaker closed his eyes, wishing the throbbing in his knee would subside.

Seraf tapped his hand, forcing him to crack his eyes open. "Take a nap. Lin and I can do the legwork. We'll wake you when we have something," she signed.

Before he could do more than open his mouth, she shook her head emphatically. He caught the glow of her Infernal eye through the black strands of her hair. She signed, "Breaker. Do it."

Instead of answering, he shrugged out of his jacket and draped it over the top of the couch's back before leaning over and taking off his shoes. "Just a few minutes," he said, only to be interrupted by a yawn.

He settled on his side, facing the back of the couch and

burrowing his face into a pillow to help block out the fading light streaming through the windows. The weight of a light blanket settled over him; trust Seraf to know that he needed some weight atop him to feel at all relaxed enough to sleep.

He fell off to the sound of Lin's murmurs and the faint clacking of keystrokes on his laptop.

Chapter 19

It was late, well past midnight. His father had sent a phantasmal version of himself to shout his son awake. Breaker jerked upright in bed, arm up in defense of his head, flinching at the sound of his father's angry voice.

He slid out of bed, throwing on a clean t-shirt and a pair of fresh sweats before padding down the stairs of the massive Greek revival mansion that housed them. Breaker shivered; somehow, the house was always cold, even on the hottest days of summer. Tonight, the chill felt even worse against his fever-warmed skin.

Seraf sat against the wall outside the study, knees drawn up and head buried in arms. She didn't look up at his approach even though he knew she'd heard him. He stopped in front of her and crouched so they were on a level. When she still didn't raise her head, Breaker reached out his hand to touch her bony elbow.

A flicker—similar to a film strip skipping a frame—and he was inside his father's study. Rain pelted the window and beat on the roof. The smell of cherry pipe smoke and burnt herbal components sat heavy over the faintest scent of lingering sulfur from a previous working. The rug that covered the working circle in the center of the room was askew, one corner rucked up.

A powerful backhand left his head ringing and his cheek stinging as the heavy gold and amethyst ring his father wore tore into his skin. Breaker staggered, nearly slamming into his father's desk, but he managed to catch his balance.

"I am not asking!" his father roared, face a rictus of fury, all narrowed eyes and sneering lips.

He grabbed Breaker with a hand threaded through with black veins and shoved him toward the circle.

"What have you done?" He wanted to reason with his father, the terror welling up inside of him. He'd never seen his father like this—and what was wrong with his hand? How long had it been like that?

Instead of answering, his father snarled at him, eyes glowing like banked embers. Breaker took a step back and tripped over the mislaid rug, landing on his ass. His father towered above him, appearing more like a vengeful god than the man who was supposed to take care of him.

Another flicker, skipping ahead. Breaker stood in the study, his blood leaking from the swollen split of his lip. His father advanced on him, the man's handsome, aristocratic features transformed into something frightening and feral.

"Pop, DON'T!" Breaker pleaded, hands held up in submission. "Please, I'm sorry!"

He didn't know what he'd done, but apologizing always helped. He licked the blood from his split lip, used to the salt-iron tang of it by now.

"You will do as you're told, and so will that monster out there!" He flung his hand at the door, and Breaker hoped Seraf had the sense to stay out of this.

He'd backed into the corner of the study—Breaker knew his father had herded him there deliberately, but he couldn't stop moving until his back pressed up against the wall, wishing he could keep going. Even at his worst, his father had never looked this furious.

The cane his father always carried smashed his upraised hands out of the way. A fist slammed into his jaw, snapping his head to the side with the force of the blow. Breaker twisted, getting a kick in the side for his trouble. The cane crashed into his back. Breaker hit the floor, chin bouncing so hard he thought he bit through his tongue. He begged his father to stop, pleading with him, his words just strings of nonsense syllables that held no meaning anymore.

Tears blinded him. He swallowed blood from his split lip and busted nose, fear nearly choking him. A shape appeared in his periphery. Maybe Seraf? He reached out his hand to her, and the heavy silver dragon head of his father's cane slammed into the top of it. The delicate bones in the back of his hand cracked and broke. He screamed.

He sobbed in a heap on the floor, all snot and drool and messy crying. Seraf took a step into the study. Her mouth opened and closed on a single word. Her normal eye was swollen shut, the side of her face misshapen from a broken cheek. She wore the marks of his father's cane as if they were nothing.

He couldn't make out what she was saying.

His father kicked his leg, and then the cane flew up, the silver dragon swooping down like an avenging angel, but Breaker didn't believe in angels because all he ever got were demons and all of them were here, in this room. The dragon flashed down in an arc, smashing into his knee with all of his father's considerable strength behind it.

Breaker howled, making noises that didn't even sound human as his father continued to beat his knee until it was nothing more than bone shards and powder and ruin.

And still his father didn't stop.

Breaker's vision faded, went soft grey around the edges, but there was Seraf, her body half in and half out of a portal in front of him. Her mouth worked, and finally, he could make out the ground glass that was her voice to understand what she was trying to say.

"Orders?"

She asked him for his command.

His father turned his fury to her. Breaker didn't know what he screamed, everything blurring together in a cocktail of confusion and agony. *Stop* was in there, and *kill*, and maybe more besides, but all he knew was if his father didn't stop, they would both die.

Another flicker, another skip.

Breathing, that was the only thing he heard: his own, hitched and unsteady, and someone else's, deep and even. The scent of blood hung thick in the air, seeming to coat every-thing in its red, meaty odor only rivaled by the earthy reek of shit.

Breaker forced his eyelids open and regretted it as the scarlet keen of his ruined knee came into blinding focus. He swallowed around the need to be sick and looked around.

Seraf sat with her back to him. Her shoulders slumped, and her clenched fists rested on the floor. The long daggers she held dripped black in the dim light spilling in from the hallway.

Where was his father?

Breaker looked past her, past the pool of sticky red around her worn-out leather boots, past her shoulders bowed with exhaustion. Past her body sitting sentinel, guarding him, to see...

...a body slumped against the wall. His father's body.

His father's head sat a few feet away from it. His eyes were open, staring, the coffee-brown color leeching away in death.

A noise escaped him, somewhere between a wail and a groan. Breaker moved without thinking, but whether it was to go to the body or try to get farther away from it, he couldn't say. The head's dead eyes stared at him, daring him to do anything.

His leg erupted in agony. Breaker curled around it, screaming between clenched teeth.

Seraf turned around. Splashes of blood crossed her face. Her human eye was disturbingly blank, but the other one, the demon eye, glowed brightly in her face, the pupil a swirling golden hurricane.

"What," he began, then choked on a sob as another wave of pain washed over him when he coughed, "what did you do?" It came out as a half-shriek.

Seraf slid over to him so fast he barely tracked it. Her hands were empty, bloody daggers put away for now. She knelt at his side, hands already reaching for his leg.

"Don't touch me!" Breaker shouted, still trying to scuttle away. Tears spilled down his cheeks. His hands hit the wall, and he heaved himself up on his good leg.

"You killed him!" His gaze flashed from Seraf's face to his father's headless body. He reached out, unable to stop the gesture. Like it would help anything.

As if anything would.

"Your...orders," Seraf managed to get out in her shattered voice.

"I didn't want him dead!" he screamed at her, taking a step. He didn't. He hadn't. He just wanted the pain to stop. What kind of son wants their father dead?

Pain flared like lightning up his leg and side. He saw Seraf's eyes go wide, and then he fell into a roaring of crimson and black.

"Breaker," came a choked, nightmare voice he vaguely recognized.

He returned to awareness straddling Seraf with his forearm pressing into the soft tissue of her throat. He blinked and jerked back as the remnants of the dream faded. His knee flared in pain as he fell on his ass, and Breaker grabbed it with both hands, memories from the nightmare still clinging to him. He rocked, hunching over it and breathing heavy, flinching when Seraf's hand touched his shoulder.

"I'm sorry," he whispered, tucking his head against his drawn-up leg. It hurt to breathe.

"It's okay," Seraf signed where he could see.

She settled beside him. "It's not," he mumbled, still refusing to look up. "It was a dream. Of that night."

Seraf said nothing but her hand shifted to the back of his neck. She began to rub at the tight muscles. He sighed and wiped his eyes on the fabric of his pants. "You don't have to do that."

The faint sting when she flicked the back of his neck made him laugh, albeit weakly. She went back to her massage, reaching her fingers up into his sweat-damp hair to dig into his scalp.

Crowley, his head hurt. Too much sun and exertion in recent days. His constitution wasn't great, so Breaker took great care to bolster it with herbs, charms, and what little healing spells he could bring to bear, but sometimes that still wasn't enough. He needed a break.

Unfortunately, this case wouldn't wait. Breaker couldn't explain how he knew they were running out of time if they hoped to get answers. It wasn't even about his contract with Domino or Unshriven's reputation; he needed to know what was happening to those missing Infernals. If they'd found a way to evade detection and get free of the threat of that new collar that was becoming the norm, did they deserve to be punished for it? And if they hadn't left of their own volition, had they deserved whatever happened to them?

Breaker raised his head, dislodging Seraf's hand. She sat at his side, waiting patiently for whatever he was going to say. So many feelings welled up in him, too many to parse. She'd always affected him like this, turning his insides into a maelstrom of hate, obligation, affection, fury, regret, and gratitude.

She had never worn a collar. He couldn't imagine her in one. Why she stayed with him, he had never understood.

"Did you uncover anything?" When he looked at the window, he saw that night had fallen. "Lin head home?"

Seraf nodded and began to sign. "A few things. Lin and I chased down two leads that sounded promising. Nothing there, except I found this on the pad of the friend's apartment Pascal was known to crash at when he got leave from the House."

Her fingers flashed through the signs quickly. "Lin went home a little bit ago. I figured you'd want to check this one out."

He took the slip of paper from her. She'd used a pencil to reveal the impression of an address pressed into the page written on the sheet above it. His heart plunged when he read the address. Dee, first the dream and now this.

Breaker sucked in a shuddering breath, pressing the heels of his hands into his eyes. Confusion and frustration cut at him, leaving him shaking and somehow fragile. While he wasn't familiar with the exact address, he knew the area painfully well. He'd grown up there.

He wanted the shower he hadn't gotten to take. He wanted to stay at Unshriven, order a pizza, and maybe make some headway in one of the spellbooks he'd bought from Yena. He wanted to lay in bed and drink until his knee stopped bothering him. He wanted a lot of things.

"You're right." He stubbornly climbed to his feet using the couch as a brace. "Let's get going."

"Now?" she signed.

Breaker straightened, unreasonably angry. Did she doubt he could do this? It was his damned job! He grabbed his cane, the phoenix head digging into his palm as he put more of his weight on it than usual.

Drawing his tattered composure tighter to him, he answered in a chilly voice. "Did I stutter?" He ignored the look of hurt that flashed in Seraf's good eye before the emotion vanished.

He knew he was being a dick and didn't care. He had a case to solve. "If there are no further objections?"

He didn't wait to see if Seraf followed him down the stairs.

Chapter 20

The Mire was still ostensibly connected to the main body of New Orleans, unlike the floating islands and waterways of New Venice. The Mire divided them, a swampy spit of mostly solid ground. The buses ran somewhat regularly though detours due to flooding were a regularity. The taxis were more expensive since they required spellcraft to travel over the questionable terrain. Breaker opted for the bus since there wouldn't be a record.

He pulled the signal to stop at an area rife with fine dining restaurants, high-end shops, and art galleries. This area was old money, the antebellum houses shored up by magic and historically accurate renovations. Breaker shuddered at the clashing of charms, glamours, and spells that cascaded over his senses. The humid air clung to him, wrapping him in the scents of the city; after a walk through his family's neighborhood, he was going to need more than just a shower to feel clean again.

He and Seraf moved quickly through the impeccably dressed politicians, mages, bankers, and socialites that mingled on the well-lit streets. Breaker knew his warding was solid enough to fool all but the most determined gazes, so they drew little attention. Few people had seen him when he was growing up—his father hadn't let him or his mother out of the compound much. Everyone thought he was dead anyway, and that was the way he intended to keep it. It was still a relief when they stepped out of the press of people and on to the quieter, less-traveled streets where the mansions of the powerful held sway.

Breaker consulted his mental map and superimposed it with the one he'd looked up online. New construction had opened a section for the newly wealthy on the outskirts, but the heart of the neighborhood remained the same. It was easy to route a path to the address listed on the note.

As they walked, Seraf's gaze lay heavy on him. It made him itch, the need to snap at her nearly undeniable. When he could stand it no longer, he said, "You are staring very loudly."

He did not look at her, continuing at an easy walk, as if he was doing nothing more important than taking in the humid night air.

She tugged at his arm. "Do you want to go and see?" she signed. Her expression gave nothing of her thoughts away.

He stopped. So did Seraf. And waited.

"No," he said after a moment. He lifted his head, sniffing at the air. Night-blooming jasmine. Honeysuckle. And there, the whisper of Spanish moss and wisteria brushing against themselves in the light breeze. His mother had kept magnificent gardens. "Maybe."

"Okay." Her fingers stilled. Neither of them moved.

He had only been back once, before the discovery of his father's body. His knee was a mess, he was high on painkillers and the hangover from healing magic that he hadn't had time to sleep off, but he and Seraf had made the journey. She refused to leave him be for even a moment.

He'd taken the essential things from the house and left everything else. He wanted nothing of his father's to follow him. Breaker still had the papers and books, the accounts of the men with whom his father had done business. He knew the attorney who held his father's will and the inheritance Breaker could claim, including the mansion. He just didn't want any of it.

"Fine," Breaker huffed when they continued to stand there, staring at each other like tools. "We can walk past it. Satisfied?"

Seraf said nothing. Her grin said enough. Breaker turned around and stalked down the street, unaccountably annoyed. He could have said no, and he wasn't sure why he didn't.

The manse wasn't out of their way, which made it all somehow worse. They passed on the opposite side of the street and stopped. Breaker could see through the iron gates and fencing that the trees were trimmed and the grounds groomed. The house itself hadn't been allowed to fall into disrepair, mores the pity. His gaze traced the roofline, stopping at a window at the very top. His old practice room was in the attic, as far from his father as possible.

He looked away, only to find his gaze settling on the window of his father's study. Breaker shuddered, hand clenching around the head of his cane. Too many lessons in that room, his father constantly pushing him to learn faster, do more with his gift, get stronger.

"Wait a sec," Breaker whispered, stepping into the street for a better look. Was that a faint light he saw shining in the study?

"Do you see that?" he asked Seraf.

No one should be on the grounds or in the house, and certainly not at this hour. The house was empty, held in trust and managed by attorneys. Tobias Winstead III was missing, presumed dead—though it was never official since they'd never found a body—and the only one with any right to the place and the memories inside it. Breaker planned to keep it that way for as long as he could.

Seraf made a questioning noise, already staring at where

he pointed. She joined him on the street, even stepping closer to the gate until Breaker stopped her with a hand on her wrist. She had just begun to shake her head when she froze. "Someone's in there," she signed.

Breaker saw it too in his father's study—a flicker of light, perhaps a flashlight or a magelight.

"What do you want to do?" Seraf signed, gaze never leaving the window that had gone dark once more.

Breaker walked back to the sidewalk, eyes still scanning the house for other signs of habitation. He saw nothing else. If someone was robbing the place, he wished them much joy of whatever they might find in their brief life before the wards on the site blew them apart. It wasn't his business anymore. Tobias Winstead III was as good as dead.

"Nothing. We've got a job to do."

"THIS IS WEIRD," Breaker muttered to Seraf as they paced up the inlaid tile walkway that led to the front door of the house. He had to admit he liked the idea—the tiles formed a sigil of protection laid out among the bricks of the rest of the walkway, giving it a mosaic effect.

Unfortunately, nothing was powering the sigil. It was useless decoration. Breaker wondered if the people who lived here even knew what it might be for or just thought it pretty. He snorted. That kind of ignorance was just begging for possession in this day and age.

Seraf's Infernal eye had begun to glow beneath the fall of her hair. Breaker proceeded carefully, lowering his wards to get a sense of the environmental signatures. He pushed his sensing outward in a wave, hoping to get a full read on everyone alive on the property.

He found nothing.

His wards snapped back, and Breaker funneled more

energy into them. Something was off. Sharing a warning glance with Seraf, he continued up the walk, ready for whatever might await them at the door. He cautiously climbed the three steps that led to the expansive wraparound porch. When nothing exploded or ripped through a portal to rend them to bits, Breaker pressed the tip of his cane to the doorbell.

No one came to the door. Raising his eyebrows at Seraf, Breaker said, "My money's on a ravening horde of demons."

"Or they could be out to dinner," she signed back.

"You have a singular lack of imagination." He quelled the impulse to stick his tongue out at her. Going by the old place had softened him up.

"I balance you out then," came her sign.

He lifted his cane to rap at the door, giving them one more chance before he had Seraf portal in via shadow and poke around. Surreptitiously, of course. The door swung open as soon as the phoenix made contact.

"Jinkies," Breaker muttered. "Think we should check it out, Scoob?"

"Why am I the dog in this situation?" Her eyes swept over him, her upper lip curling. "If you're going to be Velma, you should wear a skirt at the very least," Seraf signed in return.

"I don't have the legs for it."

Shaking his head, he wondered what had gotten into the both of them. It was like they were ten all over again. He had no idea what to make of it, but he enjoyed himself. Unwilling to waste the opportunity of an open door, Breaker shelved these concerns for later and set his mind on the job.

"Does anyone need help?" he called, hating to give away the element of surprise but not wanting to be arrested for breaking and entering. "The door is open!"

He pulled on a pair of gloves and waited. No answer. "Didn't you just hear a cry for help?" he asked Seraf.

She nodded, pulling on her own pair. Breaker pushed the door wider with his cane.

"We're coming in!" he warned as he followed Seraf.

He was surprised to find no wards, no glowing sigils, nothing to indicate a dastardly Infernal slaver ring. It was just a fancy, well-appointed house with gleaming hardwood floors covered in Oriental rugs, antique furniture, and objects d'art under glass and illuminated by museum-quality lighting. It was a showplace more than a home.

Breaker extended his senses a bit further than the immediate area, only to be greeted by the crackle of high-level shielding magic. It was focused at the back of the house and down, likely a basement or cellar of some stripe. That made more sense—most powerful mages preferred a contained and easily warded space for their work. Much easier to guard against prying eyes.

He signaled to Seraf, giving her the information she needed silently. With a nod, she slipped forward on silent feet in a crouch. Once she'd cleared an area, she waved him on. They proceeded through the remainder of the first floor this way until they reached the kitchen. Breaker stopped in front of what looked like a pantry door but said door was so warded against magic it might as well have been the entrance to a bank vault.

"This might take me a few minutes," he signed to Seraf. She pulled out her daggers and settled in to wait.

Placing his hands flat on the door, he closed his eyes. He didn't need to, but he found it helped drown out any distractions. He would need all his concentration to bypass the wards without alerting the person who cast them. If he had Seraf portal them in, they'd trigger any failsafes—and there were always failsafes—as soon as they set foot inside.

Sucking in a slow breath to steady himself, Breaker reached out with a tendril of his energy to map the matrices of the shields that guarded the area. When the divides between the planes were blown wide open, magic flooded in, but it wasn't new. Magic had always existed here; people just accessed it in different ways. Mages had affinities to certain magic or elemental power types, but there was still much to learn. Breaker loved the theoretical aspect of casting, and he spent most of his studies learning the theory behind why things worked the way they did. That knowledge allowed him not only to understand the type of spell cast but how, and then the best way to deconstruct it. Or to manipulate it.

After a few minutes of single-minded focus, he located the key to the warding. It would take hours to unravel it completely, and they didn't have time for that; fortunately, Breaker had an even better way around it. Sliding through the convoluted loops and twists of the magical energies, he added his energy signature to the ward and set it to disappear when he and Seraf exited. Few mages could aspire to such levels of detail, and they likely didn't have the taskmaster of a teacher like he'd had.

There was a price for failures.

Opening his eyes, Breaker pulled away from the wall. Checking his watch, he saw that it had taken him less than ten minutes to accomplish his addition to the spell. Seraf raised a questioning eyebrow, and he answered with a thumbs up.

Now to unlock the door. Breaker fed his power into the wood surrounding the lock, forcing the moisture in the air and the wood to harden. His breath gusted out in white plumes as the temperature around him dropped. The wood and metal became brittle as the temperature plummeted.

Hand on the knob, he gave it a quick twist while feeding even more icy energy into it. The wood cracked around the bolt with a faint snap and swung inward.

What the room revealed had Breaker pulling out his phone and dialing NVPPD, demanding to speak to Inspector Summoner Barrow.

<hr>

Chapter 21

<hr>

"What a fucking mess."

Breaker heartily concurred though he would never admit it to I.S. Barrow. The idea of them agreeing on anything struck him as fundamentally wrong, like Yankees and Red Sox fans sitting down to have a pleasant conversation about Babe Ruth.

Barrow ran a hand through his dark hair. The sleeve of his shirt rode up to reveal part of a tattoo on the inside of his forearm. Breaker couldn't make out much of it, just that it was inked in solid black and appeared somehow geometric. A strange detail to fixate on, but after the shock of seeing what was in the room, he needed something to occupy his mind.

It wasn't as bad as finding Trilya's body at the Divine. That had been jarring because it had been so unexpected. The defilement and debasement of the altar and the church itself had been shocking. The whole scene had seemed unreal, a nightmare given leave to walk the daylight hours.

The scene in the warded room was ordinary violence; the kind Breaker had come to expect of New Venice.

While they waited for the NVPPD to arrive, Breaker

confirmed that Domino's latest missing Infernal was one of the bodies. He lay on a mobile hospital bed similar to the ones in Doc Grady's clinic, body twisted in horrific angles with his death throes. He wasn't wearing a collar, though one lay on the floor beside the bed. Had he died having it removed?

Another Infernal, a female and one that Breaker didn't recognize, appeared to have attacked an ordinary-looking man before succumbing to unseen injuries. Breaker would bet those had to do with the collar still around her throat. A significant amount of blood had splashed the gurney and walls and pooled on the floor from the man's wounds.

Breaker took in the worktable that held two more of the collars favored by Domino and the other high-end pleasure palaces. There were a few other items of note that he'd like to have a look at, the man's notebooks and laptop being among them, but there was no way of getting to them without further disturbing the crime scene. He did pocket a piece of mail with the homeowner's name on it as they left the house to wait outside for the NVPPD to arrive.

Barrow rubbed at the bridge of his nose with two fingers and wished Barrow would hurry things along. The detective asked, "The front door was unlocked, you say?"

Nodding, Breaker shifted most of his weight to his good leg. "Yes. When I knocked, the door opened like it hadn't been fully closed or latched."

"So you just walked inside?"

Breaker gave a half-hearted shrug. "I called out to see if anyone needed help. I thought I heard something deeper in the house, and I wanted to check in case anyone was in trouble."

Barrow raised his eyebrows but let the lie go. "What were you doing out here again?"

This again. Breaker and Seraf had already had a once-over by forensics—again—and now he had to endure I.S.

Barrow asking him the same question just phrased differently about 200 times. Fantastic. He pulled out his phone and opened up the email Domino had sent him with the Infernal's picture.

"We were looking for him. Domino had noticed he was missing and wanted us to see if we could track him down before he disappeared. She sent this to me along with the information in the body of the email. It was late, but I had Lin pull everything he could on her Infernal's connections. The address was the first place on our list. I figured we'd ask around, see if he'd been by."

He gestured to the inside of the house. "This is what we have to show for it."

"How long had he been missing?"

"Maybe twenty-four hours, or a little less. The Infernal didn't show up for his shift, so Domino decided to put me to work." He glanced to the side to find Seraf standing to his left and step or so behind him, arms crossed in a closed stance.

"That room is warded. How'd you get past it?"

"I took it down. It must reset when one leaves the area." That was likely believable and much easier to explain than what he'd done. He'd heard of a few wealthy mages that had theirs rigged similarly. In this neighborhood, it wasn't much of a stretch to believe someone had sprung for that, especially with what this guy had been doing.

"Hmmm." Barrow hummed, eyeing Breaker up and down like he wasn't sure if he wanted to call him a liar or not. He chose 'not' for the time being. "Then what happened? Walk me through it."

"Then I called you." He saw Seraf's corroborating nod out of the corner of his eye. "We didn't go in there, and we didn't touch anything. We came back out here and waited for you."

That wasn't exactly true since he and Seraf had done a quick search of the house. Breaker found a few questionable correspondences and a journal written in code. He had Seraf stash them in a portal hidey-hole while they'd waited. Breaker doubted Barrow would be forthcoming with any information once the case became official, so he needed to get what he could before NVPPD shut him out entirely.

"Any idea who the others are?"

"I would assume the dead human is Frederick Swinburne. It's his house, after all. The other Infernal?" Breaker shrugged. "No idea."

"Doesn't match any of the others on your list?"

He shook his head. "None that I'm being paid to find." She didn't fit any of the descriptions of those he knew about either. "It's possible she came with Pascal, likely for removal of her collar. Looks like something went wrong with Pascal's. That would explain why she attacked Swinburne while hers was still on."

Barrow chewed his lower lip absently as his mind chipped away at the problem. After a few moments, he realized what he was doing, and his gaze sharpened on Breaker once more. "And the reason you broke the lock?"

"Seraf smelled blood," Breaker said, lie easily passing his lips. There was no way they could prove she couldn't. "I thought that there might be someone in trouble and wanted to offer aid if I could."

That might be pushing it. Barrow looked like that might be more than he could stomach. Thankfully, Breaker was saved from more questions by a young, uniformed officer signaling Barrow. The two conversed for some minutes before Barrow turned back to them, his body language making him easy to read. He wanted no more to do with the two of them, which was fine by Breaker. He needed time to digest everything they'd discovered before he could hope to make sense of it.

"Get lost, Unshriven. If I need you, I know where to find you."

"As always, Inspector Summoner." Breaker saluted him

and began to make his slow way down the steps. Seraf followed behind like an over-tall duckling.

When they reached the front of the lot, Breaker turned to Seraf. Body hiding his hands, he signed, "You head back and observe. I want to know what they find." He held out his hands for the items she'd hidden. "Don't get caught."

She reached in the shadows the street lamp threw on the ground and pulled out the journals they'd found in what was likely the master bedroom. "Be careful. If you think they're getting suspicious, get out of there. Remember, watch only."

Seraf nodded once, signing, "Be careful."

"I'll be fine." He grinned. "See you back at the office."

She backed away wearing a faint smile, the shadows swallowing her whole. Despite the carnage in Swinburne's home, it had been a pleasant evening. How long had it been since they'd just enjoyed each other's company without a case as a buffer? Maybe it was visiting the old neighborhood, but Breaker's shoulders didn't ache quite as much. It was almost like some heavy weight had lifted.

He made his slow way back down the street, intending to head immediately back to the office. But his feet took him in a different direction, and before long he stood in front of the gates to the mansion where he grew up. His gaze unerringly found the window of his father's study, and he remembered the light he'd seen in it earlier that evening.

Breaker pushed his hair out of his eyes. He should leave. Standing in front of the gates was asking for trouble; most people wouldn't know him after all these years, but it didn't mean he could stand here dithering either. Better to move along and forget this place ever existed.

His hand reached out and touched the wrought iron gate. The magical wardings that had sprung up around the place at his father's death lapped against his palm like a beloved hound before subsiding. Those wards recognized him as having a blood claim on the area. The gate swung open on remarkably silent hinges. Whoever was responsible for the grounds must also oil the gate to keep it from shrieking on rusty hinges.

He stepped onto the grounds quickly, trying not to think about what he was doing. Breaker hadn't set foot inside the property in over a decade. Why had he done so now? He slipped into the shadow of a vast magnolia and considered.

He should go back to the office like he'd planned to do initially. Nothing good could come of him staying here. Yet even as he thought this, his feet turned in the direction of the main house, and Breaker found himself powerless to stop them. Fear gripped him by the back of the neck and shook him hard, which seemed to wake him from his strange stupor.

He said a word of command meant to break any illusions or mind magic that might have taken hold of him. As he feared, he was unaltered. There was no insidious spell, no charm guiding his steps. Whatever was happening was entirely his own doing.

Once again, his gaze lifted to the window where the light had been earlier. He was already inside the gates; he might as well check the study. Breaker had made sure the nasty stuff was locked away where no one would even know to look for it, but it wouldn't hurt to check to see what was missing. Many valuable art pieces and books could spell a tidy profit for some enterprising and foolhardy thief, provided they could navigate the wards.

Breaker slipped quickly from pool of shadow to pool of shadow, hunching down to make his silhouette less obvious even though it made his knee ache abominably. He skirted the front of the house, avoiding the front door—the last thing he needed was a nosy neighbor or ghost hunter spotting him. Instead, he crept to the side door that led into the kitchen, a holdover from days when servant's quarters were kept on the property.

Before he touched the door, Breaker stilled and stretched out his mage-sense. The house wards were all in place, the matrices of curses and shields and keys still as solid and untampered with as ever. There were no other magical signatures in the house or the grounds. He was alone.

Was the light in the study a trick of the eyes? How to explain Seraf seeing it? A collective delusion? Breaker scoffed. Though linked in many ways, codependent insanity was not one of them.

Breaker wiped the sweat from his brow with the back of his forearm and set his hand against the door. The air clung heavily to him, wrapping clammy arms around him like the world's dampest koala. The humid breeze did little to cool his skin, and the cloying scent of whatever nonsense bloomed in the dark clogged his nostrils.

The wards gave a muted hum at his touch. The wood warmed beneath his hand, feeling almost alive and pulsing as it recognized him—or rather his genetics. There was the sense of an unraveling, of unspooling power, only for it to snap back like it was tethered to a leash once Breaker stepped inside the house.

He caught his breath, leaning heavily against the wall. The faint smell of lemon cleaner and almond oil furniture polish reached his nose, all of it overlaid with the musty smell of disuse. Lived-in places collected certain scents: candles, food cooking, perfumes, laundry detergent, and dryer sheets. The minutiae of everyday life was missing from this space.

This house held only the ashes of memories. Breaker swore he smelled the faint scent of smoke and burning as if his father lit his pipe for his evening smoke.

A stasis spell took care of such mundane things as dirt and dust, leaving everything as pristine as the day the mansion was closed up. There was no sign of dust on the hardwood floors or the carefully cultivated antiques for all that the house was empty. Breaker didn't touch anything, feeling like a ghost as he walked around the furniture his mother had lovingly chosen for her sitting room. He stood in the center of the room, lost in the faint memory of her smiling down at him, her own pale eyes shielded by her giant sun hat.

Breaker opened eyes he hadn't realized he'd closed. His father had left this room unchanged, a small concession to his grieving son. His father removed every other trace of his wife after her death, but Breaker had asked for this room to remain as it was. His father had never set foot in it again as far as he knew. Breaker and Seraf had whiled away many hours here, lying on their stomachs with the books they'd borrowed from his father's library spread out around them.

He shook his head. He'd come into the house to check on his father's study, not take a mindless stroll down memory lane. Breaker made his way out of the room and to the stairs that led to the second floor. He was amazed after all these years that he could still find his way around in the dark. It was like the house was ingrained in him, imprinted in the fiber of his being.

That thought made him want to rip his skin off and claw out his brain through his nose.

As he looked up, the staircase seemed to grow larger, swelling in length. Breaker swallowed spasmodically, his fingers clenching involuntarily around the cane he carried. He was not a child any longer and his father was long dead. He had nothing to be afraid of in this house. There was nothing here that could hurt him.

He navigated the stairs slowly, mindful of the creak on the fourth step from the bottom. Breaker remembered all the ways to move silently through the house so his father never knew where he was. He gritted his teeth around a frustrated noise as he reached the top of the steps. It was like coming back to this place had sent him back in time, to the young boy he'd once been.

He stalked down the hallway, purpose in every step. He

would check that the study was undisturbed—or note the stolen items—and leave. His hand closed around the door handle, and he pushed it open.

Breaker's mouth fell open in shock. "What?" he managed to gasp out before his world exploded into flame.

Chapter 22

A fucking fire elemental. Because Breaker's night couldn't get any shittier.

The elemental floated above the floorboards, a column of living flames. A blob at the top could have been a head if one was generous and two longer tongues of flame at its sides functioned as crude arms. The center of the elemental glowed white with the heat of its core. Even though the elemental didn't have eyes, Breaker shuddered beneath the strength of its attention.

Breaker crossed his arms in front of his face and braced, calling on his element. Water erupted and solidified around him, giving him a wall of water for a shield even as his wards took the brunt of the fiery blast. Boiling steam billowed around him, obscuring the entire hallway. Breaker reeled back from the heat, arms still up to protect his face from scorching.

The steam shivered, disturbed by someone moving through it. Without thinking, Breaker grabbed onto the water molecules making up the cloud of steam and yanked, clearing part of the hallway. He made out two shapes, one taller than the other. The shorter shape had a mass of wild hair spilling across his shoulders.

"Wait!" Breaker shouted. How had they even gotten in without tripping the wards?

The shorter figure hesitated and began to turn around. Breaker again pulled at the water molecules in the air and formed a water whip, determined to catch and question at least one of the intruders, before he froze in shock. He recognized the shorter man's profile.

"Dahrian?" What was the man doing here of all places? And who was with him?

Breaker only had a moment to revel in his vindication—he knew there was a reason the man had been hanging around him! Dahrian's eyes lit up in shades of inferno as he tapped into the summoned elemental sharing space inside his head. Fire gathered between his gloved hands, launching forth in Breaker's direction in the shape of a dragon made of flames that grew bigger the closer it got.

The dragon smashed into the floor at his feet, blowing Breaker backward from the force of it slamming into his wards. Breaker crashed into the back wall of the hallway, cane flying from his hand, with enough power to dent the drywall. As he hit the floor, he thought he heard a deep voice ordering, "Move it, Dahri!" before everything faded to nothing.

Breaker groaned as he came back to consciousness. His cheek pressed against the scratchy woolen fabric of the hallway runner, and his back throbbed from the impact with the wall. He reached out and found his glasses a few finger lengths away from his face, thankfully undamaged. Once they were on his face, he saw his cane on the hallway floor nearly in front of the open door of his father's study.

As he pushed himself to his feet, Breaker let out an esoteric curse and raked his hair out of his eyes. "The room's blocked!" he said to no one. That was why he hadn't sensed anyone's presence in the house! The study functioned almost like a magical black hole: it was impregnable to prying and scrying eyes, and it resisted attempts at sensing anyone was inside. His father often met privately with essential clients who were very protective of their privacy, so he'd designed the room accordingly.

He wanted to slap himself. How could he have forgotten? Growling, he staggered over to his cane and then into the study. Slumping into the nearest armchair, he flung his head back and tried to make sense of the evening.

Checking his watch, it looked like he'd only been out for a few minutes. At least he hadn't lost too much time. His arms ached with the mild burns from the steam, though not enough for him to do anything about them at present.

The bigger question was how the hell Dahrian and whomever he was with had managed to get into the house without tripping the wards. The protections keyed into bloodline—did that mean that Dahrian was somehow related to Breaker? Was that why the man had started popping up wherever he went? And if Dahrian was related to him, then in what way? A cousin? As far as Breaker knew, his father had no siblings—the family tree had become a trunk by his father's time. The lawyers had never mentioned any by-blows or indiscretions that might have split off the main family line.

Pushing his spectacles higher up his forehead, Breaker rubbed at tired, gritty eyes. He was only twenty-six—how did he feel a thousand years old? As he searched for an answer, his gaze wandered lazily about the room, coming to rest on the bookcase adjacent to his father's desk. The books on several rows had been disturbed, haphazardly pushed back into place. A few of the spines no longer lay neatly beside their fellows.

Breaker stood slowly, wobbling on unsteady legs. He didn't move until he was sure he would remain upright. As he passed the desk, he noted a drawer had been forced open. Pausing, he took a moment to check it. There wasn't much to see or take; Breaker had removed all of the unreasonably dangerous items to a private and well-warded location, and the estate lawyers had cataloged the rest. All that remained in the desk were stationary sheets, the odd letter opener, and some news clippings. Breaker had burned all the client ledgers and correspondence along with any mentions of himself before he'd left.

With this recent break-in, he was second-guessing his decision not to burn the entire place down. That would have saved him this headache. Ah well, nothing do be done about it now.

As suspected, the desk held nothing of interest—even its false bottom was devoid of anything exciting. Sliding the drawer closed, Breaker turned his attention back to the bookcase. He suspected they'd been looking for the entrance to his father's private workrooms.

Breaker pulled two books off the shelves. He took a letter opener from the desk and jabbed the point into the delicate skin at his wrist. Blood beaded up, and he quickly swiped it off with his index finger. Opening the book to page 114, he wiped the blood onto the page before setting it aside. He took up the second book and opened it to page 57. Plucking a hair from his head, he put it between the pages and closed it. He returned both books to their places on the shelf, then set his hands flat against the spines. The blood and hair served as the keys to the mystical lock that led to his father's workroom. As Breaker fed the keys a steady flow of his energy, the bookcase grew less and less substantial until Breaker could pass right through it and continue down a flight of winding stairs that eventually brought him to the basement.

Calling it a basement did the space a disservice, if not outright insult. Breaker's father had inherited the gaudy sensibilities of his ancestors as the décor of his workroom displayed. It looked like a sultan's harem, and a consumptive's lonely artist's garret had thrown up all over each other and took physical form.

Breaker immediately wanted to run out of there, but he forced himself to stay. It was unpleasant, that was all—nothing he couldn't handle. The white-knuckled grip he held on his cane didn't relax.

The thieves hadn't made it down here. Breaker highly doubted anyone would have been able to get in through the keys, let alone figure out how to manipulate the wardings so they didn't fry them in place. Breaker attuned to them well before he could walk.

He'd left the room mostly untouched since first closing it up after his father's death. He hadn't noticed anything missing upstairs, which meant whatever Dahrian and his accomplice had been after must be down here.

Breaker approached the low table that typically held the components his father might need when working major magic. Kneeling, he ran his fingers around, searching for a catch in the floorboards beneath it. He pressed his thumb into the pressure sensor to pop up one end of the board. Shifting it to the side, he shivered as the cold wave of the death ward flared across his arm as he reached into the space to remove the heavy book.

His father hadn't believed in taking chances with his research. Again, he'd keyed the death ward to those of his blood. While Breaker would typically be willing to trust in its efficacy, he couldn't risk it. Dahrian had gotten inside the house without dying. If Breaker hadn't interrupted them, would they have eventually unlocked this room? He wasn't willing to take that risk.

Tucking the book inside his jacket, Breaker replaced the board and stood. He'd never wanted to know just what research his father was doing in this room. Now he was bringing it home with him.

What a miserable fucking night.

SERAF WASN'T BACK when Breaker returned to the office. He took himself downstairs to the kitchen while he waited for her return. He stashed his father's book in his safe for now. He'd figure out a more permanent place for it later. For now, all he wanted was something to eat and a bed.

Even though the kitchen was downstairs, Breaker didn't use it often. The space was Seraf's, and he wanted her to have some modicum of privacy. A door separated her bedroom and bathroom from the more public areas. His presence was an intrusion without her here, like he was sneaking a look at her diary. The feeling was stupid—Seraf had nothing to hide from him.

A bowl of cereal and a glass of bourbon later had Breaker feeling up to the task of a shower. He poured himself another bourbon and began the trek to his bedroom. He stopped at the threshold, neck turning so he could stare at Seraf's partially opened door. He found himself stepping over, suddenly curious about what he might find inside.

His hand was outstretched to push it open further to look inside—how long since he'd been down here? He couldn't remember the last time he'd sat with Seraf, doing nothing but enjoying each other's company. They'd been together for so long that he'd taken her presence for granted. He shook his head as if that was enough to derail his train of thought. Going into his father's mansion had made him maudlin.

He pushed the door open. He was crossing a line here, but he couldn't muster the energy to stop himself. He'd spent so long being angry with Seraf, of hating her, of blaming her, that he wasn't sure how to step away from it. They didn't talk anymore—not the way they once had—and he missed it.

The room was spare—he would call it barren if feeling less charitable—with a twin bed pushed against one wall. There was a three-drawer dresser, and she'd installed book-shelves. She'd filled them with books though he couldn't make out any titles in the dim light. A comforter with stylized octopi covered her bed, adding a splash of color and a bit of whimsy to an otherwise stark room.

A tablet sat propped on the bed before a half-finished something. The small, knitted creatures that covered the top of the dresser surprised him the most. Only when his gaze found the woven basket filled with different skeins of yarn and knitting needles of various sizes did he realize Seraf had made these herself. When had she learned how to do this? Had she taught herself through online tutorials? And how had he not known?

He jerked back when the wards shifted to allow entrance. A slice of shadow appeared in the middle of the small dining area before Seraf stepped out, looking none the worse for wear. She took a moment to gather herself—the transition from shade to real world was always a little jarring—before she fixed him with eyebrows raised in surprise.

Breaker cleared his throat of the strange heaviness clogging it. He held up his glass by way of explanation. "Please tell me you found something worthwhile," he said to stave off questions he couldn't answer.

Walking to the fridge, she got a bottle of water. After draining half in one go, she began to sign. "Something's not right."

"Tell me something I don't know."

She shot him an amused glance. Her Infernal eye glowed briefly, and Seraf reached into shadow to pull out the items taken from the Swinburne house. She placed them on the small kitchen table and returned to her water.

"I'm going to put Lin on cracking the cipher. Dee knows he needs a project to occupy his mind and keep him out of trouble." And if anyone could break a code, it would be that tricky sort-of fae.

"Did Barrow and his team uncover anything else?"

Setting down her now-empty bottle, Seraf signed, "I followed him back to the station. They have no leads other than the ones we gave them, but one of the forensic guys said something curious." He made a go-on gesture. "Swinburne's wounds don't quite match up with either of the dead Infernals. They were going to look up their IDs in the system to see what they could find."

Breaker lifted his head, the gears in his head already whirring with ideas. "So the injuries he suffered may not have been what killed him."

Seraf tapped her finger on the table to get his attention. "Or," she signed, "whoever killed him tried to use other wounds as a cover-up."

"So it likely wasn't a collar removal gone wrong," he mused. It was a leap, perhaps, but it resonated inside him. Nothing about this case had been straightforward so far. "But something else made to look that way." His gaze dropped to the coded journal. "I think that needs to be Tamlin's top priority."

Seraf nodded. She dropped the empty water bottle in the recycling bin as Breaker made his way back up the stairs. He should tell Seraf about what happened at his father's house, but he wasn't ready to tell her about Dahrian. What would he say exactly, anyway? A strange man had stalked him to befriend him and then got caught breaking into Breaker's house? None of it made sense, and he'd sound like an idiot trying to explain it.

He'd only made it up one before her broken voice stopped him.

"Hey."

He turned, glass and journal in hand, one eyebrow cocked in question. Seraf signed, "Why were you looking in my room?"

He met her mismatched gaze even as his neck flushed in embarrassment. What the hell could he say? I was curious? It sounded pathetic. I miss you? They lived in the same space and worked the same hours. If anything, he should want less time with her. Giving her a crooked smile, he shook his head.

"No reason. Just wanted to see what you were into these days."

She cocked her head as if she didn't believe him. "You could just ask," she signed, pursing her lips.

She made it sound so easy. Nothing was ever that simple, not with them. "Yeah, I guess I could." Breaker took a swallow of bourbon before toasting her with the glass. "Night, Seraf."

Chapter 23

"Mistress Silk's on the phone for you," Lin shouted up the stairs as Breaker was already on his way down from his quarters. They'd wrapped up a minor contract yesterday with the cursed client, and he'd planned to spend some time figuring out the best way to protect his father's journal. He hadn't taken it out of the safe yet.

As he arrived at the base of the stairs, Seraf handed him a to-go cup from Witches' Brew with his usual blend, warming charm in place. "Fantastic," he said, earning a raise of the eyebrows from their admin.

"You want to take it, or do I make an excuse?" Lin prompted after a sip from his cup.

"I'll take it," Breaker told him. Seraf pointed to a bag on Lin's desk and signed, "Eat something." He waved her off as he accepted the office cell from Lin and put it on speaker. "Breaker speaking."

"I've been approached." Silk's voice sounded deeper over the phone.

"That sounds personal." He thought he heard her concierge in the background, likely saying something disparaging about Breaker's character. He smirked. "Shall I release the hounds?"

Mistress Silk released a husky chuckle that had Lin glancing at the phone thoughtfully. "Do try to rein in those asshole-ish tendencies or I'm liable to forget my reason for calling you." It was a playful threat, but Breaker heeded the warning nonetheless.

He leaned a hip against Lin's desk and rooted through the sack Seraf had indicated. He came up with some cinnamon cruller thing that was nearly the size of an infant's head. Lin snatched it from his hands, leaving Breaker to make do with the equally large muffin at the bottom of the bag.

"This is better anyway," he mouthed, earning an obscene finger gesture in response.

Turning his attention back to Silk, Breaker asked, "Am I safe to assume this is regarding your missing Infernal."

"Not quite," came her answer while he picked the liner away from his muffin. "It has to do with your Infernal."

Seraf coughed on a swallow of her cherry-flavored, white hot chocolate. Breaker raised his eyebrows and said, "You'd best explain." Seraf stared at him with eyes round with surprise. He handed her a piece of muffin.

"The fights have been put on hold for the time being due to Dempsey's unfortunate encounter with death. Certain people are scrabbling to the top of the pile to see who takes over but, at least until the fights resume, that means your little hellion is the champion."

She paused, and the low murmur of voices reached him over the line. He thought about saying hello to Chakrii to hear the disdain in those dulcet tones. Mmmmm, disdain and those cheekbones. Silk returned before he could say anything.

"I was approached by someone interested in acquiring the champion. Somehow the gentleman found out I had recommended her for the fights and smoothed your way. Since there was no way to track you or her, they reached out to me in the hopes I can facilitate a meeting to talk price."

"What name did they give? How did they contact you?"

One glance at Seraf showed him she'd gone still and quiet, her drink forgotten on Lin's desk. Her expression was empty, her lips tightly pressed together. He remembered that look well—he'd worn it himself as a child. If he could stay still and quiet enough, his father would pass by wherever he happened to be hiding without finding him.

"A phone call. Originally I wasn't going to bother with it, but I thought you might be interested in what the man had to say."

"The name." Seraf's indrawn breath was her only reaction. Breaker kept his eyes on her as he continued the conversation with Silk.

"Maurice Vanderbeck." Silk's derisive sniff was audible even over the phone. "Not his real name. He passed along his information to me in case I could contact the champion's owner. I'll send it over via email."

"Anything special about the voice?"

"It was male. No accent."

Breaker rolled his eyes. So they either didn't have one, which was rare around here, or had hidden it. "Did he say anything else?"

He imagined Silk's shoulders rising in a shrug. "Just that he was a collector and was willing to pay top dollar for someone of her caliber. He did mention he was looking to move quickly."

"Naturally." He forced down a piece of muffin even though it tasted like ash in his mouth. "That all I should know?"

Silk hummed low in the back of her throat. Lin made an interested noise. Breaker shot him a warning look which earned him a mouthed, "Fuck you," for his trouble.

"He's serious in his offer," she said after a moment's

thought. "I'd consider it if I were you. It's likely to be very generous if he's as obsessive in his collecting as he sounds—probably the most you'll ever get for one like her."

Rage washed over him like a wave breaking against the shore. He shook as it engulfed him, only to subside a moment later as he ruthlessly squashed the emotion. "If you'd send the details, I'd be most appreciative," he said, keeping his voice smooth even as his fists clenched at his sides. Silk might become a client one day; he couldn't jeopardize a potential working relationship just because she'd made the perfectly normal assumption that he'd part with Seraf for the right price.

"Certainly. And I hope you'll remember who made your windfall possible. Perhaps even a finder's fee...," Silk trailed off helpfully.

Breaker stared into Seraf's mismatched eyes. They'd gone tight at the edges, fine lines marring her otherwise smooth skin. "Yes," he said softly before hanging up, "I'll remember."

LATER IN THE DAY, Lin slapped Swinburne's journal down on the table, a triumphant smile on his icy, angular face. "What would you do without me?"

"Live my best life." Breaker lifted his head from his work. "Oh, was that supposed to be a rhetorical question?"

"I don't know how Seraf tolerates you."

"I'm an acquired taste. Seraf's had a lot of time to acquire."

Lin snorted, grey eyes the shade of lowering thunderheads before a storm. "I cracked the code on most of the entries. Do not thank me." He shuddered at the very thought.

"Wouldn't dream of it." Breaker had to bite down on 'I owe you one' because one never wanted to be beholden to any of the Fae, no matter how witty or charming they appeared. "But take the rest of the day off as a bonus."

"Way ahead of you. Try not to burn the place down in my absence, will you?"

"My affinity is for water, not fire."

Breaker paged through the book, noting every entry. "Where's Seraf?"

Lin shrugged a slim shoulder. "She said she was going out for a bit. Didn't say where."

Breaker leaned back in his chair, tipping it up onto two legs. He scowled, trying to ignore the spike of unease that pierced him at Lin's words. Seraf typically let him know when she was leaving the office, not that she often did it without him. It wasn't like she needed his permission to go out, and he knew she could take care of herself.

Leaning forward, Lin pointed to a spot on the first entry of the page. "I tried to organize it, but it just got to be too complicated." He slid his long finger down one column on the translated page. "Names here and any affiliations." He continued down to a string of numbers.

"Bank accounts, perhaps." He shook his head. "More names here, but they seem to be in a code to keep them more anonymous." Lin sniffed. "Not nearly as creative as my way."

"Not everyone can be cinephile like you, Lin." And thank Solomon for that. If he had to wade through more clever film tie-ins, he'd likely burn the office down to avoid it.

Lin gave him a long-suffering look. "More's the pity. The world would be a better place with more me in it."

The thought of multiple Lins gave Breaker hives. One Tamlin was more than enough for any plane of existence. Ducking away from that line of conversation, Breaker asked, "Cipher didn't give you much problem, eh?"

There was the proper withering look. Lin should teach a class at the local learning annex. Disgruntled, middle-aged women the world over could only dream of packing that much disdain into a simple expression.

"The Fae twist thoughts and words as easily as you folk breathe. Of course, something as primitive as that," he waved his hand at the notebook, "offered little challenge."

The Fae couldn't outright lie, but they could omit, twist, and beguile the truth and did so like it was an Olympic sport. Tamlin had learned much from his centuries with them. "I'll try and pick a more compelling subject for you next time."

Lin made a scoffing noise and slung his messenger bag over his shoulder. "If there's nothing else, I'm off to meet a rather charming young man for some kind of literary reading. See you tomorrow."

"Who's reading?"

Shrugging, Lin said, "Haven't the foggiest. Did you not hear the charming young man part?"

Breaker rubbed the back of his neck. "Yeah, well, don't do anything I wouldn't do."

"That admonition doesn't leave me many options." Lin swooped toward the stairs in the way only a Fae could. "Unfortunately, bingo and the early bird seating at the cafeteria were all booked, so we're going to go with debauched fornication on every available surface in my flat. Sorry to disappoint."

Ouch. "Hey!"

The look Lin bestowed on him was pitying as he shook his head. "We really need to get you laid." He threw Breaker a wave over his shoulder on his way out. "Night, Grandpa!"

"This from the guy who's got several centuries on me. Oh, and get off my lawn!" Breaker yelled after him, barely holding in a chuckle. He'd missed banter. He and Seraf used to snipe at each other good-naturedly when they lived on the street. They didn't have much to be happy about, but sarcasm coupled with deadpan delivery had always been a refuge.

Removing his spectacles, Breaker pressed the heels of his

hands against his eyes. Every time he blinked, his eyelids scraped across his eyes like sandpaper. He pulled a bottle of eye drops from his pocket and treated his eyes before he got back to work.

When he took Domino's case, Breaker had searched all collared Infernals reported missing in the last year. He pulled up his list of names on his computer. He'd widened his search to include all Infernals who'd gone missing. Then he'd broadened the search parameters even further, looking two, five, and ten years out. Once he had a large pool of data, he began to look for patterns.

Nothing had stood out initially aside from the staggering number of Infernals who wound up disappearing. He kept sifting through the files, hoping that some common thread would reveal itself, that he'd be able to spot some semblance of logic in the murky histories and tragic pasts.

His phone pinged at him, alerting him to a new email. Glancing over, he saw it was the message he'd been waiting for from Mistress Silk with the information on the collector interested in buying Seraf. Breaker sat bolt upright, his mind making the connections.

Lin had input everything in a spreadsheet for him, and Breaker pulled it up on the laptop. The fae had cataloged the pertinent facts, including a description of their appearance and their known Infernal traits, even attaching pictures if they were available. Breaker dove in, reading up on each missing Infernal, looking specifically for rare or highly sought-after powers or attributes. When he was unsure, he checked with the internet, sticking with the government reporting of common and uncommon physical and mental traits rather than wasting his time on fansites where people got into deep and abiding online feuds over whether feathers or scales made for better snuggling.

He was team scales. Not that anyone asked him.

Breaker divided the traits into Rare, Uncommon, and

Common and appended a designation to each missing Infernal. Once he had them all assigned, he sorted on Rare characteristics to see if they matched any of the missing Infernals from the pleasure houses.

"Gotcha," he whispered when the results came up. Every single missing pleasure house Infernal had come up in the Rare category. Along with several other missing Infernals in the past ten years.

Time to talk to I.S. Barrow.

Chapter 24

He pushed through the doors to the satellite precinct that housed the Paranormal division of the New Venice police department. A faint scent of brimstone permeated the air, the sharpness countered by the softer smell of herbs used in workings. Breaker's shoulders dropped, a bit of the tension leaking out of his muscles at this welcome bit of familiarity. Going to the police was never an enjoyable experience—fear that they would somehow glean who he was and lock him away—but the paranormal division was far preferable to regular cops. At least the PPD understood what he did.

He asked for Barrow at the desk and took a seat to wait. Breaker wished Seraf had been home when he left. He would have appreciated her company as he waited. He stifled his irritation; Seraf was allowed to come and go as she pleased—he had no right to know where she was every minute of the day.

Still, a small kernel of fury bloomed inside him that she hadn't bothered to check with him. Infernals weren't trusted or liked—even ones with a collar around their necks were treated with suspicion, if not outright hatred. Most people tolerated them but were uncomfortable when confronted with an Infernal on their own. When violence inevitably broke out, it never ended well for the Infernal.

Seraf was lucky her Infernal traits were easy enough to disguise. Her hair usually was enough to mask her Infernal eye, but if she was worried about causing an outburst, there was always an eyepatch. She had a couple lying around from the early days. Breaker could only hope wherever she'd gone that she was taking care and being smart.

"You rang?" came the Creole drawl, bringing to mind hot summer nights with frogs croaking their amorous intentions surrounded by the smells of swamp water and the things that grew in proximity to it.

"I needed to talk to you."

Barrow opened his mouth, but something on Breaker's face stopped him. Perhaps he'd gotten used to the banter, the casually tossed barbs to keep the other sharp, and he wasn't expecting such seriousness. Whatever the reason for his sudden change in mood, Breaker was grateful for it. He wasn't up for an exhausting round of pointless sniping at the moment.

"Come on back." Barrow waved him inside the bullpen. He walked up to a large whiteboard hanging from the wall and wrote his name next to Interview Two before he beckoned Breaker to follow.

"This should be pretty quiet," he said as he led Breaker to the room.

Breaker nodded, unsure of what else to say. Fortunately, he didn't have to come up with a lot of the conversation because Barrow talked enough for two people, seeming to suffer from an aversion to comfortable silences. He didn't stop until they were seated on opposite sides of a metal table. Finally, he leaned back and asked, "Why're you here, Unshriven?"

Folding his hands together on the tabletop, Breaker took a deep breath and began. "The missing Infernals. I may have found something."

Barrow raised his eyebrows but stayed silent. He made a 'go on' gesture with one hand.

"Someone's been trafficking Infernals. Rare ones, with traits not often seen and thus highly prized among collectors. It's been going on for at least ten years, maybe even longer than that. Swinburne was involved in it but only for the last couple of years."

"How'd you come to that conclusion?" Barrow asked, eyes narrowed.

Breaker kept his gaze even, unwavering. He wasn't about to admit he tampered with a murder scene. "Once I had Swinburne's name, I followed the money. Bank accounts rarely lie."

"We're still going through his financials."

Breaker allowed a dark grin to spread his lips. "I don't have to follow procedures or wait on pesky warrants. My admin had what I needed in an afternoon." He propped his elbow up on the back of his chair. "Mistress Domino told me he's the one who supplies her with those custom collars of hers. I tracked her payments down, then noticed there were numerous payments to Swinburne from another account—an offshore shell corporation—in the same amounts. They closely correspond to the dates rare Infernals went missing."

"That's not enough." Barrow ran a hand through his hair and then down his face. His eyes had the dark circles and redness that came from too much stress on too little sleep. If he hadn't been a cop, Breaker might have sympathized.

"You asked for me to share information with you," he reminded Barrow. Breaker hadn't forgotten the drink and conversation they'd shared at the bar all those weeks ago. "This is me sharing."

Barrow shook his head. "It's thin. Circumstantial. All you're telling me is a guy took orders for collars meant to keep Infernals in their place. That's not illegal. Hell, some people might give the guy a posthumous medal."

"He likely helped sell Infernals into Crowley alone knows what!" Breaker snapped, hands slapping flat on the table.

"Yeah, Infernals. Not people." When Breaker opened his mouth to disagree, the Inspector Summoner held up a hand. "I know what you're going to say, so I'm going to save you the trouble." He rubbed absently at his mouth before continuing. "Swinburne might have engaged in sketchy behavior, but he was a respected doctor murdered by two Infernals. *That's* what people care about, not that he may or may not have been involved in some shady shit. That's what the brass wants me looking into."

"He was being paid to remove the collars too. By Infernals. I think your brass might care about that." Breaker folded his arms over his chest and set his jaw.

Barrow spread his arms. "Then he got what he deserved—at least that's the way the press will paint it. And his death will serve as a warning to the next guy who wants to make some money getting Infernals out of their collars." He shrugged. "It's all in the spin."

"You can't honestly think that Swinburne messed up taking off a collar that he designed?" Breaker scoffed. "It makes no sense that the other Infernal would kill him before he removed her collar!"

"Right now, the evidence points to one Infernal dying on the table and the other flying into a rage and attacking the man she thought was responsible for it. They're dead, Swinburne's dead, and that's all we have to go on. Maybe the Infernal had too much of the junk they pump through those collars in his system. Maybe they got there too late—who knows? I have to go off pesky facts, not indulge in wild speculation." His smirk infuriated Breaker.

Gritting his teeth, he managed to get out, "What about the missing Infernals? Are you going to try to tie them to Swinburne?"

Breaker saw Barrow cast a glance to the corner of the

room before he looked back at him. Breaker risked a peek and saw a camera's red light blinking before he focused back on the summoner. So they were being watched or at least recorded for review later.

"Why would I waste time doing that? They're Infernals."

Breathing out, Breaker saw a plume of white leave his mouth as the temperature around him dropped in the manifestation of his icy wrath. He got ahold of himself; this was possibly the worst place to lose his iron self-control. "It's your job," he growled, consciously forcing his fists to relax.

"My job is to protect the people of New Venice. People." The detective enunciated the word as if Breaker was an infant. "The government hasn't ruled that Infernals even qualify as such. Until they get that status in the eyes of the law, I've got too much on my plate to go poking into that mess in what amounts to an animal cruelty case." His smile was an ugly thing. "That's what you problem solvers are for, am I right?"

Breaker stood, vibrating as he fought not to encase the building in a layer of ice. "Right," he snarled.

Barrow rose as well, bracing his hands on the table and leaning forward. His hazel eyes were intense as they stared into Breaker's before they shifted to the camera then back again. "Like you said, you're not bound by pesky warrants and following procedures."

Ah.

Someone still watched. With a huff, Breaker threw his hands up in frustration. "Thanks for being a complete waste of my time, Inspector Summoner."

"Always happy to be of service," Barrow said, offering a lazy salute as Breaker turned on his heel and stormed out of the room as fast as his bum knee and cane allowed. All the while, gears turned inside his skull.

Barrow wanted him to follow up on his hunches because the police couldn't, for whatever reason. The detective had hinted around it—someone high on the food chain didn't want anyone looking into the mystery of the missing Infernals and had handed down their decision. Breaker couldn't count on help from the police quarter, and he was happier operating without the police even knowing his existence.

Exaggerating his limp, Breaker left the precinct and let Barrow's words simmer in his mind. The summoner wanted Unshriven to keep looking into it—whoever had given the order from on-high, it tied the summoner's hands. Swinburne had been a respected researcher; he worked at the university doing something with Infernal blood and its effects on various chronic diseases. Breaker had Lin do some digging into the man himself along with his forays into his finances.

Someone didn't want this nasty side gig of Swinburne's to get out. Breaker wasn't exactly interested in finding out who that was just yet, but he stuck a mental pin in it. Once he had solved Domino's case, he'd get back to it. He knew most Madames had at least one cop on their payroll and likely several judges. Corruption ran rampant through all public administration and government levels in New Orleans and New Venice. Palms got greased, bribes paid, and people profited. You didn't rise to any height in this city without selling a part of yourself to it.

So he couldn't count on any information from the police. They had their narrative for Swinburne's death ready and weren't going to look any further. Barrow had made it clear that any investigation into a trafficking ring for Infernals was a non-starter.

He stopped at a bridge and leaned over to look into the swampy water below. The onset of the evening did nothing for the heat, though the sun did pound less mercilessly on the back of his head. Breaker breathed in deep and pulled out his phone. He tapped the cool metal against his forehead as he wrestled with his guilt.

He dialed the number Silk had sent him. After a few rings, a voice as deep as the Marinas Trench answered. "Yeah?"

"I was told there was someone interested in procuring my champion Infernal at this number." Breaker rubbed the back of his neck, feeling the sweat collecting at the ends of his hair.

"One minute."

"Certainly." Breaker rested his elbows against the sun-warmed stonework and waited, mind wandering. Where had Seraf gone? Shame made him shift—he didn't even know if she had any other, what, friends? They'd been together for so long that he assumed he knew everything about her but her crocheting habit had surprised him. What else had he missed? No, that wasn't right.

What else had he not been interested in finding out?

He kept her at arm's length, not fully trusting her, not after what she did to his father. Yeah, if she hadn't done what she did, Breaker was sure his father would have killed him, killed them both. But it didn't make it any easier to look at her every day. He still remembered the way his father's face would soften from its severe lines every time he gazed at Breaker's mother. He'd hoped that one day he'd catch his father looking at him like that—like he loved him.

"Do I have the honor of speaking with Mr. Stadler?" The voice on the phone was male and lightly accented—Eastern European was Breaker's best guess—when he spoke. So this was likely not the same man who contacted Silk; that man had no discernible accent.

Breaker pulled the phone away from his ear as it crackled and spat with interference. A spell to alter his voice. Technology didn't play nicely with magic, interacting in strange and, sometimes violent, ways. "You do," he said after the static subsided.

"Am I to assume Mistress Silk reached out to you?"

"You are."

"Wonderful. I saw your Infernal fight, and I was singularly impressed with her skill and ferocity. Tell me, is she intact?"

Breaker closed his eyes, nausea rolling over him in a wave. His answer came out steadier than he expected. "She is. You looking to breed her?" Crowley, he was going to need a Silkwood shower after this.

"Perhaps." Breaker could hear the smile in the man's voice. "Though I'd want her to get a few more wins under the belt. Drives up the price."

"I wasn't planning on selling her." Let the man think he was driving up the asking price.

"And yet you called me. Which leads me to believe that you are at least curious about my offer."

Breaker wanted to knock the smug look he knew the man must be wearing off his face. "I am. But I'd like to know who I'm doing business with first."

"Forgive me, how rude of me to forget to introduce myself. For this transaction, you can call me Santiago."

Not a name Breaker recognized and likely a false one. It didn't matter. All that mattered was the meeting. "I haven't said I'm willing to sell."

"I'm not worried. I can be very convincing," Santiago's voice dropped into a purr.

Breaker shuddered. Forget the Silkwood shower; he would take a bath in lye. "I'm waiting to hear your offer," he said instead of violently retching.

Santiago's chuckle made the crackles pick up again. When they subsided once more, he said a number that had Breaker blinking in astonishment. It was an obscene amount of money.

When Breaker didn't respond immediately, Santiago prompted, "You're quiet. Did the amount surprise you?" He sounded pleased.

"No. I'm just trying to figure out how much you think you can charge for each breeding attempt and if you're deliberately lowballing me because you think I'm an idiot." There, that should open negotiations nicely.

Santiago laughed outright. "You are a canny one, Mr. Stadler." A sigh. "Fine." He trotted out another number, magnitudes higher than the last. Breaker grinned, all teeth. He'd enjoy taking this Santiago down.

"Acceptable."

"Wonderful." He paused. Breaker could make out a muffled conversation with someone on Santiago's end, but that was all.

"I'll wire the money to an account of your choice when you bring me my asset."

"Acceptable. When?"

Santiago once again consulted someone else on his end. Finally, he said, "Two days. I'll contact you with the location."

"Fine." Breaker didn't like it much, but he didn't want to make the man overly wary. He needed him overconfident, secure. He'd be more likely to make a mistake. He should still have plenty of time to scope out the location and ensure there were no surprises.

"Done then!" Santiago's voice vibrated with pleasure. "I look forward to the conclusion of our business, Mr. Stadler."

"As do I, Mr. Santiago."

"Until then."

Breaker ended the call and lowered his head. Bracing his arms on the bridge rail, he propped his chin on his hands and looked out over the canal. Water taxis ferried in tourists and locals alike. Lights glittered in the water, the darkness of approaching night making everything look softer and beautiful. Night hid the city's sins, making people feel safer committing them.

His phone buzzed, pulling him from his dark thoughts. Seraf had messaged him.

Where are you?

Went to talk to Barrow. On my way back now.

Meet you?

He sighed, wiping the sweat beading his brow. He'd bargained with Seraf's life and safety, and he hadn't told her yet. He hadn't even asked. He was such an asshole.

No. I'll be at the office shortly. We need to talk.

Chapter 25

Seraf put her chopsticks down and signed, "Who do you think gave the order to Barrow?"

Breaker finished slurping the noodles he'd lifted with his chopsticks before answering. He'd stopped to get pho on his way back to the office for him and Seraf, and they were having a pleasant dinner on the couch. It would be too awkward to suggest eating at the table in the kitchenette downstairs after getting caught snooping in Seraf's space.

He took a sip of the Vietnamese iced coffee that he'd also ordered for them. "Police chief, mayor, concerned citizen with a lot of money to throw around? Doesn't matter. All it means is the cops are of no fucking use in this."

"But they aren't going to get in your way?"

He reached for the condiments and added more basil and another squeeze of lime to his pho. "So long as we're relatively quick and quiet, no. Barrow is focused on Swinburne and doesn't care about anything else. We should be left alone." That wasn't precisely correct about Barrow, but Breaker didn't feel particularly charitable. The police force's attitude about Infernals stuck in his craw, and he wasn't in the mood to forgive.

Seraf added a few more chilis to her bowl, and Breaker set aside his utensils. "I contacted Silk's buyer."

She raised her eyebrows but said nothing, just stirred the broth with her chopsticks. Breaker shifted where he sat, waiting for her to respond. When she didn't, he sighed and continued. "He offered an obscene sum of money for the champion of the ring."

"Should I be flattered?" she signed, a rueful smirk on her face.

"I told him I accept."

Seraf's human eye—the only one he could see—went wide. Her gasp came out as if it had been through a cheese grater. She set aside her chopsticks and folded her hands in her lap. Breaker watched as the surprise on her face faded to a kind of weary acceptance. It made him want to chew steel and spit out nails.

"I'm not accepting, of course," he assured her, hoping to get that deadened look off her face. "He might be able to lead us to whoever is dealing in Infernals."

"What about Swinburne's journal?" she signed.

"Lin is still working on tracking those strange payments, but that might take some time. Madame Domino will probably be satisfied to know that Swinburne isn't around to remove any more collars, but there's more to it. Infernals have been disappearing for years and nobody seems to care. If there's a way to find out who is behind it, don't you want to know?"

She shrugged, not looking at him. "It's your case," she signed. "You're the boss."

He dragged fingers through his hair, clenching his fist in the strands at the back before dropping his hand to the couch. "Look, it's just a meeting. If there's anything you don't like, you can bamf us out of there, no questions." He caught her gaze, hoping she would see that he meant every word he said. "It won't be like the fights. I won't let it."

The silence stretched painfully between them until she finally nodded. "Okay," she signed though Breaker could read the tension in the lines of her shoulders. She wasn't happy, but she'd go along with it because he needed her.

"Where'd you go earlier?" he asked her, hoping a change in subject would lighten the tense mood. He gestured for her to eat with his soup spoon.

Seraf fiddled with her chopsticks, not picking them back up. "I went to talk to Father Lyle," she signed. "I wanted to see how he was doing after the," she waved her hand.

Breaker picked up a bit of tendon with his chopsticks. He hadn't even thought about checking on Father Lyle after the nightmare discovery in his sanctuary. He was too busy thinking about the case—and then the break-in at his father's mansion—that the priest had slipped his mind.

"How is he?" he asked as he chewed.

Seraf finished her bite of noodles and signed, "Seems to be doing well. He scrubbed down and purified the sanctuary once the cops let him back inside. He's even started masses again, although the turnout isn't what you'd expect."

"What, like nobody's showing up?"

She shook her head, giving him a glimpse of her Infernal eye. Her fingers moved quickly. "Tourists. They even added The Divine to one of the murder tours. It's keeping the local parishioners away."

"Pretty sure the dead Infernal did that."

Seraf gave him a sour look. He sipped at his drink, looking as innocent as possible. "He asked if we knew her."

Breaker set his drink down. "Why did Lyle want to know that?"

"I don't know. Maybe he thinks all Infernals know each other." She shrugged when she'd finished signing.

"What did you tell him?" Breaker did his best to keep his worry from his voice.

"Just what the papers already said. Father Lyle said something interesting."

"Related to our case?"

"No. Father Lyle said Dempsey and then Trilya being so close to each other—their deaths— it was like God was abandoning New Venice." Seraf spread her hands out on the table.

"God would have had to have been here to abandon it," Breaker told her.

"I'm worried he might be losing his faith," Seraf signed, frowning.

"And you want to help him look for it?" He dodged the cuff aimed at his head. "We can't do anything about his spiritual crisis or whatever it is he's having. People die all the time, and it has nothing to do with God or the Devil. It's just people."

"You don't understand." Her hands twisted sharply with her frustration.

He went back to his food. "You're right. I don't understand that kind of faith because I've never had it in anything in my life. As far as I can tell, Father Lyle's lucky he's been able to cling to it for this long, especially living here." When Seraf didn't say anything, he asked, "You guys talk about anything else?"

"This and that. He offered me a chocolate pudding." Her smile was wistful.

"That's nice."

She grabbed another bunch of noodles with her sticks, shoved it into her mouth, and continued. "Did you ever figure out what was going on at your father's house?"

Breaker was glad he had already finished his food when she asked; otherwise, he likely would have choked. He hadn't told her he'd gone back to the mansion, and he certainly hadn't shared what he'd found there. He hadn't even looked at the book since he hid it away behind seals and wards of protection.

He wasn't sure what he would tell her. That the guy they'd met in the apothecary might be some long-lost family member? That he was trying to steal something of his father's? He had no answers and it wasn't her business. He was the last surviving Winstead, and he intended to keep it that way. The name was a curse, same as the family.

He wiped his mouth on a napkin and stood, suddenly needing the comfort of movement. "I'm going to go leave a message for Ari at Witches' Brew. We're going to need two more of her glamours for the meeting."

"Hang on," she began to sign, moving to climb to her feet.

Breaker waved her back down. "Finish your food. I'll run down there and be back in a jiff."

She watched him warily like she was expecting a trick of some kind. He gave her a double thumbs-up, then grabbed his cane and began to walk down the stairs, breathing a sigh of relief at ditching that conversation without making anything worse.

NIGHT HAD FALLEN as he stepped out of the coffee shop. He'd lingered over a café au lait and a plate of beignets after he'd left a message for Arinayah, not wanting to go back to the office immediately. Breaker made patterns in the powdered sugar as he pondered what to do about Seraf.

He needed space from her. They'd been together for practically their whole lives, and he resented her as much as he required her. Yet every time he tried to drive her away, guilt raked at him, which fed into his resentment. Then he thought about what his life would be like without her constant presence, and he couldn't even imagine it. Seraf's presence was so much a part of him that her absence in his life was beyond his comprehension.

Is this what codependency was? If so, then what was Seraf getting out of it all?

He'd left the shop, his head still in a muddle. Breaker could hear the revelry carry on the air from New Venice as he strolled down the street. The Mire sat hard beside it, and the streets closest to New Venice held shops that closed when the worst of the debauchery occurred. Now that the French Quarter no longer existed, New Venice had become the new Bourbon Street. The few proper neighborhoods within the Mire were at the other end of the swampy spit of land, closer to New Orleans proper.

Breaker walked over to the canal side, grounding his cane and leaning on it as he stared in the direction of New Venice. Madame Domino's place would be busy, no doubt, as would Mistress Silk's. He shuddered, unable to scrape the filthy feeling that clung to his skin off. Even if he found out who was behind the disappearances of Infernals, what good would it do? They would still be commodities to be sold and traded. They would still be collared and kept.

Those collars were terrible creations. Breaker didn't know how to stop their use—wasn't sure he could stop it even if he found a way. Too many people feared Infernals, thought they were unstable, susceptible demonic influence in their DNA. He wished he could go back in time and stop the geneticist who was too excited by what he could do that he didn't stop to think if he should.

The faint tingling at the back of his neck alerted him that eyes watched him. Breaker swept out his sensing in a quick pulse and frowned at what he perceived. He didn't say anything, but he straightened from his lean, spine stiff and shoulders back, as he waited.

"Sorry about the fire," Dahrian said as he stepped up beside Breaker.

"No, you're not," Breaker grumbled, gaze fixed on the water and the bulky, squat shapes of New Venice in the distance. "Lies cheapen the both of us—you for attempting it and me because you think I'd believe it." He settled both hands atop his cane. "What do you want?"

Dahrian threaded a hand through his thick hair. He reminded Breaker of a hedgehog with how his hair bristled outward as it fell past his shoulders. "And if that's what I want? To apologize?"

"I don't have time for this bullshit," Breaker snorted and turned around, intending to walk back to the office.

Dahrian dashed in front of him, one arm outstretched with palm extended. The fire summons he carried was quiet—Dahrian's eyes only held the faintest glow of red around the iris.

"Wait."

Breaker's fraying hold on his temper snapped as a headache stabbed him in the eyes. Snarling, he stilled. Fine. Dahrian wanted to know what he was thinking? Breaker would be more than happy to enlighten him. "How did you get into that house? What were you doing in there? And who was with you?"

"I could ask you those same questions."

"But you haven't." Breaker narrowed his eyes behind his glasses. He hadn't trusted Dahrian, but there was something—a camaraderie perhaps. Not friendship yet, but possibly the beginnings of one. Breaker allowed himself few friends, and now even that was gone. "Which tells me you already know the answers."

Dahrian flushed and dropped his hand. Breaker put his free hand on his cocked hip, the other one still gripping the head of his cane. Dahrian looked away. With a disgusted snort, Breaker began to walk away from the man. He didn't have space in his life for this nonsense, possible relative or not.

"I'm not who you think I am." Dahrian's voice sounded subdued, a bare whisper in the darkness, nearly lost beneath the lapping of canal water.

Breaker stopped but didn't turn around. "I don't care."

"You should." His voice was louder now and closer. Breaker shivered despite the heat. "I know who you are."

"I'm no one of any importance." He forced air into his lungs despite the feeling that an elephant sat upon his chest.

"You and I both know that only someone with Winstead blood can gain entrance to the family mansion." Dahrian crossed in front of Breaker again. "You're supposed to be dead, Tobias."

Breaker couldn't help but flinch. "That's not my name," he insisted. Because it wasn't, not the one he chose. Tobias Winstead was as dead to him as his father.

"Maybe not anymore, but once it was." Dahrian sounded so sure. Breaker wondered how he'd figured it out. He peered at Breaker's face as if searching for something. "Your eyes *are* blue."

He snorted. "I told you that already. Albinism does not give red eyes. It's the light reflecting through the blood vessels that makes them appear red." Why was he telling Dahrian this, as if his eye color mattered at all? Had the admission broken his brain? He thought he'd be far more terrified of someone knowing his secret, but calm blanketed him as if he sat in the eye of a hurricane.

"You look nothing like your father."

Breaker didn't respond to that, unwilling to even tacitly confirm Dahrian's belief of who he was. Instead, he repeated, "How were you able to get into that mansion?"

His answer surprised Breaker. "I was with someone who could access it."

"Is that who you've been following me for?" Breaker narrowed his eyes, the anger that surged into him comforting after the cold shock of hearing his birth name. "They set you on me like a bloodhound."

"Hey!" Dahrian sounded offended. Good. It might make him careless with his words and give Breaker something useful. "It was a favor for a friend, not some kind of sleazy business venture." He sniffed. "I leave that kind of stuff for you."

Breaker lips lifted in a slow smile. Dahrian thought himself above the work that Breaker and Seraf did? Typical. The man likely had no idea what it was to sleep beneath discarded cardboard or dumpster dive for dinner; no idea how to beg or busk on the streets for a few stray coins from people who just wanted you to go away.

"I'm done with this conversation." Breaker stepped around Dahrian, only to lift an eyebrow when the man placed a hand on his arm to stop him.

"I'm not related to you. But my friend is. You're right. That's why I was following you—for him."

That hurt him in a way Breaker wasn't prepared. Dahrian had only reached out to him as a favor to a friend. Stupid, not to expect such a thing, even more ridiculous to think someone would reach out to him of their own volition. Even Seraf was with him because of what she was.

"Go away, Dahrian," he said without looking at him, shaking free of his grip. "I'm not interested in anything you have to say."

"Would you just wait a sec--," Dahrian said, once again grabbing his arm.

Breaker spun, bringing the cane up to break his grasp. Ice crackled in its wake, the frigid sting making Dahrian jump back with a yelp of shock. "Don't ever touch me without my express permission again, or I'll freeze your arm and shatter it into pieces while you stand there gaping like the idiot you are." His father's reputation was frightening; since Dahrian knew who he was, Breaker may as well make use of it.

"Don't cross me or you'll learn just how like my namesake I can be."

He swept away down the street. Dahrian did not try to stop him again.

Chapter 26

Breaker slept poorly. He put Seraf off the night before by claiming he was tired and just wanted to rest but knew he couldn't stall her forever. He'd spent most of his free time digging up whatever he could on Dahrian. Most of what he found was frighteningly normal—at least for The Mire. He was a summoner, from a solid family, and he worked at an acquisitions firm. There was nothing that Breaker could find that linked him to one of Breaker's extended family members, not that there were many left. He promised himself he'd come back to it once he resolved the current case. He didn't like not knowing.

He also didn't like that Dahrian knew who he was. Breaker tried to take comfort in the knowledge that no one would believe him should he decide to announce that the missing Winstead heir had been working as a paranormal problem solver for the past decade instead of claiming his inheritance. It might sell a few papers, but there was no solid proof. He'd deal with it after meeting with Santiago.

Breaker was beyond ready to get this case and everything related to it off his books.

"Want some overtime, Lin?" Breaker asked as he came down the stairs, straightening his tie.

"Tonight?"

"Early evening. Five o'clock. I don't see it taking more than a couple of hours."

The admin shrugged. "Sure, why not?" He went back to scanning something on his laptop, eyes flickering across the screen.

"Find anything interesting in Swinburne's accounts?" Lin was still practicing his hobby—raiding other people's financials with the determination and zeal of a Hun.

"Still tracking down a few things. But," here Lin spun the laptop around and pointed at a spot on the screen, "I found something you might be interested in."

Seraf walked over to join Breaker, and they peered at the screen together. After a few minutes of being utterly baffled by the rows and rows of numbers and lists of names, Breaker blinked and raised his head. "What am I supposed to be seeing?"

Lin sighed. "You are utterly hopeless," he chided. "What would you do without me?" When Seraf began signing, he held up an admonishing finger. "Rhetorical question, my glorious thorn."

"Lin?" Breaker prompted, rubbing at his eyes.

"Right. I've tracked the payments to Swinburne's account and followed the wire transactions back to their source. Some of them are pretty easy and not all that interesting," he indicated a printout that Breaker had already taken a look at, "but there were a few that were far more complicated. This one right here went through a couple of shell accounts."

"Okay?" It made sense, but Breaker still didn't know why Tamlin had flagged it.

"Other payments were made to various places, but this one in particular," he pointed to a line, "is what got my attention. This payment is to a nonprofit organization here in New Venice." Lin switched tabs, and a website appeared.

Breaker scanned the webpage. Typical nonprofit verbiage, photos of the good works they provided, details of how one could help. He signaled for Lin to scroll lower and sucked in a breath. A familiar meeting room with several Infernals, their faces too distant to be recognizable, sat around in a circle with the nondescript Peter in sharp focus.

"Wages of Sin," he breathed.

"Yup," Lin said, popping the 'p' sound. "It's one of the many nonprofit outreach programs supported." He clicked a link that led to a page listing all the programs alphabetically. "There we are," he said as he scrolled to Wages of Sin.

"Quid pro quo," Breaker murmured. "Wages of Sin gives out Swinburne's name to Infernals who want their collars removed, then Swinburne pays a percentage to the nonprofit in a 'donation' as a kickback." He shook his head. "Elegant arrangement."

Seraf signed, "Do you think someone at Wages of Sin had him killed?"

"Seems like bad business to kill someone who gives you money."

Lin took the laptop back and continued with his work. "I'm working on finding out the names of those affiliated with the main nonprofit. And I don't just mean the ones listed on the website."

"The whole thing could be a front," Seraf signed.

"It's New Venice. That's practically guaranteed." Breaker stretched. "Lin, you're not back-up tonight. I want you to film the building, see if we can get video of our buyer. Mistress Domino might recognize him."

"No problem, boss. I'll find a happy little rooftop and lurk like I'm Batman." He swept his arm across his body like he wore a cape. "I am the Night!"

"Glad to see you're treating this with the proper level of

professionalism," Breaker said, slanting a look at Seraf, who was openly grinning at Lin.

Breaker walked to the file cabinet drawer that functioned as the office supply cabinet and pulled out the padded box containing their tech. "Lin and I will have earpieces."

He set the small disks down on the desk and laid out the piece of blue silk cloth that had Breaker's sigils inked in white. Magic was a touchy mistress, especially this close to planar portals. Breaker had little to worry about when working with his elemental affinity; that came as easy as breathing to him. But for complicated spellwork, he liked to be careful. He'd inked this focusing cloth on his own, even going so far as to create the ink himself to make sure there were as few conflicting signatures influencing his work as possible.

He set the disks on the center sigil and put his hands on either side of it, palms settling into place atop two other inked sigils. Light flared briefly as the power inked into the cloth activated, cued to his magical signature. Breaker whispered the spell's words, forcing his intent through the labyrinthine thought patterns required. The magic roiled deep inside his guts, swirling up and out, taking the shape he willed.

He opened eyes he hadn't realized he'd closed to catch the fading flare of magic on the disks. Breaker took a deep breath and stepped away. He lifted his hands from the cloth, shaking the pins and needles from them before glancing at Lin. The admin wore an impressed expression.

"I forget you're actually a competent magic worker," the fae-man said.

"Right," Breaker said, shoving hair out of his eyes, " and I forget you're an asshole."

Lin blew him a kiss. "Charmer."

Breaker handed him one of the disks. "There's body glue in the cabinet. Affix it so it sits behind your ear, and you'll be able to hear everything I say. If you speak, I'll be able to pick up your words."

"How long does the spell last?"

"Only for twelve hours. I didn't think we'd need longer." He could adjust the spell's duration at will upon casting. Breaker didn't think they'd need much beyond four, but he liked to be as prepared as possible. "And don't put it on early and decide to fuck with me, you troll."

"Perish the thought," Lin replied, although the grin on his face did not fill Breaker with hope for Lin's restraint. "Ooooh, should we have a code word? You know, just in case things go bad?"

"Pretty sure you'll be able to tell that everything's gone to hell. But if you want one, how about, 'ohshitohshitohshitoh-fuck?' That good?"

"You possess the whimsy of a sea cucumber."

Breaker ignored him, instead returning his silk cloth to the supply drawer. He pulled out another padded box, this time removing thick silver cuffs. He handed them to Seraf, who studied them with distaste.

"I know you don't like them," he said. "But the buyer wanted assurances you wouldn't freak out during the sale."

"Fine," Seraf signed. She put them on the desk as if she couldn't bear to touch them for longer than necessary. They were dampeners. Once activated, they would cut off her Infernal powers for a limited time, and she wouldn't be able to access her shadow portals.

"You remember how to get them off?" At her nod, Breaker picked up the cuffs. "Show me."

He thought she was going to protest. He recognized the mulish set to her jaw—she'd looked that way whenever she thought his idea was crap when they'd been on the streets. When she stuck out her arms, wrists held forward, he blinked in surprise at the lack of protest.

Breaker snapped the cuffs over each wrist. They were three inches wide, covering her wrists in wide circles, and solid silver. He pressed a button on the inside of the right cuff, and the two stuck together in front of her body.

"Okay, now."

Seraf twisted her wrists in opposite directions. The cuffs unlocked and fell away. Lin whistled, impressed.

"Breakaway cuffs. Ingenious."

"I hate those things," Seraf signed. "They make everything fuzzy."

"It was either that or a collar, and there's no way I'm putting one of those on you."

"Appreciated." She gave him a wry smile as she signed.

Breaker was not a good man, and he didn't pretend to be one. But some things ran counter to how he wanted to live his life, and collaring people—and he believed Infernals were people, despite their demonic heritage—was not a part of it. Even for a case.

"You ready to scout?"

"As I'll ever be," she signed.

Breaker checked that he had everything he needed. Ari's glamour sat tucked in his pocket, ready for use. After one last check with Tamlin, he stuck the disk to his ear and led Seraf down the stairs.

They had a suspect to meet.

THE PLACE WAS NONDESCRIPT, surprising for New Venice. The city rarely subscribed to subtlety, choosing instead over-the-top gaudiness and questionable taste to draw the attention of tourists. The building was a dry dock, housing boats and crafts of various sizes and styles needing repair or replacement. Part of the back of the building opened directly into the canal, allowing small boats to drive right in so long as the metal access doors and the ramp were deployed.

There was nothing out of the ordinary—a few wards to

deter thieves but nothing that set off Breaker's internal alarms. He didn't sense any dormant magic, and Seraf had done a sweep and found nothing to arouse their suspicions. That was more than enough to rouse Breaker's. Still, there was little to be done about it; he would simply have to wait and see.

When they returned at the appointed time, it was on a private ferry. Breaker and Seraf's glamours ensured that they looked the way they did on the evening of the fight. Seraf's wrists were bound and her eyes downcast. Breaker had his cane, spelled to resemble a showpiece rather than a functional walking aid, the phoenix turned into a Kraken.

He rapped at the door with his cane. After a few tense minutes where Breaker wondered if they'd somehow scared Santiago off, the door opened. A large man, easily a head taller than Breaker and almost twice as broad, filled the doorway, a questioning look on a face the size of a Thanksgiving turkey. "Can I help you?"

His voice was surprisingly soft, almost light, and not deep at all. It was inconsistent with the man's appearance.

Breaker inclined his head and said, "Mr. Stadler to see Mr. Santiago. I'm expected."

"Of course, come inside." The man moved the grace of a ballet dancer, light and easy on his feet despite his bulk. He stared at Seraf curiously. When she stepped forward, he simply shifted his weight, allowing her to pass by, close enough that she could have easily touched him if she'd wanted to. The man didn't seem bothered by her proximity. Odd.

"Thank you," Breaker said, stepping over the threshold.

They were led through a simple office and a series of doors and then down a flight of stairs. As they walked, Lin spoke in his ear. "There's a boat headed in your direction. Fancy, speedy thing. Thinking it might be your fellow." He heard the machine gun clack of keys—Lin typed like he was trying to obliterate the keyboard.

"I'm almost through, I think," he said. "Once I have it, I'll let you know. Good thing the password to the wifi in this building was so easy to crack. Whoever thought 'i<3b00-bies69' was a secure password needs their head examined."

Breaker pushed his hair behind his ear, tapping his earpiece as he did so. Maybe the static would shut Lin up; he did not need the half-fae's voice in his head while he worked, especially if he was going to give him a play-by-play of every moment of his stakeout.

The large man opened the door to reveal two more men, all in suits, all looking various levels of dangerous. They stood at the open bay door, canal water lapping at the dock. Breaker, Seraf, and their guide stood on the raised platform above the work area. There were no boats docked for repair currently, further evidence for Breaker's conclusion that this place was simply a front for less savory business.

"Boat inbound," Lin said. "Rounding the corner."

Breaker could hear its approach. He glanced at Seraf. She kept her head down, but her focus stayed on the two men. The tension in her body was unmistakable. She was ready for a fight.

"The boss should be here in a minute," their guide said, gaze resting on the entrance. The wedge-shaped bow of the boat slid through the opening, engine cut. Two lines were thrown out by the pilot and caught by the two on the dock. They swiftly tied it off to the cleats on the dock, stepping aside as the driver hopped off the boat.

"Mr. Santiago, I presume," Breaker called out.

"Oh shit, oh shit." Breaker would have said Lin sounded panicked if he didn't know better. "I got him. You're not going to like it."

Breaker gritted his teeth. He didn't need the distraction, not now. The pilot peered up at them. He was a nondescript-looking man, of middling height with a cap of mahogany curls. When he spoke, it was with a thick Creole accent. "He'll be up in a second."

He resisted glancing at Seraf. Something wasn't right here. He wanted to place his hand on her arm, partly seeking reassurance and partly to quell her trembling. She was a hairsbreadth away from twisting out of the restraints. He kept his gaze on the big man, trusting Seraf to watch the other three.

"You won't believe who's the money behind it all," Lin continued, not knowing what was going on inside the building. "You know him!"

A hatch opened on the deck of the ship. As if that was a signal, magic flared, not around the building but him. Breaker tried to counter whatever spell hit him, but his brain turned to pudding. When he reached for his magic, it was like his metaphorical hands were bound. Spellbinder, his brain supplied too late to be of help.

At the same time, Seraf snapped the cuffs, the dull clang of the metal hitting the floor loud in the sudden quiet, and hurled herself at the three men below. The large man they'd come in with lunged with a speed that surprised Breaker, slamming into him and carrying him to the floor, nearly smothered beneath his bulk. His cane rolled from his grip.

The man jerked Breaker's arm behind his back, nearly dislocating the shoulder in his enthusiasm. He held Breaker's wrist in a hammerlock to emphasize his point and shoved his head down with his other hand.

Breaker struggled briefly, stopping when his shoulder popped alarmingly. "Ohshitohshitohfuck," he ground out, hoping that the binding hadn't interfered with such low-level pre-existing magic. When he got no response from Lin, he assumed the message hadn't gone through.

He heard the sounds of fighting below as Seraf unleashed on the three men. There were gunshots and the occasional grunt of pain. Breaker wished he could see, but the crushing grip on his skull hadn't abated so he was only able to see the weave of the carpet beneath his cheek. He'd hoped that Seraf would be smart enough to portal out of there and get to Lin if things went south—she said she would—but perhaps the binding extended to her too.

A gun cocked next to Breaker's ear. He froze in place, fear sliding along his nerves like ice. He hadn't even registered that the pressure on his head had lessened.

"Oi!" The man's voice wasn't soft anymore, and there was a cruel edge to it as he called out to Seraf, loud enough to be heard over the fighting. "Keep on fighting, and I'll be getting a good look at your boy's brains when I splatter them all over my shoes."

The man let go of Breaker's arm and dragged him up by his hair so that he swayed on his knees. Points of pain flared: in his shoulder, his wrist, his scalp from the harsh grip, and most especially his bad knee that did not like bending with so much weight pressing on it. He tried to shift to alleviate the strain, but the man's grip on his hair tightened in warning.

He could see the dock now. And Seraf. She stood, surrounded by the three men. All of them looked the worse for wear. The driver held his arm at an awkward angle. One had blood leaking from his lip while the other's eye was swelling shut and his nose broken.

That's my girl.

Seraf appeared unhurt. She stood in a fighting stance, ready to defend against all comers, but she paled when she caught sight of Breaker with a gun to his head. Breaker glared at her, willing her to portal out and get Lin, to get Barrow, to get anyone. If he ever wished for telepathy, it was in this moment.

Instead, Seraf lowered her hands. Her gaze never left his.

Gods damn it, Seraf. If he could have shaken his head, he would have. He should have known better than to think she'd leave him.

Chapter 27

He could do nothing but watch as they grabbed Seraf by the arms to hold her still.

One of the men holding Seraf turned his head toward the boat. Breaker followed his gaze, straining his senses to discern anything. He saw the top of a man's head clear the decking. He was too far away to make out any features. Shifting his focus, he saw Seraf's eyes widen in shock as she caught sight of whoever was exiting the boat. The noise that left her throat sounded like a dying whale.

Breaker didn't need a clear view or better eyesight to know who was stepping off the boat.

"Long way from the Divine, Father Lyle," he called. "Or is this a different kind of outreach?"

His head rocked to the side as the big man backhanded him. At least he did it with the hand not holding the gun. Breaker didn't fancy a broken jaw. It made being an irritating smart-ass much more difficult.

"Ow," he said, deadpan. He spat out the blood from his teeth cutting into his cheek. "Rude."

Big Man drew his arm back again but stopped when Father Lyle tutted. "No need for that Montclare. We're old friends, Breaker and I." Montclare dropped his hand, gun still trained on Breaker's skull.

Lyle walked over to Seraf, studying her intently. He stared through her like she was a specimen on a slide beneath a microscope. Lyle made a noise of appreciation before turning and climbing the stairs to Breaker.

"My compliments to the fae who handles your glamours. Their skill is impressive."

"I'll pass it along."

"I don't believe you'll be able to do that." Lyle's voice lacked its typical rich warmth. There was an oiliness to his tone that had never been there before.

"It's a shame Seraf didn't die in the ring. I paid a significant sum of money to make it happen." His smile was almost fond. "It doesn't do to underestimate you two."

Of course, Lyle was at the fights or watching remotely on a private stream for the reclusive high rollers. Breaker gritted his teeth and cursed his stupidity.

"I needed definitive proof of Tiberius' asking price. When Seraf defeated him, my deal went to shit. But a female champion fighter?" Lyle grinned hugely. "That more than made up for the shortfall."

Gone were the cleric collars and the short sleeve black shirts, the chinos bought off the rack. Lyle wore an expensive custom-fitted navy suit with a gray Oxford shirt and extravagant tie. His usually shaggy hair was neatly styled and slicked back from his face.

He looked like a different person.

Lyle reached out a hand to pat Breaker's cheek. "I should have known you'd be the one to figure it out. The police are thick as bricks and only care about humans—not that I can fault them for that." Lyle leaned in close until they were nearly nose-to-nose. "You were always too sharp for your own good."

"I thought that the Church frowned on magic users in

their ranks." The Holy See wanted to be the only ones in the miracle business. "Yet you're a Spellbinder."

Spellbinders were rare, even among mages. They bound and blocked magic just by their very presence. They were a sort of walking black hole or energy sink. When around a working Spellbinder, spells were useless.

"With the right ingredients, a charm can be made that even fools the examiners," Lyle explained, a cheeky grin on his face. Breaker wanted nothing more than to punch his fist through it. "So long as you can afford the cost."

"Looks like you can afford a lot of things," Breaker commented with a sardonic raise of his eyebrows. "That suit is a touch more expensive than a clerical collar."

"You think I planned to live out my retirement in priestly squalor?" Lyle snorted. "Hardly."

Seraf made a growling sound, attracting Lyle's attention. He faced her with a mocking smile and said, "I haven't forgotten about you, Miss Seraf. I've got a buyer your brand of violence is perfect for."

He brushed invisible lint from his lapels. "He's waited quite a long time for the perfect Infernal—patient man, that one. I confess," he leaned heavily on the word, a delighted smirk on his lips, "I hadn't thought of you for him, but since you're here, you'll do."

As Breaker watched closely, he saw the tell-tale tightening of Seraf's features as she locked down her reactions, stifling the turbulent emotions churning inside of her. Her eyes narrowed almost to slits as she surveyed the man before her.

"Collar her."

Seraf lunged, nearly wrenching free of the men holding her. Lyle took a step back, his surprised expression almost comical. What had he expected to happen? Breaker would have laughed if not for the gun pressed against his temple.

Just as suddenly, Seraf went still. Her gaze flicked to

Breaker, then back to Father Lyle. "Free. Breaker." Her voice came out clotted and strange. "I w-won't. Fight."

"Always so concerned for each other." Lyle shook his head. "Your care of him, Seraf, could almost convince me that your kind aren't lesser creatures." She flinched at his words.

The collar snapped around her neck with a damning click. The men holding her stepped back warily. Breaker gritted his teeth around the puke that rose in the back of his throat. The keening noise that escaped Seraf's clenched jaw tore into his gut as if it had claws.

Lyle took out a small remote from the inside pocket of his tailored jacket. He pressed a button with his thumb. Seraf's eyes pinched closed, and her face scrunched as she scrabbled at the collar around her throat.

"Perfect," Lyle purred.

Breaker watched, helpless, as Lyle closed the distance between him and Seraf. The ex-priest raised a hand to her cheek. She held herself still, revulsion in the lines of her body. "Then again, even animals can show signs of care for their young, and we *eat* animals."

The crack of his slap echoed in the suddenly too quiet room. Breaker managed to hold himself still—barely—as he watched Seraf's head snap to the side with the force of Lyle's blow.

"It's a shame there is not as neat a way to control humans." Lyle continued, speaking as if he hadn't just smacked the taste out of her mouth.

"You set Swinburne up to take the fall for you." Breaker's gaze slid from Seraf's agonized expression, unable to bear it. "The last loose end to tie up."

"Not quite the last," Lyle said, gesturing at Breaker.

"You were the one that killed the Infernal in the church." Breaker's mind sped through the details of the case, drawing the lines where Lyle intersected them. Lyle simply smiled, which was answer enough.

"And Philip. From the support group. He fed you the names of Infernals that matched your list for a cut, right? Tell me, did you set up Wages of Sin as a front, or did you just take advantage of what was already there?"

Lyle's measured him with something akin to pride in his gaze, and his mouth split into a broad grin. Breaker didn't think he could feel dirtier after his time in Purgatorio, but here he'd found something even filthier than that cesspool dressed in diamonds.

"How many?"

"Hmmm?" Lyle blinked lazily, like a sleepy tiger in a nature video. "How many what?"

"Infernals. How many Infernals have you sold over the years?"

Lyle stepped closer to Breaker, gripping his chin tightly, hard enough to bruise his sensitive skin. "Do you ask God how many vermin he's killed in famines and fires and floods over the centuries?" He wrenched Breaker's head around until he was staring at Seraf again.

"You're not God," Breaker growled despite the punishing grip on his jaw. "You weren't even a particularly good priest."

Lyle chuckled, glancing over at Seraf, who watched them with wide, pain-clouded eyes. "People who live in glass houses," he said, lips quirking into a cruel smile. "Really now, Tobias, I think you, of all people, would appreciate a good cover when he saw one."

Seraf surged forward, but the men were ready for her. The drugs in the collar had done their work well. Lyle sniffed dismissively once she sagged in their arms, turning his attention back to Breaker. Breaker's limbs went cold and heavy like they were encased in frozen lead. He had no idea of the expression he wore, but it made Lyle laugh to see it.

"You thought I didn't know?" He released Breaker's face to pat him on the cheek. "It took me some time and a fair bit of digging to find out you were Winstead's son, but I got there eventually."

"You knew my father?"

"By reputation, just like most everyone in my line of work." He didn't specify which line of work he meant. "We met in passing only once, and he was as formidable as everyone said he was."

And just as crazy. However, Lyle didn't know that. Probably.

Lyle continued. "I imagine he'd be disappointed in you, though."

"That's the nicest thing anyone's ever said to me."

"At least in death, you'll live up to his fearsome reputation." Lyle beckoned Montclare over. "Open the portal."

The big man nodded and began to chant. Breaker clenched his fists, pushing against the binding that locked up his magic. Even his element was inaccessible. He glared at Lyle, brain desperately working for a way out of this mess.

"Get her on the boat," Lyle ordered the men holding Seraf. "Tobias Winstead's long-lost son found dead after opening a gate to release Hellspawn in the very midst of our own private Sodom," he tutted. As Lyle stepped away, Montclare sagged, his energy spent.

The portal was a smudge of shimmering grey hanging in the air. Breaker watched as a three-fingered hand, mostly claws, passed through the portal, followed by the rest of the first demon. It had massive shoulders and stood upright on bear-like legs. It lumbered forward as more demons pressed their way through the portal.

Breaker stared, fascinated. One with a scrunched face like a bat with enormous ears and five eyes scuttled around on wingtips that ended in massive hooks. Another resembled an armored beetle with the serrated mandibles of an ant. Still another sported a horse's head if the horse had huge lower fangs and bulbous eyes in the front of the elongated skull.

Lyle kept on droning, but Breaker barely paid attention.

"He misjudged the strength of those he summoned and was torn apart before the brave men and women of the NVPPD could disperse them."

Breaker finally tore his gaze away from the demons to look at Father Lyle. The false priest grinned at him. Then, with a slow nod of acknowledgment, he ordered, "Kill him."

The summoner gave the order in demonic syllables, his finger pointing like an arrow at Breaker. Breaker didn't bother watching the demons gather; he stared at the two men muscling Seraf toward the boat. She fought them every step of the way.

"Seraf," he yelled to her, uncaring of who heard. It was just the two of them—one last time—as it had been since they were kids. "Thank you!"

Genuine gratitude, unfettered by any resentment or pain or rage or obligation. Had he ever said it this way to her and meant it? "For everything all these years."

She stilled her struggles to listen to him. As they dragged her closer to the edge of the dock, Seraf lashed out, her Infernal eye aglow. A wash of crimson light illuminated half her face. The men lost their grip on her, and she tore free, sprinting for Breaker.

The demons, five in total, closed on Breaker with rage and death flickering in their burning brimstone eyes. She wouldn't make it in time. But she might still get away, get to Barrow or Lin and get that damned collar off. She might yet live.

"Get out of here!" he ordered, but as with so much else, he didn't get what he wanted.

He closed his eyes as a clawed appendage descended. The smell of sulfur and blood wreathed him in its heavy, sickly perfume. Breaker braced himself for that first sharp bite of pain that would signal the end approaching. *Be seeing you real soon, Pop.* He could finally tell the man to go fuck himself in person.

A horrible guttural cry rent the air with its force, tingling along Breaker's taut nerves. It tasted of magic, old and strange. It slithered like oil along his mage-sense, and he gagged at the feel of it.

He cracked open an eye when he didn't feel his blood spilling down the front of his shirt. All five demons stood frozen in place, silent snarls creasing their strangely angled faces. Breaker opened both eyes and took a wary step back, gaze automatically finding Seraf. She stood at the top of the stairs. One hand pressed white against the steel collar, the other outstretched in the demons' direction. She swayed on her feet, but she was *on* her feet.

When she opened her mouth, unintelligible words spilled out in a language Breaker didn't know. It sounded similar to the tongue used to summon and contract with demons but subtly different. That wasn't what had him gaping like a boy seeing his first pair of breasts.

Seraf spoke clearly. Gone was the painful gravel and ground glass sound of her voice. This language was uniquely suited to her strange vocal cords. The words spilled out of her in a flowing stream. Though he couldn't understand a word of what she said, he marveled at the harsh beauty of hearing her voice as it was meant to be heard.

As one, the demons' gazes shifted from him to her. Breaker's stomach twisted in fear. What was she saying to them? They weren't moving or attacking him. Was she communicating with them or controlling them? Was the power of her voice only realized when speaking the proper tongue?

Seraf said something else in that evocative, bewildering language, and the demons bounded away. Two turned to go after Montclare, who'd collapsed from the strain of the portal summoning. The big man crawled as fast as he could, sweat streaking down his florid face. He shrieked when one demon hooked its claws into the meat of his calf and pulled him backward. Montclare twisted, bringing his gun up and firing wildly before the other demon pounced on him.

Breaker flung himself at Seraf, catching her around the waist and bearing them to the floor. Bullets cut through the air as Montclare emptied the clip. Breaker covered Seraf with his body, feeling the shudders rip through her frame as the man's screams increased in pitch and volume before dying out with a liquid gurgle.

Seraf made a choking noise. She writhed beneath him, her hands clawing at the metal collar. Breaker raised his head to see Lyle with the button in his hand as he hurried to the boat, leaving his men behind to deal with the other three demons. One of the demons grabbed for Lyle. The ex-priest juked to the side, barely evading the strike.

"Hang on, Seraf," Breaker whispered, pressing his palms on her shoulders so she wouldn't knock him in the face with her spasms. "I'm going to get that remote."

Mismatched eyes cracked open, the glow of her Infernal eye dimmed. The iris spun like a fiery hurricane beneath the lowered lid. She panted around her pain, grabbing at his hand while the other clung futilely to the collar. "Off," she croaked.

"That's the plan." Breaker tried for a bracing grin but was sure he fell short of the mark given the circumstances. "Be right back.'

He pushed his body up and into a run despite the howling protest from his knee. He scooped up his cane and raced to reach Lyle. He passed the knot of demons and men fighting for their miserable lives without incident. The monsters didn't look away from their meal. Whatever commands Seraf had given them, she must have considered his safety.

The disruption in the air beside his head pulled Breaker from his grateful thoughts. Lyle had pulled out a gun of his own and had it trained at Breaker even as he edged backward toward the boat. *Oh no, you don't, asshole.*

Breaker broke into a shambling run. His knee began to buckle beneath him, so he threw himself into a slide along the floor. His half-controlled skid had him stopping in front of

Lyle. He clutched his cane in steady hands, the tip of it pressed against the priest's chest.

"Don't you fucking *twitch*," Breaker growled from between pain-clenched teeth.

Lyle grinned down at him. The gun's barrel shifted until Breaker stared into the black muzzle. After a moment, Lyle's face slipped into the warm lines Breaker remembered from the soup kitchen years ago.

He murmured, "You could always step aside. How many times have you wished she'd," he tilted his chin in Seraf's direction, "just disappear? How many times have you prayed for a bullet or a spell to strike true?"

"I don't understand." Breaker stared into Lyle's eyes, trying to see signs of the man he and Seraf had known for years. It was stupid to want to know why. It wouldn't help anything, and learning wouldn't change the fact that the man had sold people as if they were things.

"Selling Infernals into slavery? That's a pretty big departure for a man who fed homeless kids."

Lyle frowned, shaking his head like Breaker was a recalcitrant toddler. "You know better than most that they aren't innocent. They aren't even human. Those not culled outright were likely to be killed in hate crimes or wind up selling themselves in those whorehouses. I was getting them off the streets. I saw a need. I filled it."

"And the ones already working at the pleasure houses with plans of their own?"

"They sought *me* out," Lyle said, gaze shifting to take in the carnage of the demons tearing into his men. "To be free of that life."

"Ah yes, your Wages of Sin front. Nice name," Breaker finished. "But you never gave them the freedom you promised."

Lyle stared at him with the open gaze of someone without guilt or regret, who believed that they were right.

Breaker saw someone who had sacrificed part of his soul for what he thought were legitimate reasons. Or maybe the guy was just an asshole with a clever way to rationalize his greed.

The road to hell *was* paved with good intentions.

Breaker wondered what paved the road to Heaven. Broken promises?

Lyle laughed, brittle with bitterness. "Like what you are doing is so much better. Just what have you promised Seraf?" The gun in his hand never wavered. "Admit it, Breaker. Wouldn't it be a relief to be rid of that monster after all of these years? There are enough suppressors in that collar for five Infernals. Just let me go, and you can walk away, free and clear."

Putting one hand on the silver phoenix head that adorned the top of his cane, Breaker dared a glance at Seraf. She stared at him with mismatched eyes glazed with pain.

"Monster she may be," he told Lyle, meeting the priest's gaze with a determination born of pure spite and pettiness, "but she's *my* monster." A feral grin stretched his lips.

Lyle's face went alternatively pale and red with rage at Breaker's words. "How are you going to stop a bullet, eh?" he asked, scorn in every word. "You're nothing without your magic."

"I don't need magic to deal with you." Breaker twisted the phoenix's head. A foot and a half of sharpened steel slid out from inside the cane. He pushed up, slipping the sword between Lyle's ribs and up into his heart.

The gun clattered to the floor. Lyle used both hands to scrabble uselessly at the length of steel jutting from his chest. His mouth opened and closed on a silent scream, his eyes wide with shock.

Breaker watched it all from his spot on the floor, hands wrapped tight around the wooden shaft. Blood soaked through Lyle's expensive shirt. With a vicious smile, Breaker twisted the sword inside Lyle's body. A small groan escaped the man's slack lips.

"I hope all the Infernals you betrayed are in Hell and just waiting for your sorry ass," Breaker whispered. Lyle's eyes closed as he slumped backward.

He pulled the steel sword out of the priest, letting him crumple to the ground. Carefully, Breaker picked up the gun, checked the chamber and magazine, and took stock of the room. The demons had made short work of Lyle's henchmen. They stared at him, red eyes glowing like cinders deep in their skulls. Swallowing down his fear at their stone-faced regard, Breaker nearly melted at the tingle of his magic returning. With the spellbinder dead, he had access to his power again.

Reaching down, he pulled the remote control from Lyle's limp hand. Checking that the safety was engaged, Breaker tucked the gun in the back of his pants and stood up. He had to get to Seraf.

His knee was not interested in cooperating. Wiping the steel of his cane sword on Lyle's jacket, Breaker twisted the phoenix head, and the blade disappeared inside the housing. He'd have to clean it thoroughly later, but for now, it would do. He hobbled over to Seraf as quickly as his body allowed.

She'd managed to crawl over to a wall and pull herself into a sit. Her head lolled to the side. Breaker fell beside her, already reaching for her neck when one of the demons spoke.

"We followed your command." The demon with a horse's head stepped closer on thick, furred legs. Breaker could understand the language with his magic back now that the translation seal tattooed on his skin was active once more. "Release us, half-spawn."

"Come on, Seraf. You have to dismiss the nice demons before they get bored and decide to eat our faces." Seraf's eyes remained closed. He rubbed her shoulder soothingly.

"You are off-limits, caster," the horse-headed demon rumbled. "She who speaks the tongue said as much."

Joy.

"You have completed the task set before you. Disperse back to your own plane," Seraf slurred in their tongue.

With a nod, the demon signaled to the others. They leaped as one through the roof, leaving a gaping hole and raining debris on them. The detritus bounced harmlessly off Breaker's warding. They would head to the gate and back to the pull of their home plane.

"Let's get that nasty thing off you," Breaker whispered to her. She hummed her agreement, her breathing shallow and quick.

Pulling the remote from his pocket, he scrutinized it. A large button would deliver a dose of the drug used to incapacitate Infernals. He found the smaller button that likely unlocked the collar from around her throat on the opposite side.

"Ready?" he asked.

She nodded slowly, demon eye cracking open to watch him. "Okay."

He shrugged out of his ruined jacket, handing it to her. The collars all had an injection needle embedded in them that pierced the skin when attached; removal would leave a wound that could leave behind genetic traces they didn't want the NVPPD to find.

Breaker pressed the button. The collar clicked open, but as he leaned forward to remove it, Seraf gasped in pain. Both hands came up, clutching her throat. A rush of bluish-red blood spilled over her fingers as the collar fell away. Then Breaker saw the needles.

They were longer and slightly thicker than the typical needle, and there were a helluva lot more of them. They ringed the collar like diamonds on a necklace. Breaker remembered seeing something similar—on Trilya's head at the Divine. Breaker wrapped the coat around her neck and tried to apply pressure, all the while looking around wildly.

He needed help. These things had been buried in Seraf's neck, opening much bigger wounds and likely hitting an artery. If he tried to put the collar back on to block the blood flow and didn't line them up exactly right, he'd open more wounds or make the ones she had already bigger.

It was Lyle's last gambit, something to ensure that even if he lost, he still won. Seraf's demon eye was wide and dimly glowing. Her other was terrified as she searched his face.

"Hold this," Breaker said, ignoring the way his voice shook. He pulled her hand up to replace one of his. "Press as hard as you can." She shuddered beneath him. "I need to get help." He moved her hands into place so he could search for a phone.

As he searched, he tried the earpiece. "Lin, do you hear—"

He didn't get to finish his question. A fire elemental blasted through the door leading to the office and juked inside. Dahrian followed a step behind, and Tamlin a step behind that.

"I hear you," the fae man said, the smirk on his face fading when he caught sight of them.

Breaker deliberately didn't address or look at Dahrian. He had questions—why was he with Lin, how had Lin found him, what did he hope to prove with this stunt—but they would all have to wait until Seraf was safe.

"I need to get her to Doc Grady."

Tamlin was beside him in an eyeblink, taking over compression duty. "Phone's in my pocket. Let him know you're coming."

"Seraf's in no shape to shadow travel us," Breaker said, bloody fingers pawing for Lin's phone with little grace. She'd slumped onto Lin's shoulder from the drugs and blood loss.

"Nobody's using that boat." Dahrian's deep voice came from behind Breaker. He thought he hid his flinch, but Lin's gaze shifted to him anyway, eyebrows raised. "I'll drive."

Breaker gave Grady a quick rundown and ETA before pocketing the phone and swapping places with Lin. Their admin was better able to carry the unconscious Infernal while Breaker kept up the pressure on the holes in her neck. They had to move slowly as Breaker's knee made walking difficult, and Dahrian had grabbed his cane when he'd taken off to get the boat started.

Lin settled Breaker on a bench seat when they finally made it aboard before arranging Seraf in his lap. Breaker's hands shook as his jacket became heavy with Seraf's blood.

"Let's go!" he shouted just to have something to do.

He looked up at Lin, desperate enough to plead. "Can't you do something?" God, it was like he was fourteen all over again—powerless and useless and depending on someone else to make things better.

Tamlin's grey eyes were filled with sorrow as he stared down at the two of them. "I'm afraid my skills don't work that way," he murmured before turning away to join Dahrian at the wheel.

Bowing his head, Breaker pressed his forehead to hers. Lyle should have just shot him—it would have been less painful than watching Seraf slip away, inch by inch. She was his oldest friend—the only one still left who knew him before he became Absalom. He couldn't lose her.

"I didn't claim you all those years ago to have you leave me like this."

Chapter 28

Breaker didn't remember much of what happened after they got in the boat, probably for the best. He only came to awareness when someone tried to take Seraf from him. He snarled at them, water spikes materializing from the air. Tamlin pursed his lips, unimpressed, and Breaker reluctantly let him take her.

Tamlin hopped off and raced the distance between the closest canal and Doc's clinic with Seraf in his arms. Breaker and Dahrian followed at a much slower pace. Dahrian slung one of Breaker's arms across his shoulders and took more and more of his weight the closer they got to Grady's. Breaker's vision surged and whited out with each step, his knee a red keen inside his head. His face throbbed from Montclare's punch, and his whole body ached from the fight.

The worst, though, had to be the magical backlash that came from having his powers bound. His nerves sparked and twitched at odd times, and his elemental sensing rose and fell like the tides until he thought he was going to be sick from it. It was like being tossed about on a tiny boat in a massive storm.

"Absalom, I—," Dahrian began as they limped down the street.

The leash barely holding Breaker's temper in check snapped. "How many fucking times do I have to tell you? You call me Breaker."

Dahrian's sigh made Breaker long to hit him somewhere soft and painful. He had no right to sound long-suffering. Not after what he'd done at the Winstead house. "Very well. Breaker--,"

Breaker dropped his arm back to his side and swung around, ignoring his body's protests. "We. Are. Not. Friends." Satisfaction curled hot and low in his belly when Dahrian took a step back at the menace in his voice.

"I never said we were." Dahrian put his hands up as if that would appease him.

Breaker raised one disbelieving eyebrow. Dahrian had the good sense to look sheepish. "Did your friend," he sneered, he couldn't help it, "send you after me again? Or were you being a stalker all on your own this time?"

The rage that towered inside him like a tidal wave needed a place to crash, an outlet of some kind. Dahrian was in its direct path. Breaker tore into him with the delicacy of a tsunami. "Go home and tell your master that you ran me to ground like a good hunting hound."

"You're a real asshole, you know that?"

Breaker bared his teeth in what might—if someone wished to be generous—be called a grin. "Didn't you know? It's a family trait."

"Tonight had nothing to do with Chane!"

Chane. Breaker filed the name away, too consumed with rage to spend too much time thinking about this mysterious family member he'd never met. Instead, he focused on the water of the canals at his back. He reached for it, fingers twitching. Dahrian's contract was with a fire elemental. How would it fare against his water? It was suddenly imperative that he find out.

"I came," Dahrian snarled, black eyes taking on a molten bronze glow, "looking for you on my own. To apologize and explain if you'd let me!"

"Liar." Breaker's voice held fathoms, the cool deeps of the ocean. It didn't hurt, and he didn't have to think about Seraf and what it might mean if Grady couldn't help her. Much better to drown the pain and anyone who caused it.

Dahrian rolled his eyes, the heat rolling off him causing the air around him to shimmer in waves. His hair began to floof out around his body like some kind of sentient, hairy halo. "Not lying, you epic dickhead." He crossed his arms over his chest and scoffed, "Why the hell else would I be here helping you save that mess of an Infernal you call your partner!"

Breaker barely recognized the howl that wrenched loose from his throat. He raised his arms above his head. The canal waters rose with them. He would smash it down on the ridiculous summoner's skull for even daring to mention Seraf, who might be dying even as they spat insults at each other.

Pain exploded along the side of his face. Breaker, already off-balance, lost his footing and fell to the ground. It took him a moment to reorient himself, cheek throbbing. Dahrian's wicked hook had caught him and sent him flying.

"You going to try and drown me again?" the fire summoner asked, breathing hard. Steam plumed out of Dahrian's mouth as he spoke. "Stay down."

"Don't you ever mention her again," Breaker growled, pushing himself into a painful sit. Slowly he shifted until he thought he could get to Dahrian with a lunge and bring him to the ground and smash his stupid-haired head into the sidewalk.

Before he could put his plan into motion, Tamlin stood between them, looking perturbed. "What by the Sidhe king's knobby staff are you two assclowns doing out here?" He turned his stormy glare on Breaker. "Grady is doing his best to keep Seraf from dying, and you're out here brawling with the human equivalent of a hedgehog!"

Lin pointed an accusing finger at Dahrian. "And you had one job—get him to the clinic! You couldn't even manage that?"

"Not when Mister Emotionally Constipated decided to conjure a damn water wall!" Dahrian tossed his head with an affronted sniff.

Lin reached out and hauled Breaker to his feet, ignoring his pained hiss at the bruising grip. Breaker thought he heard him mutter, "Lord, what fools these mortals be," but was too busy being dragged behind the fae man like a poorly behaved child to be sure. Dahrian shuffled along in their wake, hair falling back around his face and hands shoved into his pockets.

"Try not to behave like a raving lunatic, will you?" Tamlin warned as he shoved him through the clinic's door.

Breaker tumbled onto the couch, barely remaining upright as it sagged beneath his weight. "What did Grady say?" His gaze darted to the closed door that led to the clinic's treatment area. When he shifted to push himself off the couch, though, Tamlin shoved him back down.

"Sit." The note of command in Lin's voice had the hairs on Breaker's arm standing at attention. His reptilian hindbrain recognized the danger present and chittered wildly in warning. Lin's lips stretched wide, too wide, and Breaker was sure there were more teeth than there should be.

He froze, eyes wide and heart pounding. Lin's smile took on more normal proportions once more. "Good boy." He shifted to see Dahrian and ordered, "Staying or going?"

"I'll stay. For a while, at least." Dahrian edged deeper into the room, clearly wary of Tamlin. Breaker couldn't blame him. It was easy to forget that Lin had spent centuries in the Fae Lands and had acquired strange powers while there.

Lin waited until Dahrian had settled into an armchair before continuing. "Grady will give us an update as soon as Seraf is stable. And he said he'd call us if he needed help. If you decide to act on your unhinged and hysterical thoughts, you'll only end up in his way and compromising Seraf's care. So you will sit your ass down, and you will behave yourself until Grady comes or calls for you."

"Yes," Breaker said, nodding. Now that his adrenaline ebbed, the reaction crashed over him. He shouldn't have raised the waters like he had, not with his magic still recovering from the binding. His hands shook where they curled in his lap.

"Same goes for you," Lin said, shooting a look at Dahrian over his shoulder.

"I got it, yeah," Dahrian grumbled.

"Fantastic. Will you two behave if I step out for a bit?" At Breaker's quizzical look, he said, "The boat."

Breaker nodded. They needed to get rid of it, and he trusted Lin to take care of it. "I'll play nice," he assured his admin. Glancing at Dahrian, he saw the man nod as well.

"Wonderful. Now be good and don't do anything to make you regret your life choices, and I'll be back in a trice." He was gone before Breaker could even protest.

"Is he always like that?" Dahrian asked after a few minutes of incredulous silence.

"No," Breaker told him, laying down on the couch and making himself as comfortable as he could with his head spinning. "Usually, he's worse."

Breaker uncoiled when Dahrian snorted, some of the tension that he'd carried since Lyle had bound him seeping out of him like rain into dry ground. First Dempsey, then Trilya and Swinburne, and now this. There was no way Barrow would believe his version of events when he got wind of Lyle's death. He needed to go back and scour the site of his and Seraf's presence.

Dahrian shifted in his chair, seeking the most comfortable position. "You want to tell me what happened in that warehouse?"

Breaker propped his leg up on some cushions, made more difficult when he realized he hadn't let go of his cane. When he tried to set it aside, his heart jumped and his stomach twisted. Instead, he kept it close, tucking it against his side even if the phoenix dug into him.

"Do you want to tell me who Chane is?"

Dahrian's jaw firmed. He glanced away.

Breaker ignored the sinking of his stomach. He shouldn't be disappointed--he knew better. It still surprised him that he'd wanted to know anything about this Chane. Since the day Breaker had left his family name behind, he hadn't been interested in his few surviving relations. Now shouldn't be any different.

"What were you doing in my house?" he asked when it became clear Dahrian wasn't going to answer his first question. "You said you wanted to explain."

"Look," Dahrian began. Breaker rolled his eyes, remaining silent to fully absorb the idiocy of whatever next came out the man's mouth. "I apologized already. It's not my place to say anymore. Not about that."

Breaker drew in a deep breath, ready to protest, and then let it out in a slow sigh—no point in pressing for more information. Dahrian wasn't going to give him anything outside of the name, and even that had been a slip. He pinched the bridge of his nose. His head and face pulsed in pain.

"Your, ah, Seraf. A collar did that to her?" Dahrian's asked, voice subdued since the first time Breaker met him. Breaker turned his head at the faint clang of medical instruments from the back. He focused on the rhythm of Dahrian's steady breathing as a distraction.

Breaker nodded tightly. When he was confident he could

speak without his voice shaking, he said, "It was one of the new ones popular in the pleasure houses. Nasty things."

"Clearly." Dahrian leaned forward, digging his elbows into the tops of this thighs. He steepled his hands in front of his mouth. The circles around his irises grew brighter as his summons came closer.

Breaker held still, every muscle tensed in anticipation of an attack. After a long moment, the glowing red faded from Dahrian's eyes until there was nothing but banked embers in his stare. "My friend—Chane. He was able to get into the mansion because he's your half-brother. Your father's youngest son."

Breaker blinked, the words seeping into him like spilled ink on porous stone. A half-brother.

Before he knew it, a chuckle burst out of him. Once he started, Breaker couldn't stop. Of course! This night just kept on giving! The hilarity bubbled up from a spring of mirth somewhere deep inside of him, so sharp it could cut. If an edge of madness colored his laughter, well, the only person who would know was being worked on by a doctor in the next room.

"Breaker," Dahrian began, then pursed his lips when Breaker only laughed harder. He snapped his fingers. "Come on, man."

Breaker stopped laughing abruptly, like all of the humor drained out of him instantly. He could only stare at Dahrian with hollow eyes, unable to process anything else. In a hoarse voice, he ordered, "Get out."

He didn't know what the summoner saw in his face, but it must have been terrible because he said nothing else as he stood. Breaker didn't watch as he opened the door and left the clinic, pulling it shut behind him. He sat with his hands threaded into his hair, gazing at the tips of his shoes as he tried not to puke on them.

He didn't know how long he sat there, contemplating his

footwear. He only stirred when he heard someone softly calling his name. When he looked up, Doc Grady stared down at him, looking like he'd aged three decades since the last time Breaker had cause to see him.

"Seraf?" he asked.

"You and I need to talk."

Chapter 29

When it came to ominous conversation starters, "We need to talk" was right up there with "Don't be mad" and "I've got to be honest with you." Nothing good ever came after those sentences.

Grady watched him closely, his eyes hollow and dark skin sallow with exhaustion. Breaker waited, but the man wasn't speaking. "Is she . . .," he began, and then stopped, unsure if he wanted to know.

Grady nodded, a tired dip of his head. "Out of immediate danger. By no means is she stable. I just needed to take a break. It's...a lot." He flopped his long body down in the nearest chair. "I nearly lost her a few times already. She was dosed with was some nasty shit."

Breaker sank back, whole body shaking. "But she's going to be okay?" His voice came out sounding younger than it had in years.

"Absalom," Grady began, using Breaker's first name. He never did that, though he was one of the rare few who had permission to do it. "Seraf was full of poison. It would have shut down her organs, destroyed tissue, and could have done irreparable damage. And that's if she didn't bleed out first."

"Lyle put those around the necks of the Infernals he sold to private collectors. They thought they were getting freedom and just got sold into worse slavery." Breaker wiped his hand across his mouth, feeling the sickness rise at the back of his throat.

"Then I'm glad he's dead because that was some of the worst shit I've seen when it comes to Infernals." Breaker watched as Grady passed a shaking hand over his eyes. Then the doctor met his gaze with a sharp look of his own. "Let her go, Absalom."

Breaker blinked. "What?"

Grady shook his head. "Look, I don't pretend to understand what it is between you two, but I've patched you both up enough to know that you're going to get her killed one day. And she'll *let* you. So let her go before you do. Whatever you're punishing her and yourself for, she doesn't deserve it."

Grady paused, then stood up. Breaker's mouth opened and closed on words that would not come. Grady set a firm but strangely gentle hand on his shoulder and said softly, "Neither do you."

Bowing his head, Breaker blinked against the sting in his eyes. How long since he'd cried? He couldn't remember. His father hadn't been a big one for tears. They never helped solve anything anyway. Blinking rapidly, he cleared his throat, suddenly gone dry and scratchy.

"We . . . I mean, I don't have a contract with Seraf. It's not like that between us. I freed her, you know, after my father."

Grady snorted. "For someone so smart at spells, you are absolute shit at people."

Breaker half-laughed, half-*something*. He wasn't going to call it a sob, no matter how it sounded. He remembered Father Lyle in that kitchen years ago. One of the good ones, or so he'd thought. And all that time, he'd been selling Infernals into Crowley alone knew what. "That should come as no surprise to you."

Something lit in Grady's eyes, and his expression turned vicious. He moved faster than Breaker expected, jumping out of his seat and crossing to haul Breaker to his feet by his shirt. Grady shook him so hard his brain rattled in his skull.

"Do you know what she did for you that night?" Grady's voice was tight with fury as he all but spat his words in Breaker's face. "After carrying you on her back to my clinic? Did she ever tell you?"

Breaker didn't get a chance to answer or even shake his head before Grady barreled on. "As I was working, I talked to myself—I don't pay attention to what's coming out of my mouth. She must have heard me wonder how you two planned to pay for my services."

Grady loosened his grip on Breaker's shirt. He sagged where he stood. Breaker didn't remember him ever looking so exhausted. "So when I went out to the waiting room to give her an update, she dropped to her knees and tried to unbuckle my belt."

Breaker jerked away from him with a grunt. "Did sh—did you?"

Grady's frosty glare could have turned Texas into an iceberg. "Think real careful about the next words that come out of your mouth, boy." His tone promised a particularly bloody brand of rebuttal if Breaker's thoughts continued on that path.

"I pulled her to her feet." Grady rubbed at his jaw, the memories still raw. "And she shrugged and began to take off her top. As if it didn't matter!" He shook his greying head. "When I stopped her, she said she needed to pay me and she didn't have any money."

"Dee," Breaker breathed, stumbling back until the back of his knees hit the couch.

"She was a child—couldn't have been fourteen, if that! When I told her so, she just looked at me as though I was speaking fucking Urdu." Grady pushed Breaker to sit down, keeping his hand on his shoulder for a long moment.

"I don't know what happened in that house, and," he held up a hand when Breaker tried to speak, "I don't want to know. What I do know is that Seraf has no sense of self beyond what you've given her—not that you have that much either. Just, please, for an old man who cares about the both of you, fix whatever it is between the two of you or cut her loose so you can both figure out who you are."

Breaker reeled. "Grady," he said but stopped when he couldn't think of anything to say.

The medical mage let go of his shoulder. "I'll be getting back to it. Think about what I said, yeah?"

He nodded dumbly, his whole body numb. Breaker pressed the heels of his hands against his eyes until colors flashed against the darkness of his lids. Listening to Grady had hollowed him out until he was sure nothing would ever be able to fill him up.

Seraf had never told him what she'd offered the doctor in exchange for patching him up. He remembered so little of that night. One of the few memories he did have was screaming at Seraf, blaming her for everything that happened.

He scrubbed a hand down his face. Even after he'd done that, Seraf had gone to her knees to try and pay for Breaker's medical treatment. Thank Dee for Grady. If it had been someone like Lyle, well, Breaker had enough nightmare fuel, and he didn't need more.

Old gods, he was tired. He flopped backward, sighing when the couch cushions cradled him. His brain and heart ached with everything he'd learned today, and it still wasn't over. Breaker wanted to see Seraf, to know that she was out of danger. He had to wait for Lin's return. He needed to figure out what he would tell Barrow when the cop inevitably came by with questions. He only meant to rest his eyes for a moment.

BREAKER WOKE TO GENTLE SHAKING. He flailed at the contact, surging out of deep, exhausted sleep. Rolling off the couch, it took him a moment for his brain to make sense of where he was. Right. The clinic. Seraf.

Lin stared down at him, an impish smile tilting his lips. "Wha-what time is it?" Breaker asked him, hauling himself back onto the couch.

The fae man closed his eyes for a brief moment before saying, "Two-thirty. In the morning."

"Any trouble?" Breaker rubbed at his gritty eyes and bit back a yawn.

"Nothing we need to worry about yet. I ditched the boat and came back here. Dahrian was gone, and you were asleep. That was a couple of hours ago."

"And you stayed?" He dropped his hands in his lap to stare at Tamlin.

Lin shrugged. "I wanted to see how Seraf was doing." He glanced over his shoulder at the examination room. "Grady came out a few minutes ago. You should be able to go in and see her shortly."

"Fucking finally," Breaker muttered before he could stop his tongue's flapping. Gods below, he needed about a gallon of coffee to even approach coherence. "Did he say anything else?"

Lin sauntered over to the door with a grace that was closer to unearthly than human. "She's stable and should recover with careful rest. And with that, I'll take my leave."

"You can stay and see her. Since you waited and all." Damn, that came out more condescending than he meant — he needed to wake the hell up before he alienated one of the few people who tolerated him.

"I don't think so," Lin said, the ghost of a smile haunting his lips. "Besides, I should check on the office and then head to bed. I'm taking the day off. I suggest you both do the same. If Grady lets you leave, that is. He didn't sound very pleased."

"Hey," Breaker said, stopping Lin' s progress to the door. "Your help has been invaluable." It was the closest thing to thanks he could offer.

"Wonderful. But I'm still giving myself a ten percent raise." He was out the door before Breaker could retort. He stuck his head back in after a second and said, "Take your time here and don't fret about Unshriven." Once again, the front door of the clinic closed with a click.

Breaker took himself to the small bathroom just off the reception area to splash some water on his face to wake up. The icy water was bracing against his sweat-tacky skin. He grabbed a fresh towel from under the sink and wiped his face.

The sleep was welcome but not nearly enough to stop the exhausted tremors that shook his body whenever he moved. Running a hand through his still-damp hair, Breaker studied his reflection in the small silvered mirror. Tracers of magic edged his skin—another sign of the healing. His wounds had been relatively minor compared to Seraf's: bruises, cuts, more damage to his already messed up knee, and magical exhaustion. The bags beneath his eyes had bags of their own.

He looked like hot buttered shit. But at least he was alive. Lyle and his boys weren't. That was good enough for Breaker.

Pulling a face at his reflection, he hobbled out of the bathroom to find Grady standing in the open doorway that led to the back. If Breaker looked bad, Grady looked like something a necromancer might have summoned on a bad day.

"You can come back and sit with her," he croaked.

Breaker walked over, mindful of his knee. He left his cane where Lin had placed it on the sofa after he'd finished cleaning it. Breaker knew that if Barrow tried to find evidence to tie him to Lyle's death, the cane would show up clean. Tamlin deserved every dollar of his self-appointed raise.

"She's stable," Grady told him as he passed. "Finally." He

rubbed at a jaw gone scratchy with stubble. "I'm going to catch forty winks. Don't hesitate to get me if you think she's in distress."

"Are you--," Breaker wasn't sure what to ask. "Okay?"

"Just energy drained." The medical mage managed a crooked smile. "You know how it goes."

Breaker glanced away, his next question heavy on his tongue. "How is she?" A vague question, but he couldn't find the words to encompass everything he wanted to know about Seraf.

Grady heaved out a sigh. "She's going to need a lot of rest. Those drugs wrecked her system, and it is likely going to be a while before she's herself." The warning Breaker saw in his eyes made him shudder. "You think about what I said?" he asked as he grabbed Breaker's arm so he couldn't move past.

"Done nothing but," Breaker answered.

Grady nodded and let him go. "I'll check on you both in a little while."

"Get some sleep, Doc."

Breaker limped into the examination room, relaxing at its familiarity. If there was one place that felt like home from their time on the street, it was this place, more than even the soup kitchen. Here was safety and healing, even if delivered with dry humor and rough care. As he pushed back the curtain that separated Seraf's bed from the rest of the room, Breaker breathed in the icy scents of antiseptic rubbing alcohol and the sharp smell of plastic from the IV bag.

The small, pale figure on the hospital bed shocked him. He'd never seen Seraf so still, so subdued. Grady had unbound her thick, unruly hair, and it spread out on the pillow in a nimbus against the white sheets. Her sharply angled face held little color, even the normal brown-pink of her lips bleeding into the ashen tone of her olive skin. A swath of bandages covered her throat, wrapping around her neck and down her chest to disappear beneath the light blanket. He cataloged the bruises and cuts on her face and arms as he watched her breathe for a few quiet minutes.

Grady had a chair pulled up next to her bedside. Breaker folded himself into it and took her slack hand in his. He rested his forehead against their joined hands. If he'd been a praying man, he might have said one, but instead, he spent an unknown amount of time counting Seraf's breaths. In, out. In, out. A living metronome for him to measure time.

When the rhythm of her breathing changed, he wasn't sure. He'd been breathing in time with her, entering a fugue state where his mind wandered from one thing to another without really sticking on any one thing. It wasn't until her long fingers twitched against his face that he sat up. Seraf blinked, gaze hazy and unfocused as she tried to get her bearings.

"Have a nice nap?" he whispered, unable to keep the relieved smile from his lips.

Seraf looked confused for a moment before taking in where she was. Her eyes widened when she saw the IV pole and the curtain surrounding the bed. She licked her lips. "Doc's?"

"Yeah." He let go of her hand and pushed the chair away from the bed. "Let me get you some water."

Fetching a cup and filling it from the pitcher on a table beside the door, Breaker thought about getting Grady but decided to let him sleep a little longer. Seraf seemed to be doing all right for the time being. "How are you feeling?" He asked as he put the straw up to her lips.

After a few sips, she turned her head away. Her eyes narrowed, raking over him briefly before she turned her body away as much as she could. "Why are you here?"

Breaker cocked his head, unease coiling in his belly. "Where else would I be?" He set aside the cup and reached for her hand.

She slid it out of the way. "Seraf?"

"Heard. Father Lyle." Her broken voice didn't waver as she spoke slowly so he wouldn't miss a word. "Want. Me gone." When she met his gaze, her own burned with accusation. "Chance. To be. Rid. Of me."

"Seraf, you're confused. The drugs Doc has you on are probably pretty in—"

"Heard!" There was no give in her voice; she was utterly unyielding. "These. Drugs. Suck."

Breaker took a step toward the door, intending to fetch Grady. "Are you in pain? Is that it? I can ask Doc to get something stronger—"

She cut him off. "Answer." Her voice deepened with her growl of anger.

"I don't know what you want me to say."

"Truth. Idiot." She rubbed at her palm with her opposite hand. "All I. Ever. Wanted from you."

Breaker rubbed at the back of his neck. "I'm here because I didn't want to be anywhere else, not until I knew you were going to be okay."

She stared at him with pursed lips.

Breaker ran a hand through his hair. "You don't believe me?"

Seraf tried to nod her head and hissed in pain as the wounds on her bandaged throat pulled. She took a moment to rally before answering. "Hard. To believe."

The lash of her words made his chest burn with hurt. Breaker took a deep breath and held it before exhaling slowly. "Why is that?" He needed to understand, to know what she meant by that. Didn't she trust his words?

She furrowed her brows as if she couldn't believe he was seriously asking her that question. Finally, she began to sign. "I killed your father. I know what you see when you look at me. I know why you hate me sometimes."

He stumbled over to the chair, dropping into with a low groan. "I am too sober for this conversation," he murmured, wishing he had a bottle of bourbon to help ease the pain of lancing the hurt between them.

"Tell Grady you need the good drugs," she answered in sign, expression tight.

He chuckled at the joke. Then he grew serious. Breaker set his hand, palm up, on the bed beside Seraf but made no other move. Disappointment arced through him when she didn't reach out immediately. "I don't hate you," he said softly. "I've never hated you."

He rubbed the bridge of his nose against the headache forming. They were going to get rain. "I hate me."

He shook his head. "I gave the order to you to stop him. I remember screaming it at you. He was out of his head that night, completely unhinged. He wouldn't have stopped with just my knee. I know that. And I didn't want to die. There was only one way to save me. So you did it. You were just the bullet in the gun. I pulled the trigger."

Covering his mouth, Breaker took a steadying breath. "I was angry and scared and so many other things. He was my father. He wasn't supposed to do the things he did to me—to us. I know he was an asshole. But he was still my dad."

Breaker blinked rapidly against the rising ache in his chest, wishing he had alcohol to make the memories less immediate. "And he's dead. Because of me." He dropped his head into his hand, resting his forehead in his palm. "I wasn't only punishing you. I was punishing me, too."

Another deep breath, and he looked up, meeting her questioning gaze. "I'm sorry, Seraf. I'm so damn sorry. It isn't right what I've been doing." He turned his hand over, palm flat to the sheets. They'd been washed so much they were like silk beneath his fingertips. He could do this. He owed it to her. "You're free to leave if that's what will make you happy."

A grating noise filled the small space like stone grinding on stone. Breaker blinked. Seraf was laughing at him. Why was she laughing?

"Fuck. You," she said after she got a hold on her bitter mirth. "J-just go. Fuck. Yourself." The snarl in her voice was unmistakable even without the expression that crowded her face.

"What? Why?" He didn't want her shackled to him out of obligation or some other warped sense of responsibility carrying over their original contract.

"Leave?" He could tell she wanted to shout, but her injuries wouldn't allow it. Her whole body bristled with her rage. She resorted to signing again, every movement sharp. "Where am I supposed to go? Infernals can't just leave— you've seen what happens."

She shifted her body away from him as much as her injuries would allow. "You should have just left that collar on me if you wanted me gone—it would have been kinder."

He gasped, the hurt at her words opening him up like a gash. "No," he whispered. Not that. Never that.

Seraf jerked back around, shoulders flinching as she moved too fast. Her eyes were furious, the Infernal one spinning slowly with all the drugs still in her system. It glittered faintly with her unshed tears. She managed to push herself into a half-sit, but Breaker could see what the effort cost her in the way her arms shook as they supported her weight. He shifted the pillows so she could sit up easier.

She signed, "You say you're sorry and then speak of me leaving. I'm a monster, Tobi." It was his turn to cringe at the use of his old nickname. She gazed at him, a challenge in her eyes. "Where is a monster supposed to go when no one wants them anymore?"

Breaker stared at Seraf, the bottom dropping out of his world. Everything they'd been through since that first day they'd clasped hands on that dirty street spooled out in his mind. If he'd never met her, his life—if he even still had one —would be a very different thing.

How much damage had he done to the both of them over

the years of shutting her out? How could he genuinely hate her when what he saw was so much of himself? Of what he'd made her? Yet, he'd made her think that in every way that mattered.

He truly was an astounding asshole.

Her not being in his life wasn't something he wanted to think about anymore. He was better with her, and his life was better for having her in it. He *never* wanted that to change.

He'd never said as much to Seraf. Grady was right. What other way out did she have except to throw herself in front of him in the hopes that one day he'd wake the fuck up or that this time she wouldn't walk away? What other choices had he given her?

Breaker reached out and placed his hand over hers. Seraf's eyes narrowed, but she didn't try to punch him, so he took it as a good sign. Holding her gaze, he told her in his gentlest voice, "You're not a monster. Not to me."

She snorted in disbelief—or would have it hadn't turned into a sound of pain when she moved her head wrong. Breaker urged her to relax, lowering her back against the pillows.

"I know you don't believe me." He perched on the edge of her bed. The wariness in her expression gutted him. He'd put that caution there, no one else. How many times and in how many ways had he been unkind, thoughtless, hurtful in his need to punish? His father didn't deserve this kind of loyalty.

But Seraf did.

"I know I haven't given you much reason to," he began. "But I heard something once, a long time ago." He stared into her firestorm of an eye, walls down, masks missing. She knew him better than anyone else. Breaker only hoped she could read the sincerity in his gaze.

"When is a monster not a monster?" Breaker asked her.

She blinked, brow furrowed in confusion. She shook her head.

"When you love it." As understanding broke across her face like the dawn of a new day, Breaker smiled. "You're my best friend in the whole world, Seraf. I can't imagine my life without you in it."

He leaned forward until his forehead touched hers. "I love you, Seraf. I always have." Breaker drew in a deep, shaking breath. "I'm sorry I've been such a raging asscravat about it. I promise I'll do everything I can to earn your forgiveness. If you'll let me."

Choices. It was about choices, and Breaker could start by giving Seraf this one.

Her hand rested on the back of his head for a moment before she ruffled his hair playfully. Gods, when was the last time she'd done that to him? When was the last time he'd let her?

"Idiot," she whispered, closing her eyes. "But my idiot." Her fingers twined his hair gently, just holding the strands, never pulling. "Forgiven."

He blinked away the moisture gathering in his eyes. "Just like that?" he murmured.

She nodded, eyes still closed and forehead tucked against his. "Best friends. Forgive."

Seraf opened her eyes and smiled hugely. "That doesn't mean you're not going to make it up to me, though," she signed.

"Fucking finally," Grady interrupted from his spot at the door. "Now, if you're both done with the dramatics, I need to check on our patient."

Chapter 30

Breaker pulled his father's journal out of the safe with careful hands. It was the first time he'd gotten a pocket of time to examine it since he'd brought it home with him. Seraf's recovery and the discovery of Lyle's trafficking ring—thanks to Lin's superb ability to seed technological breadcrumbs that led the police to the man's offshore accounts—meant extra work for Breaker.

Domino was so pleased with Unshriven's work that she'd dropped off a bonus with her final payment; despite being unable to return her employees, Unshriven had ensured that more were unlikely to meet the same fate. NVPPD promised to look into the matter to see if they could track down the buyers, but Breaker didn't have high hopes for Barrow and his team. Silk was more impressed that they'd managed to unravel the mystery of years of missing Infernals.

Inspector Summoner Barrow had already been by to ask his questions. The NVPPD had tracked the demons' departure through the Gate and traced it back to the source. The bodies had been found, along with the summoner, and they'd chalked it up to a spell gone wrong. That Lyle's wounds didn't match the other demonic violence present on the bodies was something they didn't have time or interest in solving, not after his financials came to light.

Seraf had spent a few days with Doc Grady. The only way he released her was with Breaker's promise that she would rest and not do anything suicidal or stupid—Doc's words—until she fully recovered. Breaker had readily agreed while Seraf pouted in her wheelchair.

He'd invited Lin to stay for dinner on her first night back at Unshriven, and they'd all shared a celebratory banquet from one of the best Italian restaurants in the city. Tamlin had polished off two bottles of expensive Sangiovese all by himself, though the alcohol left him largely unaffected. Lucky fae bastard.

Breaker set the journal down on the kitchen table. Seraf was asleep in her room, the door shut, so the light from the kitchenette didn't bother her. He'd taken to doing most of his work down here during her recovery in case she needed anything. Not that there had been much work—he wasn't accepting new clients until Seraf was back in fighting trim.

"Okay, Pop," Breaker murmured as he opened the cover with gloved hands. "Let's see what you were hiding."

He could feel the pulsing magic even through the spelled leather gloves he wore for protection. Breaker shouldn't have been surprised, not with the pains his father took to secure it, nor the effort Dahrian and Chane had taken to procure it. He did not doubt that this journal was what Dahrian and Chane had been looking for that night at the mansion. The question was, how had they even known about it? Breaker only knew of the journal's existence because he'd seen his father with it. As far as Breaker knew, the journal had never left his father's study.

At first glance, the journal was like any other mage's: notes on spellcraft, results, research, lists of substitute ingredients.

But with each page turned, Breaker grew more and more unsettled. His father's notes were not haphazard, each experiment leading to the next, and then the next, methodical and plodding.

It wasn't until he got to his father's notes on reanimating Breaker's mother's pet cat, Viola, that he hissed out, "Shit. Pop, you knew better."

Necromancy. The one art that resulted in instant punishment—usually death—for the practitioner. The art of raising and controlling the dead.

It looked like his father had easily cracked that particular conundrum, and there was still at least half of the journal to go. As Breaker read on, he had to change into a new pair of gloves as whatever magical protections Pop had placed on the book ate away at the wardings embedded in the leather.

He sucked in a breath as he reached the final set of notations. His father hadn't just wanted to raise and control the dead. He'd been trying to create a gate into the plane of the dead to bring back the souls of those gone beyond the mortal plane. Or to leave this plane to rule over the other. His motivations and endgame weren't precisely clear, but one thing was certain.

His father had figured out a way to do just that.

And somehow, his half-brother, someone he'd never met, had been searching for this very journal.

Breaker breathed deeply, mindful of Seraf sleeping in the next room. He couldn't give in to the panic rising inside him as he slammed the book shut and shoved it as far away as the table would allow. He pushed himself out of the chair with trembling hands and braced himself on the table.

"Shit."

-FIN-

UNSHRIVEN'S ADVENTURES continue in Book Two, coming in 2022.

Acknowledgments

To Molly and Lish—A huge thank you for all reading this monster in various stages and offering criticism and encouragement. Love you guys to pieces.

To my readers—I hope you enjoy this world and these characters as much as I did while writing them.

To my family—Yeah, I'm sorry about the laundry.

About the Author

Jeanette Battista is the award-winning and Amazon best-selling author of The Moon Series, These Violent Delights, Masquerade, Long Black Veil, and several other series. Holding an MA in Medieval English literature, she's been a technical writer, a software project manager, and a freelance educational writer. She's taught college freshman how to write and occasionally still talks writing with high school and middle school students.

Her household includes several humans and three cats, one of whom is missing an eye. He is, unfortunately, not named Odin, a choice that will haunt her forever. When she's not writing, she's running, reading anything that falls into her lap, and playing PS4 games badly on Twitch. She lives in North Carolina.

Also by Jeanette Battista

The Moon Series

Leopard Moon

Jackal Moon

Hyena Moon

Hunter Moon

Fox Hunt - short story

The Demon's Gate Series

The Iron Bells

The Stone Golem

The Demon's Gate

The Books of Aerie Series

An Unkindness of Ravens

A Murder of Crows

A Parliament of Rooks (forthcoming)

Long Black Veil

Played

These Violent Delights

Masquerade